Praise for *Where I Can't Follow*

"Haunting and hopeful, a hard story full of shocking warmth and unexpected beauty. The little doors of Blackdamp are the kind of make-believe that feels true, a magic so vivid it feels more like a memory than a work of fiction."

—Alix E. Harrow, *New York Times* bestselling author of *The Once and Future Witches*

"*Where I Can't Follow* is a powerful and unflinching look into emotion, place and its people, and what binds you even when not fully belonging. Ashley Blooms has written a haunting testament to the survival of self and family in a struggling, desperate Appalachian community."

—Kim Michele Richardson, *New York Times* bestselling author of *The Book Woman of Troublesome Creek*

"With wisdom beyond her years, Blooms illuminates human frailty and elevates the humble journey. Her mountain tale of hardship comes wrapped in delicious language. I highlighted favorites phrases so I could reread them and be stunned all over again. Her original voice is captivating and unique and delivers an ethereal story about trust triumphing over self-doubt. Congratulations, Ashley Blooms, on propelling our imagination toward a new dimension."

—Leah Weiss, bestselling author of *If the Creek Don't Rise* and *All the Little Hopes*

"Ashley Blooms novels have this in common with the tallest of trees: they are deftly rooted in the land of their origin, and yet their crowns, dappled with starlight, define a much broader world. In *Where I Can't Follow*, the twined themes of magical escape and what it means to be left behind build a brilliant stage on which Blooms's luminous cast of characters is transformed. A captivating novel that is at once personal and universal."

—Fran Wilde, double Nebula Award–winning author of *Riverland* and *Updraft*

"Bloom is the best we have at combining magical realism with the grit and grace of the best documentary. The Blooms of *Every Bone a Prayer* continues to flower in *Where I Can't Follow*."

—Robert Gipe, author of *Pop*

Praise for *Every Bone a Prayer*

"*Every Bone a Prayer* is a difficult, important, and beautifully rendered story of generational trauma, survival, and healing. The characters I met within its pages have stayed with me, their names and stories etched on my memory."

—*NPR*

"*Every Bone a Prayer* evokes the magic of my favorite childhood stories—thrilling, but eerie—but it's also a painful, beautiful, and necessary examination of trauma and autonomy."

—*BuzzFeed*

"An exploration of faith that borders on fanaticism, belief in the unseen wonders of this world, the fear that lives deep in the heart of girls whose innocence is stolen from them, and the resilience built by refusing to be destroyed are all beautifully, heartbreakingly, and magically at work in the brilliant *Every Bone a Prayer*."

—*Seattle Book Review*

"This is the kind of book we need to set literary expectations for a new decade. It's so textured, so layered with love, and so wonderfully terrifying, intimate, and magical."

—Kiese Laymon, author of *Heavy: An American Memoir*

"Haunting and healing, *Every Bone a Prayer* is a powerful debut that will leave its mark on readers' hearts."

—Kim Michele Richardson, *New York Times* bestselling author of *The Book Woman of Troublesome Creek*

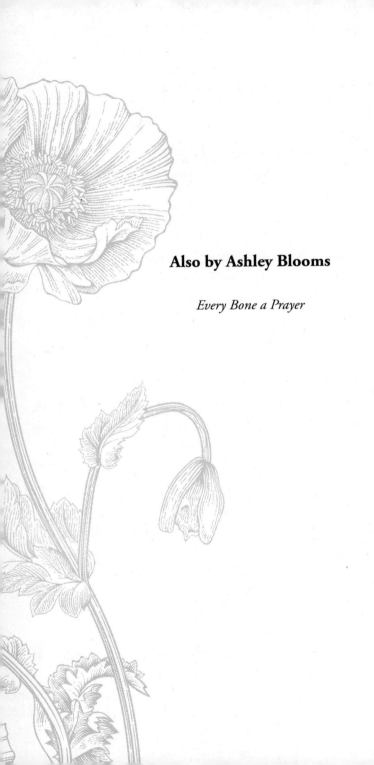

Also by Ashley Blooms

Every Bone a Prayer

Where
I Can't
Follow

A NOVEL

ASHLEY BLOOMS

Copyright © 2022 by Ashley Blooms
Cover and internal design © 2022 by Sourcebooks
Cover design by Sarah Brody
Cover images © Jena Ardell/Getty Images, Olga Korneeva/Getty Images

Sourcebooks and the colophon are registered trademarks of Sourcebooks.

Published by Sourcebooks Landmark, an imprint of Sourcebooks
P.O. Box 4410, Naperville, Illinois 60567-4410
(630) 961-3900
sourcebooks.com

Library of Congress Cataloging-in-Publication Data

Names: Blooms, Ashley, author.
Title: Where I can't follow : a novel / Ashley Blooms.
Other titles: Where I can not follow
Description: Naperville, Illinois : Sourcebooks Landmark, [2022]
Identifiers: LCCN 2021039373 (print) | LCCN 2021039374 (ebook) |
    (trade paperback) | (epub)
Classification: LCC PS3602.L667 W48 2022 (print) | LCC PS3602.L667
    (ebook) | DDC 813/.6--dc23
LC record available at https://lccn.loc.gov/2021039373
LC ebook record available at https://lccn.loc.gov/2021039374

Printed and bound in the United States of America.
VP 10 9 8 7 6 5 4 3 2 1

For you, Mom.

Dear Reader,

Please note that this book contains depictions of drug use and addiction, alcoholism, mental illness, and mentions of suicide. For a more detailed breakdown of these warnings, you can visit ashleyblooms.com /triggerwarnings.

chapter one

When I was little, my cousins and I used to pretend what it would be like when we got our little doors. Even then, we knew not all of us would get a door. Maybe none of us would. Most of our parents hadn't, and none of our parents had taken their door even if they *had* gotten one. Not yet, anyway.

No one really knew how the doors worked, only that they showed up from time to time and seemed to appear to people who really needed them. The doors found the hurt, the lonely, the poorest, and the most desperate. They seemed to have the same taste in picking partners that I would develop when I grew up.

No one knew where the doors led. They may have taken everyone to the same place—some pocket of some world where the sky was green and the grass tasted like Peach Nehi. Or maybe they took people through time. Shunted them forward or dragged them back. Maybe they were dream doors, leading us to the place we wanted most. Some people claimed the doors led to Hell, of course, but those people claimed most things were portals to Hell—talking during church service, smoking menthol cigarettes, wearing a thin T-shirt over a dark bra, or worse, not wearing a bra at all.

The doors never looked the same, either, and only the first one ever witnessed had been a *little door* at all. Everyone in Blackdamp County knew the story. Elizabeth Baker, 1908. A door three inches high appeared on top of the piano she played at church. When she'd asked who had placed it there, no one else could see it, so Elizabeth pretended she'd made a joke. Even then, she knew what happened to women who claimed to see things no one else saw.

She'd gone through her door two weeks later, after she'd asked her father to baptize her for the second time, just in case it would help her wherever she was going.

Since then, the doors had come in all shapes and sizes: a well that appeared in the center of Donna Gail's kitchen; a hole in Ida Ross's bedroom wall that slowly grew bigger and more ragged and warmer by the day; a ladder that stretched past Mr. Coleman's apple trees and into a low fog that never moved and never thinned; a length of rope that led between the trees in Tanya Ross's backyard and into the darkest darkness she had ever seen. My favorite doors had always been an empty teacup with a chip in its handle; a skeleton with the teeth still stuck inside its jaw, the mouth opened just enough to show something glimmering inside, like light skipping across a pond; and a book lying open with big, looping scrawl across its pages like a child's handwriting when they were pretending to write a story.

No matter what they looked like, every door after the first was called a *little door*. Like many things in Blackdamp, that would never change, no matter how little sense it made.

The most important thing I'd ever learned about doors was that they didn't go away on their own. This seemed the best part of all to me. Something that would never leave you. Something guaranteed to stay. It seemed that doors had to be sent away by their owner— closed, really, once and for all. Though no one was entirely sure how this worked, either. Some people said they'd simply closed their eyes and willed their door away while others composed lengthy goodbyes.

One woman claimed she'd danced with her door in the summer-long grass of her backyard and that the door had left her midtwirl because it simply knew she could never walk through it.

And while all these stories were lovely, they were also incredibly frustrating to anyone who wanted simple, solid answers. In that way, doors were a lot like love. No one could really tell you exactly what they were or how they worked, but everyone was sure you would understand if you were ever lucky enough to find one.

But that summer when I was nine, for me and my cousins, our door was an old hollow-core one that Uncle Tim had taken off an unused shed and set in concrete in the field behind Granny's house. The door's frame was old and soft with wet rot. It smelled like damp earth, and it gave beneath our fingers when we gripped it too hard. All that only added to its magic. The door was a frail thing, shooting up out of the ground beside the bloodroot and goldenrod like they'd all grown there together. We let the door swing open and took turns running through it, shouting where we thought the door might take us.

Dollywood.

Wisconsin.

The ocean.

I'd shouted the last one and then jumped through, standing triumphant in the tall grass until I realized I didn't know how to swim.

"I'm drowning," I'd cried and fallen to the ground in a heap.

The grass swayed above me, and my cousins ran around delirious with heat and imagination. That's when I'd noticed my mother standing at the top of the hill watching us. Her arms were crossed over her chest, and she had a strange blue flower tucked into her hair. I wonder now if she'd already made up her mind and knew that in two months' time she would be gone, walking through her own door and into some other world, leaving me behind with no parents, no home, no explanation.

I'd wanted a door more than anything back then, but after Mom left, I'd begun to doubt the doors. They seemed meaner once they'd taken her, little magic thieves who didn't care about daughters at all. Then I moved in with Granny, and she rarely talked about Mom or the doors. She had this way of ending things like weeding a garden— she'd snatch them up by the roots, pull hard, let go.

But it wasn't that easy for me. I kept thinking that if the doors could lead anywhere, maybe my door could lead me back to Mom. They had taken her from me, and then they became the only chance I had of getting her back.

So a part of me wondered. Waited.

But of all the ways I'd imagined I might get my door, and all the shapes I thought it might take, I never expected to find it the way I did.

chapter two

I knew something was wrong as soon as I pulled into the driveway that night. Every light in our house was on. The windows glowed a mix of gold and white, even the one in my bedroom that was spiderwebbed with cracks and mended with duct tape to keep the cold out. The curtains in the living room had been half torn down so they hung crooked on one side and reminded me of a shoulder peeking out from beneath a dress strap, a girl nervous of her own skin. The front door was thrown wide open, casting a beam of yellowish light onto the porch steps, revealing the unmown grass still stunted by the winter but fighting stubbornly to return. I always let it grow out because I loved the way it felt when it snuck up between the steps and tickled the bottoms of my feet, like it had been waiting all season long to see if my skin still tasted the same.

I probably should have been more afraid as I sat there in the driveway, worrying at a tear in the fabric of the driver's seat. But sometimes when things got really bad, I just kind of stepped away from myself, and it's like nothing was happening to me, exactly, but to someone shaped just like me, with the same wild, dark hair and untrimmed eyebrows and scar on her chin. Besides, this wasn't the first time I'd come home to find things strange. I knew something was wrong with Granny. I knew it was getting worse, too, but so far, I'd been able to pretend it was a worse I could handle.

I'd forgotten all about the cell phone in my hand, so when it buzzed, I nearly threw it across the car. A text from the man I was supposed to go on a date with that night. The first date in more months than I could count. I didn't even like him, really, but I was lonely, and he was tall, and when he asked me if I'd go see a movie with him with his head all dropped down and a hole in the collar of his work shirt, I had felt like I was coming out of winter, too, somehow.

A little part of me mourned him as I put my phone in my pocket. I would forget to text him back until the next morning, but he wouldn't respond. He would stop coming into the store where I worked to get a cold Pepsi, and when I saw him a month later, it would be with a girl who was in pharmacy school, the two of them walking out of the Dairy Queen, smiling.

The air smelled like burnt metal and cold, wet earth as I stepped out of my car. I walked over to the light cast through the open front door of the house and shivered. Even though I lived there, I still felt like an intruder when I peeked my head inside.

The living room was all messed up. The cushions pulled off the couch, the coffee table pushed to the far wall. The television was turned on, but the volume was too low to hear. The doorway that led to the kitchen showed more of the same—cabinets thrown open with what little they held inside scattered across the counter.

Even though I knew it was the work of Granny's failing memory and her unpredictable moods, some part of me still hoped it wasn't her who had torn our house apart but instead someone looking for pills or money or something to pawn. Break-ins had become more common on the mountain. There were more people out of work, more drugs than ever. And here Granny's house sat, twenty miles from town with every mile more long and winding and dark than the last, and I felt the distance then, felt the switchbacks between us and the hospital if Granny needed something more than a warm bath and a cup of buttermilk to soothe her, felt the weight of everything between us and the help we might need.

I took one slow step into the house.

"Granny?" I asked and felt just like a little girl. A memory tried to shake loose from me, but I fought it down.

I searched the house just to be sure Granny wasn't hiding somewhere and then called my oldest friend, Julie. I couldn't wait the ten minutes it would take her to get to the house, so I grabbed Granny's coat and the only flashlight I could find and headed into the backyard, through the field where I played as a little girl. The concrete Uncle Tim set was still there, but the door of my childhood had long since rotted away.

Granny's yard was wide and mostly even with a gentle slope downward to the woods. I skirted the edge of the tree line, hollering her name every few steps, listening for her voice, but only the whip-poor-wills answered each other in the dark. I crossed from Granny's yard into my cousin Cheryl's, where the grass was littered with children's toys, the bright plastic almost glowing in the dark. I heard the back door squeal open and then Cheryl's voice shouting, "Everything all right?"

"Yeah, I'm just playing hide-and-seek," I yelled. "Did you check in on Granny like I asked you to?"

"Well…"

"Well what, Cheryl?"

"Well, you ain't got to be like that. I had a flash sale on my Jazzy Jemstones page, and it really blew up. I was on live, so I couldn't just leave in the middle of it. I have a business to run."

I opened my mouth to say a dozen things, each meaner than the last, but I couldn't spare the energy, so I just rolled my eyes and kept walking. The first couple of times Granny had wandered off, I'd been able to find her within a few minutes. I'd never had to ask for help, but I'd come close the last time she disappeared—three months ago, middle of December, snow on the ground. I'd searched for an hour before my fingers went numb. I'd trudged back home, resigned to calling Uncle Tim and telling him what happened, when I walked inside and found Granny sitting in the living room watching television as though she'd never left. The only proof I had that she'd really been missing was her boots by the front door, crusted with snow, and the coat I now carried in my arms. I'd found mud shoved in the pockets and more mud dried under her fingernails, though she'd never told me what she had been doing that night.

After I'd gotten her cleaned up and tucked into bed, she'd said, "Don't tell the others. Tim and my babies. I don't want them to worry."

Granny didn't have many babies left. My uncle David, the oldest, had died before I was born. Mom had taken her door, and Aunt Forest had moved away not long after and rarely came to visit. That left Uncle Tim, who lived a few miles away, and his oldest daughter, Cheryl, who lived next door. We didn't have many people to tell about Granny's memory, but I'd promised her I wouldn't tell anyone at all. And I'd kept that promise, too.

Granny's troubles had started even before that night, though. Two years ago, she'd had a small stroke, and I had abandoned community college to help her get back on her feet. She hadn't lost any permanent function, but neither of us fully recovered—Granny from the illness, me from the debt I racked up trying to take care of her. Before her stroke, we always seemed to manage, just barely scraping by. After, everything got harder. Like when the water heater went out in January. It had taken all of Granny's social security check to cover the cost, even with Uncle Tim installing it for free. I'd had to let the phone and electric bill slide that month and had been cutting corners and skipping lunches at work so we could get caught back up.

Granny had changed, too, after the stroke, and especially after the issues with her memory began. She used to be out all the time. Visiting people, going to church, raising money for this or that. She had more friends on Facebook than I did and could tell me about every one. But then she stopped going out so much. Stopped answering the phone. I knew it was because she was afraid someone else might notice she had changed, but it still scared me. She seemed to draw a little more into herself every day. I'd only convinced her to go to church a few days before, and she'd seemed happier after, more like herself. But just when it seemed like we might be okay, something else would happen, and I would be out in the woods again, throat raw with the cold, searching for an answer in the dark.

I kept following the hill behind Cheryl's yard as it sloped steadily downward, the grass growing higher with every step. Soon, the ground evened out again and led to a place that looked something like a bowl surrounded on three sides by trees and shadows. I'd played there sometimes as a girl, but we usually left this place alone. It always felt like it was a mistake that it was covered with grass instead of water. The field should have been a pond instead, and it felt like the field knew it, too, and was bitter about it. The ground was uneven and littered with fire ant hills and snake holes. It was the kind of place that made it clear it wasn't made for people like me to go stumbling across in the dark, but that's where I went, because that's where I saw Granny. She stood right at the center of the field in her favorite blue housedress, her arms held out by her sides, chin tilted back so she could stare up at the sky.

And that's where I saw my little door for the first time.

chapter three

It happened between blinks. First, I was standing there, weak with relief at having found Granny so soon, and then I was looking not at her but at the thing floating above her.

My little door was mostly round and small enough that I might have surrounded it with my arms, had I tried. It moved, spinning in a slow circle like someone had pulled the plug in the air, the world was being sucked through a drain, and the center of the drain was the center of my door. It was deep black there, an endless kind of black that hurt my eyes to look at too long because it felt too big, too sure of itself, like that color could creep behind my eyes and replace every other color until all the world was darkness. Around the edges of the circle, where the spinning was the slowest, the air was tinged pale blue and purple, streaked with white, like there were stars hanging there, close enough to touch. The colors faded as they moved toward the center, turning black and picking up speed. The door looked almost liquid, as if I could dip a cup inside and drink it down.

It reminded me of a picture of a black hole I'd seen in one of my high school textbooks. I wondered if the door drew its shape from my memories. If every door was plucked from the mind of the person it belonged to.

I wanted to touch it. Badly. I wanted to sink my arms to the elbow inside it and pull them out drenched and dripping blue and purple light, my skin glittering with stars. I wanted to look like my door. I wanted to glow.

Some part of me sang with the fact that this was *my* door. Mine, only and ever.

Mine.

I'd never really owned anything in my life. The car I drove had belonged to Granny before; the clothes I wore were secondhand from the Christian Mission; my bed was a hand-me-down from one of my cousins. There were so few things in my life that someone else hadn't touched before.

Mine.

But then my stomach twisted with some mix of fear and anger. After Mom left, I used to pray to get my door. I'd begged God to send it to me so I could find her. Nine years old and crying in the dark. I told myself that if I was good enough, then it might happen—if I said my prayers and listened to Granny and went to church and didn't do anything wrong, then my door would find me. I tried so hard to be good enough for my door, for God, for Mom.

But it never worked.

So to finally find my door sixteen years after Mom left... It felt both too much and too little. I wanted to yell at it, ask it why now, of all times. Why like this? I wished I could fight it somehow, draw back my fist and feel it connect with something real, but I worried that touching my door would mean *taking* it. And I couldn't do that.

Not yet.

Granny swayed suddenly like she was about to fall. She caught herself at the last second, her hair bouncing loose from the bobby pins I'd put in that morning before I left for work.

"Granny," I said, too loud, so I said it again, softer. She didn't always recognize me in moments like this. Sometimes she thought I was her sister or one of her children. Sometimes she didn't know me at all. "Hey, Granny, whatcha looking at?"

She turned toward me slowly.

"Oh." She blinked. Her eyebrows had grown wiry and white over the last few years. They hunched over her eyes like two disgruntled caterpillars, and the sight of them always made me smile. "When'd you get home, little britches?"

"A little while ago," I said. I kept looking between Granny and my little door like my eyes couldn't decide which was more important. I felt guilty and small for being able to think of anything that wasn't Granny, and I tried to force myself to focus on her. "What're you doing all the way out here?" I asked. "Not running off with some younger man, are you?"

Granny laughed. "Not hardly. Unless it's that new mailman. I might give him a try."

"Is it them little shorts he wears in the summer that does it for you?"

I held Granny's coat between my hands as she stepped into it, laughing, shivering. I took one of her hands in mine, and they were frigid, the joints stiff and swollen with the early March cold. I zipped up the coat and tried to pull the hood over her head, but she wouldn't let me. She was at least a foot shorter than me and thirty pounds lighter, but no one did anything for Granny without permission. I settled for rubbing my hands against her shoulders as she stood there looking more like an outline of a Granny than the real thing. My little door cast a faint, ghostly light over her graying hair so she glowed around her edges.

Behind me, Julie whispered, "Maren. *Maren.*"

I smiled. "Look who else came all the way to see you."

I stepped to the side and waved Julie closer. She was wearing the same bright-green shirt she'd worn to work that morning. "You look like a highlighter," I said as she wrapped her arms around Granny.

Julie stuck her tongue out at me and fussed over Granny.

"Jules is going to take you back home, all right?" I squeezed Granny's shoulder. "I'll be there in a few minutes." When Julie looked at me, I mouthed, *I need a minute.* She nodded and helped Granny up the hill, taking slow, small steps.

I waited until I couldn't hear the sound of their voices before I turned back to my little door. I knew no one else could see another person's door, but it still bothered me that Granny had been standing there looking right through mine. She couldn't have known it was there—it just didn't work that way—but I still felt like I did back when I'd been caught kissing the preacher's daughter in the church parking lot. Scared, ashamed, but more excited than anything else. Maybe even a little hopeful.

"I don't know what I'm supposed to do with you," I said.

A door slammed behind me, and Cheryl's voice called out, "That you, Maren? I just seen your granny walk by with that girl you work with. You sure everything is all right?"

"For Chrissake, Cheryl, go to bed!"

"You know you're standing in my yard. I have half a mind—"

I turned to face her and said, "Half a mind is all you'll have left if you don't get in the house and leave me alone."

Cheryl hurried back inside. She was eight years older than me, but she'd never acted like it.

I turned back to my little door and sighed. "Well, *I* have half a mind to take you just to get away from Cheryl."

The door didn't respond. I waited for it to shift or move or do anything at all. I stepped into the place where Granny had been standing a few minutes before.

"Are you going to stay here?" I asked the door. "Or do you follow me? There might be some kind of magic word I'm supposed to know. If there is, nobody taught me." I shifted from one foot to the other. "Well. I have to get going now. Don't swallow nobody while I'm gone, all right?"

I took a few steps and then paused. I wasn't sure which kind of door mine would be—some were fixed in place, never moving from where they appeared, like that very first little door stuck fast atop the piano in Elizabeth's church. Some doors followed their owners, like the bright-red ball that rolled behind Tom Franklin wherever he went until he finally picked it up and was transported wherever little doors go. One door appeared as a tarnished hair clip in the shape of a dragonfly, its wings shimmering with something like glitter, but finer. The wings would move from time to time in a slow, steady beat, like they were dreaming of flying.

I wanted my door to be a following door. I didn't want to keep threatening Cheryl every time I came to the field, though I would, if it came to that. I took a deep breath and turned around. The door hovered a little closer than before, still spinning slowly, almost thoughtfully, about six feet away. The light it cast seemed brighter as the night grew darker around me. I smiled. It would follow me, then, wherever I went for as long as I wanted, and it wouldn't leave until I told it. If I told it.

I took the long way back to the house that night, stumbling because I kept looking back to make sure it was still there, but with every step I took, my little door followed.

chapter four

The light from our house looked different when I walked back into the yard. It wasn't bleeding from the edges anymore but held carefully inside like a hand hovering over a flame, hoping the wind won't snuff it out.

My door hovered closer now, just about a foot from my shoulder, like it wanted us to see eye to eye even in the dark. I still wanted to touch it, to drag my finger through the brightest edge and part its surface like water. I wanted to know if it was warm or cold. If my mouth would fill up with some strange taste at that first touch, something I didn't have a name for, something that would rewrite my memories and have me speaking in a new tongue. I clenched my hands into fists to keep from reaching out to it. I wasn't sure how it worked yet. If I touched it, would I be gone? Or did it need me to *want* to leave before it would take me away? Somehow, the last one felt right—the door seemed respectful, after all—but I was too tired to test the theory right then.

"Well, this is Redlick," I said to my door, then opened my arms to take in the trees and the narrow two-lane road. People claimed Redlick got its name from a shoot-out that happened on the land decades ago that ended when the creek ran red with blood, but others said the name was changed one summer when coal runoff had poisoned the water, turned it a dim sulfurous brown. The mountain that Redlick ran through didn't really have a name—it was more an intersecting series of named roads and hollers that branched here and there until the roads met the town of Wyland to the west and Sterns, where I worked, to the east. The nearest actual city—the kind with good hospitals and Indian food and more stoplights than you could count on one hand—was more than two hours north. I turned toward my front porch and dropped my arms to my side. "And this is my house."

My door spun slowly in response.

"I guess it's our house now." I sighed. "That's all I need. A roommate that don't pay rent."

Back inside, the living room had already been put back together— the curtains rehung, the photo albums back on the coffee table so Granny could pull them out at a moment's notice, flip to a picture of me as a toddler standing naked in the backyard, and yell, "Look at how flat your butt was! Like a tiny little pancake," whenever I started to get on her nerves.

Julie was on her hands and knees scrubbing the kitchen floor. Her blond hair was tied back with a ponytail, a handful of bobby pins, and at least one paper clip. She leaned back on her knees and said, "I was about to come looking for you. I've got the kitchen handled, but I need you to put them pictures back up before Granny gets out of the bath."

I ran my hand over the empty wall to my left. It was normally covered in twenty years' worth of framed photographs of Granny and her favorite rosebush. Granny must have taken them all down during her episode and stacked them neatly on the floor. I wished I knew what she had been looking for when she tore the house apart, what chased her through each room, drove her into the dark of the woods. But she rarely remembered an episode after it was over, and she didn't like talking about the parts she did remember.

I glanced back at my little door to make sure it was still with me. It hovered silently by the front door, and I wondered if they recognized each other somehow, if they could talk among themselves about door worries that no one else understood. It made me feel better just to see it floating there, to know that it was with me. So I turned back and picked the first photo from the floor. It was from last summer. Granny stood with one hand blocking the sun from her eyes, frowning because I was taking too long to take the picture and because I kept telling her to show a little skin for posterity. I smiled at the memory. Then I turned the picture over to get to the hook on the back and stopped. There was a small sheet of notebook paper taped to the back. Granny's thin, scratchy cursive looped across the page. The letters were so narrow that I had to squint to read them: *Summer 20—. There was too much rain that year and the roses were pink instead of red. Maren was teasing me and laughing so hard I could see the fillings in her back teeth. It was a good day.*

Tears welled up in my eyes. I glanced at the kitchen, but Julie was humming to herself as she wiped down the refrigerator doors. I hung the picture back in place, reached for another, turned it over.

There was a message there, too. A message on all of them, all written in Granny's wavering letters, all brief descriptions of the day the photograph was taken. Things like: *I was frowning because I burnt the biscuits on the first morning David came to visit in months. Tim had just poured motor oil on the road to keep the dust from rising since he'd waxed his Camaro, but Maren wandered right through it in her bare feet and I had to scrub her with a kitchen sponge.*

The last picture in the stack was the only one without a complete message. It read: *I kept telling Nell.* The sentence died there, the words shifting abruptly to blank space, the white of the page glaring like a grave. I flipped the frame over and found the glass cracked in one corner, spiraling out from a single point as though it had been struck with something small and blunt. It was the only photo that included my mother.

She wasn't there, exactly—just one arm reached out from the left-hand side of the frame, her fingers straining toward one of the biggest, brightest roses. She was always picking them, even when Granny told her not to.

After Mom took her door, Granny rarely spoke about her. She shoved away everything that might remind us of Mom—took down all the pictures except the one I held, gave away all Mom's clothes and knickknacks, and scrubbed Mom's old friends from our life, even Thelma and Karen, who had been more like sisters than friends. They'd sent me letters at first, birthday cards and Easter baskets, but no one could hold up to Granny's stony silence for long, and eventually they stopped reaching out until there had just been Granny and me, carrying on with the ghost of Mom between us, pretending we couldn't see her.

That's why I learned how to keep Mom inside me instead. I carried her like a torch through the dark, this bright, shining phantom who always said the right thing and always knew just what to do. I didn't remember enough about her to really know who she had been, so I made up the rest, filling in all the gaps with my own visions of who Mom had been. I used to imagine she'd been forced to take her door, chased to it by some terrible evil, and she'd stepped through it thinking of me, swearing one day she'd find a way home to her little girl.

I ran my finger along the web of cracks over Mom's hand before I hung the photo back on the wall. I tucked all those thoughts of her away and thought of Granny instead—a habit so old that it felt like second nature. I knew Granny was forgetting things, but I hadn't known how badly she wanted to remember. I felt a wave of guilt so strong that it made my fingers curl into a fist. The guilt settled in my stomach and made me feel sick with failure. I didn't know what I was supposed to do to help Granny take care of herself, but I knew I had to.

"You all right, Maren?" Julie asked.

I could see her from the corner of my eye, her shadow as thin as a slip hanging from a doorknob. I touched the edge of one photo like I was adjusting it, cleared my throat, and tried to say something clever, but it came out as a strangled sound instead.

Julie was at my side in an instant. She looped her arm through mine and pulled me tight against her. "Hey, it's okay. We're going to get through this, all right? Just like we always do." She pressed a quick kiss to my shoulder. "I was going to give this to you at work, but I think you need it now." She pulled something small and dark from her pocket and held it up for me to examine.

"Is that a lump of coal?" I asked.

Julie smiled. "I thought the same thing at first. But then I turned it over." She shifted her hand to reveal the other side of the stone—a mass of thin, glittering crystals grew along the back in jagged lines that shone dull purple and gold in the dim light of the living room. She twisted it back and forth to let the light arc here and there. "It reminded me of you."

"Which side?"

Julie laughed. "Both of them. This plain one is what you show everybody. Try to scare them off being all tough and mysterious, but if they hang around and get to know you"—she turned the stone over again—"there's so much there that they didn't see at first."

My throat tightened as I took the stone from her hand. I twisted it this way and that, so focused on the stark difference between the two halves that I didn't notice someone else was in the room until he spoke.

"That a Maren rock?" he asked.

The voice sounded familiar, but it wasn't until he stood beside me that I recognized Julie's older brother. My brain did a strange little stutter at the sight of him. He was Carver, but different. He seemed taller. His cheeks were covered in stubble so thick it verged on a beard. He'd moved away three years ago, and I'd heard little from him aside from the occasional update from Julie. Seeing him there in my living room felt perfectly normal and perfectly ridiculous at the same time.

"How can you possibly know that this is a Maren rock?" I asked.

He touched the crystal side of the stone, rocking it back and forth against my palm. "It looks just like you."

I pulled my hand away and tucked the stone into my pocket. I felt off-kilter—confused and irritated and, worst of all, happy to see Carver in my house again, standing there smiling like someone who hadn't gone away and never called, not even once. "What're you doing here?"

Julie shook her head. "He showed up this evening. I found him in the living room watching *Jeopardy* and eating all my Grippos."

"What're you doing back?" I asked. "I thought you said you wouldn't set foot in Blackdamp until you had something worth bringing home."

Carver spread his arms out at his sides. "You're looking at it."

I rolled my eyes. He was still Carver then. "At least you finally grew into that nose of yours. Well. Mostly."

"And I see your mouth is still running away with you," Carver said.

"Well, I'm glad the two of you haven't changed at all." Julie walked back into the kitchen. "Now, Maren, what do you want me to do with these? They expired last week." She held up two bottles of pills and shook them a little.

I took them from her and frowned. "Well, shit. Don't let Granny see these."

"But they're hers," Julie said.

"I know, but she refuses to take them. The doctor gives them to her for her fibromyalgia and her bulging disks. The woman is falling apart and refuses to take anything stronger than Advil. She makes me swear not to fill the prescriptions, but I'm always worried she'll hurt too bad one day and change her mind, so I keep a bottle or two nearby. I'll have to refill these."

"You think she's that way because of your mom?" Carver asked.

I sighed. Mom had had a drinking problem, and it had always been a sore spot between her and Granny. I remembered that much on my own—the cups I wasn't allowed to drink from at home, the parties Mom went to on weekends, the time she had driven into Granny's front porch and how Granny had refused to repair the damage for over a year just so Mom would have to face what she'd done over and over again. I shook my head. "I'm sure that's part of it."

Carver took the bottles from my hand and examined their labels. "At the very least, you ought to be careful with how much of this you keep around. There's people in this county who would break into the house just for a handful of these. You can make a lot of money selling these things."

"How would you know?" I took the bottles back and shoved them into the corner of the tallest cabinet, the one Granny couldn't reach.

Carver said, "How else you think John Edward got that dinky little task force set up? I drove by his new headquarters on my way into town. You should have heard the way the women down at the BP was talking about it."

"I wish the county would stop giving him more power. He shouldn't even be deputy. That man scares me." Julie shivered.

"What's there to be scared of?" Carver scoffed. "He was a chickenshit in school and now he's a chickenshit in uniform."

Julie frowned. "You know what happens to the boys who get picked on and beat up and called names in high school? They take it out on the girls. They always do. Ask any girl from school what she thinks of John Edward, and she'll tell you."

"She's right," I said. "We knew never to be alone with him. And now he's got a gun and keys to a cell."

"Shit," Carver said. "I didn't know."

"You never had to." Julie crossed her arms. "I don't want to talk about this anymore. Carver, go make yourself useful and lay out some clothes for Granny. One of them flannel nightgowns and some thick socks. And, Maren, go lay down. It's almost midnight, and you're opening the store in the morning. And why do you keep looking over your shoulder like that? You scared of something?"

For a minute I didn't know what to say. I *had* been looking over my shoulder where my little door floated in the living room. I couldn't stop looking at the damn door no matter how hard I tried.

"The only thing I'm scared of is your attitude," I said to Julie, which seemed to be the right answer because it got everyone moving again. Julie went back to cleaning, Carver went to fulfill his orders, and I lay down on the couch and pulled one of Granny's quilts over me. I told myself it wasn't the right time to tell anyone about my door. We had Granny to worry about first. I would tell them later, when it was right, when no one would worry.

I also told myself I would only lie down for a minute to satisfy Julie. I still needed to help Granny out of the bath and into her clothes and under the covers where I would tuck her in so soundly that she wouldn't be able to move until morning. Only then, when she was safe, could I rest.

But then my door floated through the air until it stopped about two feet above me. It swirled in its slow, liquid way, and from this close, I noticed there were even more colors along its edges—a deeper blue that wasn't quite purple and a dusty pink and a pale, pale yellow. I watched them blend and blur together, watched it spin its slow, unending circle, until I woke in the dark with Carver standing beside the couch.

chapter five

I sat up in a rush. Carver said something, but I couldn't make out the words. My door wasn't above me anymore, and I panicked. Some part of me already began to mourn it in the seconds I searched for it in the dark, thinking, *Of course it left. Everything leaves.* Then I saw it floating by the living room window. I leaned back against the couch. I wasn't entirely sure where I was or why, and part of me was convinced that Granny was on the roof for some reason, her arms spread out like wings.

"Sorry," Carver whispered. "Bad dream?"

"Bad day," I said. "Bad *life*."

He snorted and set a glass of water down on the coffee table. "I didn't mean to wake you."

"It's okay. Where's Granny and Julie?"

"Asleep. Granny in her bed, Julie in yours. You wouldn't know Julie was sleeping by the way she's talking in there. You know she has actual conversations in her sleep?"

I smiled. "I woke up one night at a sleepover, and she was talking to me on the phone. Even had her hand held up to her face like she was holding the receiver."

"That girl ain't right." Carver shook his head. "Anyway, I was about to head home."

"What time is it?"

"About two."

"Shit."

I scooted over, and Carver sat down in the empty space I left behind. He smelled like the cheap floor cleaner I bought at the Dollar General, which reminded me of work, which reminded me that I would have to get up and face the day like none of this had happened—not Granny, not the door, not anything. I groaned.

"You all right?" Carver asked.

"Not really."

"Can I help?"

"Not really." I drew my knees up to my chest and looked at him. My little door cast the living room in pale, shifting blue light. There was something watery about the way the light moved, like a river ran beside us that we couldn't see or hear. "Does the Reverend know you're back?"

Carver frowned. "No. I figured I'd wait until I had a job and then go see her. She's easier to deal with if you have good news."

I nodded. The Reverend was Julie and Carver's grandmother. She and her husband had all but raised Carver and Julie after their mother died in a car accident. Carver's grandmother had been given the nickname "Reverend" as an insult by a man she'd made angry for some reason or another. It was meant to make her feel bad about the way she got involved with people in the town, how she'd judged everyone, how she was always the first one at church and the last one to leave. But Tabitha Greene wasn't the type of woman to be insulted, and she'd taken Reverend as a mark of honor. Now everyone in town called her that, including the pastor of her church.

"Well," I said, "are you going to tell me the truth about what you're doing here or not? I remember how angry you was when you left. I really thought you'd never come back."

"Did you miss me?"

"Sometimes."

The smirk on Carver's face disappeared. We had teased each other for as long as I could remember, bickering like cousins, so the easiest way for me to catch him off guard was to be honest.

"I missed you, too," he said. "I missed Julie and Granny and gas station hamburgers and sitting in the parking lot of Martin's Grocery on Saturday nights. I missed Blackdamp."

"Really?"

"It surprised me, too." He lifted his ball cap and ran a hand through his messy hair, then fit the cap back on his head a little lower than before. "But I had to leave."

"Why, though?"

A long moment of silence stretched into another, and Carver stared at the floor like the answer was lost there among the dust and scuff marks. I nudged him with my shoulder.

I said, "Even Julie didn't know why you left like that. And it's not like you ever called or texted to tell anybody what was going on." Saying it made my chest ache a funny, hollow little ache. I never really acknowledged how much never hearing from Carver had hurt my feelings, and I had no plans to admit it then, and especially not to him.

Carver pulled the cap down lower over his eyes. His hair had grown out shaggy and dark, long enough to curl around his ears. "I wanted to."

"Why didn't you, then?" I'd assumed Blackdamp and Julie and I were all baggage he wanted to leave behind. I never expected Carver to come back, and I didn't realize I'd wanted him back until he was standing in my living room.

"I don't know. I wanted to call. You especially. But it felt like I couldn't unless I had something good to say. I couldn't call and tell you—" He shook his head. "I just didn't like who I was up there, and I didn't want anybody else to know it. But it's different here. I know tonight was a mess, but it's the best I've felt in a long time. I like knowing that if you or Julie or Granny needs something, I can be there to help. I like being the kind of person who makes things better, not worse."

I leaned back and sighed. Part of me wanted to keep pushing him, but the rest of me was too tired, so I said, "You liked cleaning my house?"

He laughed. "I loved it."

"You want to come back next week and do it again?"

"I'll come back whenever you'll have me."

"Oh, hush," I said.

"What? You think I forgot about how you kissed me before I left?"

My face warmed. I'd avoided mentioning that part so far because part of me was afraid Carver had really moved to get away from me, desperate to rip loose the stitches between us before they set in place. I couldn't help how high my voice rose when I said, "I was drunk!"

"You'd had two light beers! Even Granny wouldn't be drunk after that."

"Granny's more woman than I am," I said.

"Yeah, and she's more man than me, but that's beside the point."

He leaned his weight against my side until I had to lean in to him or be tipped over by the pressure. I met him in the middle, but I couldn't meet his eyes.

I *had* kissed him before he left. He'd thrown a going-away party at his and Julie's house, and half the town came. It had been fun for the first few minutes, but then there were too many tipsy people I'd known for too long, so I'd snuck around front and crawled into the back of Kaylee Joe Osborne's pickup. We'd dated for a while after high school, so I figured she wouldn't mind. Carver had come looking for me, climbed up, and talked for a while. He had always been pretty—doe-eyed and slender—but he looked even prettier when I thought he was leaving. So I leaned over and kissed him. It was nice as far as surprise kisses go. Soft. He'd started smiling halfway through, and then Julie showed up and we pretended nothing had happened.

I'd wanted to kiss him since we were in middle school, and I think I felt safer kissing him knowing he would be gone soon. There would be nothing to clean up afterward. A coward's kiss. But I think, too, that I wanted to send some part of me with him when he left. I figured the imprint of me on Carver's lips would be the farthest I'd ever get from Blackdamp.

He said, "It should have been me that kissed you. I'd wanted to longer."

"Since when?"

"Fifth grade. We were waiting for the bus, and Tammy Stidham started making fun of my new T-shirt because she said it had belonged to her big brother. They'd donated a bunch of clothes to the Mission and I didn't know. I loved that shirt until she told me it was charity. And you got so mad that you punched her. Bloodied her nose."

"Sprained my thumb, too."

"Which one?" he asked.

I held up my right hand and wiggled my thumb. He took my

palm in his fingers, lifted my thumb to his mouth, and kissed it softly. The hairs from his beard tickled my skin, and I flushed. His gentleness always surprised me, even after all these years. I don't think he realized how much power those touches held—how he was always one sweep of my hair or grazing of fingertips away from undoing me, how all my carefully constructed defenses couldn't withstand a kiss on the forehead. And I could never let him know, so I had to look away. I watched my little door from the corner of my eye. Its shifting light made the shadows long and lean and dancing. A familiar voice inside my head whispered, *You shouldn't want him; he's not for you.* I thought of that voice as a fog. It settled over me often. Warned me away from things that might hurt me. Reminded me of who I had to be in moments when I was tempted toward some other life that was never mine and never could be.

Carver placed my hand back on my knee and said, "That's why I should have kissed you first. I'd been saving it for a decade, at least."

"You're not going to let this go, are you?"

"Do you want me to?" he asked.

"It don't matter what I want."

"Of course it does," he said, half laughing. "Who ever told you it don't matter?"

"The world told me." I rubbed my hands across my face to try to chase the fog away. "I don't want to go to work, but we have bills, so I have to. I don't want to spend the rest of my life as a grocery clerk, but every time I try for something better, I get knocked back. I don't want Granny to be…to be *sick*, but she is. 'Want' has nothing to do with any of it."

Carver leaned forward until he caught my eye. I didn't look away that time. His face was so familiar to me even though he'd changed.

We'd known each other since we were seven and nine. I'd invited Julie home from school with me one day, and Carver tagged along, trailing us like a shadow, and Granny had treated them like they were her own. Since then, we'd spent our summers in the field behind my house, growing long and gangly and awkward together. Three children who thought nobody wanted them—nobody but each other.

"It matters what you want," Carver said. His voice was soft but insistent. "Even if it don't matter to the world, it matters to me."

I sighed.

"So I'm going to say it again. If you want me to, I'll never mention that kiss. I'll drop it now and forever. Find me a nice Pentecostal girl and get reformed." He smiled, but he glanced down at my mouth and was slow in returning to my eyes. "All you have to do is tell me so. Is that what you want?"

I almost kissed him again right there, but the fog swelled up in me and said, *He doesn't know what he's saying. He'll be gone again soon and you'll be alone.*

"I should get some sleep." I stood and stepped away from the couch. The room felt colder without Carver pressed against me.

"You never answered me," he said.

"Didn't I?" I smiled. "Just sleep on the couch, all right? There's no use in you driving home this late."

"I won't fight you on that."

"There's more quilts in the closet there if you get cold. Good night, Carver."

"Good night, Maren," he said, toeing off his boots. "And hey— just think. You got one more person on your team now that I'm back. Things can only get better."

chapter six

Three days later, I sat in the hospital waiting room with my little door floating nearby. Granny had pneumonia, which I'd known the day before, and suspected the day before that, but I could only force her to the hospital that morning when she started coughing and couldn't stop. I'd listened to the sound of her breath wheezing through her lungs for the whole half-hour drive into town, and I felt like I might never stop hearing it.

She was being admitted to a room—poked and prodded, forced into a gown—and I was waiting outside to speak to the doctor. I was supposed to be at work, and I kept counting down the half hours, thinking, *If they admit her now, then I could go back and get five hours of my shift, which would be at least thirty dollars after taxes, which means I could still pay the whole phone bill as long as I skipped lunches for another month...*

My stomach growled. There'd been no time for breakfast that morning, and Granny was the only one with the good sense to grab her purse. I didn't even have change for the vending machines that sat across from me, reflecting my frazzled image in their sticky glass.

I turned to the ceiling-length windows behind me to distract myself from my hunger. Sterns was the largest town and county seat of Blackdamp County, and it was quiet this early in the morning. Fog still clung to the tips of the highest trees, and the sky was hazy, half-asleep without the sun there to remind it that it was morning. A river cut through the center of town, winding its way behind the courthouse, the police station, and the discount shoe store that also printed flyers and signage, served as a meeting space for the Shriners, and had adult videos in the basement if you knew who to ask. I'm not sure who would need all those things in one space, but I knew I wouldn't care to meet them. Just out of sight was the high school I'd attended, the library, a few restaurants and businesses, and houses dotting the hillside like wary creatures crouched between the trees. Sterns was pretty from a distance, but I'd only ever seen it up close.

My little door floated over like it wanted to see what had captured my attention. Somehow, my door appeared even brighter next to the faded pastels of the waiting room, as it cast swirling, colored shadows on the dingy tile beneath us. Everything it touched seemed prettier. I could only imagine what it would feel like to go through, like being baptized, maybe, only better. Realer. I'd wanted to leave Blackdamp a thousand times, but I'd never had a chance like this before. Julie and I had even made plans once or twice, picked out apartments in Lexington, got brochures for colleges, and found applications for jobs online. I was going to be a nurse, and she was going to be a librarian and then a counselor and then a principal, but there'd always been some reason to put it off another day, another weekend.

My phone buzzed in my pocket, and I looked down to see Julie's name on my screen. Guilt flared in my stomach. Here I was thinking about leaving, about some new and shining life, when there were people who needed me in this one.

Any news yet? Julie asked.

Nothing, I typed. She was at Martin's Grocery on the other side of town, covering the shift I needed.

Nothing here, either, she replied. Except Arlene. She keeps singing Old Rugged Cross and I'm about to find one to hang her from.

I smiled. Now, now. What would your therapist say about that?

Nothing anymore. She left.

What? When?

Couple months ago. She got a job at some fancy therapy center up north. The clinic hasn't replaced her yet.

What're you going to do?

I knew I'd asked the wrong question when the little dots didn't appear on my phone to show that Julie was typing. She was always quick to respond, known for sending a dozen messages in a row. She'd even turned on my receipts so she could tell when I read her texts because I was so bad at responding. *At least then I'll know you're alive*, she'd said.

But she wasn't saying anything now.

Julie had been in and out of treatment since we were fourteen— sometimes because she chose it, sometimes because the Reverend did. She'd been diagnosed with many things, but mostly bipolar. When she'd come back from the last psychiatrist, we'd stayed up most of the night looking for information on my beat-up Acer laptop, drinking chocolate milk and eating Grippos until our tongues went numb. By the end, neither of us had felt much better, but we'd worn ourselves out enough to sleep.

The last six months had been better for her. A new therapist, new meds, but now her therapist was gone and things suddenly felt shaky. It could be that way with Julie. We would be going along fine until I glanced down and noticed there was nothing but air beneath our feet and we were falling before I could even try to help.

My fog crept in, made me feel heavy and tired. *Can't help Julie, can't help Granny, can't help yourself—why do you even try?*

I opened my text messages again, hoping Julie had responded, but she remained stubbornly silent. So I opened the last text Carver had sent me instead. It was from this morning—a picture of a box turtle's grim and blurry face. Beneath it, Carver had written: stopped and picked this fine gentleman out of the road this morning. his mean face reminds me of julie when she wakes up. how're you?

I smiled. He'd always been good at those little things, drawing pictures and slipping them into my locker between classes, leaving notes with little puzzles taped to the bathroom mirror when I spent the night at their house. I hadn't responded to his text yet, so I pecked out: at the hospital with Granny. pneumonia. could you bring me something to eat? no pork rinds.

The last line was a reference Carver would understand. He'd stolen a bag of pork rinds from a gas station back on the mountain when we were about ten. This was the summer their mother was back in town and convinced that Julie would make the perfect Miss America. She was shuttling Julie back and forth to pageants, getting her gigs modeling clothes for local stores, which left me and Carver alone for most of that summer.

We'd run off like pirates through the woods and down to the creek not far from the store to assess our bounty. We ate the whole bag of pork rinds in ten minutes, and I don't know whether it was the humidity, the greasy food, or the guilt, but we made ourselves sick. After our stomachs were empty, we walked home together, taking the long way around to avoid the store. The thing I remember most is Carver spotting a walking stick for us both, digging one out of the underbrush and tearing another from a dying ash tree.

We'd used them all summer long, carrying them everywhere, and when my stick had snapped clean through the middle, Carver had given me his.

But even with a joke there to soften the message, I still felt nervous texting him. Raw and exposed. I was hungry and alone, and part of me said I should stay that way. I was fine, after all; I'd been hungry before. *Toughen up, Maren, toughen up.* But there was another, smaller part that didn't want to toughen up. It wanted Carver to bring me a chicken biscuit and take magazine quizzes with me so we could find out which shade of lipstick we were. I hit Send before my fog could catch up and tell me all the reasons why I shouldn't ask Carver for anything. I fidgeted in my seat and wished I were at work so I could rearrange the chip rack or drag the mop out of the utility closet, throw all these feelings into my body, and work them out.

Instead, I watched my door as it moved at eye level around the waiting room. It floated back and forth, pacing gently, casting a faint, shimmering shadow over the worn tiles below. From this angle, my door was thinnest at its edges, maybe two inches thick, but it grew toward the middle, bulging out to about four inches. It looked like a cluster of small, glowing bugs swarming together, or maybe starlings flying in formation from miles and miles away.

The door eventually paused in front of a display of pamphlets on addiction—every drug known to man was written in boldface across the front with high-resolution before-and-after photos of addicts below. The same materials were strewn all across town, though they didn't seem to be helping. Three people I'd gone to high school with had overdosed in the last couple of years, and at least that many had gone to prison for manufacturing and distributing. I wondered if the hospital had any better material that might help me figure out what

I was supposed to do with my door, even though I knew there were only two options: take it or leave it. Maybe I could pick up *On the Care and Feeding of Your Personal Void* or *Five Signs You Should Enter Your Black Hole and Disappear Forever.*

My phone buzzed, and I fumbled for it, hoping it was Carver telling me he was on his way with three bags of food, but it was Julie instead. She'd completely ignored my question and had asked one of her own instead. You were acting kind of funny the other night. You all right?

Yeah, I typed. Just worried about Granny.

IDK. You kept looking behind you like you were waiting for something. Or somebody.

It was my turn to avoid answering now. I'd hoped she hadn't noticed anything different, but it was Julie—she always noticed. I wasn't sure what to say, so I squeezed my phone back into my pocket as a nurse walked through the room and directly down the center of my little door. She never flinched, but the door shimmered, seemed almost to dissolve where she had touched it. When the nurse passed, a bit of color and light trailed after her, slowly floating through the air until it rejoined my little door and made it whole again. My mouth dropped open at the sight, and the nurse squinted at me.

"Who are you here for?"

"Dr. Owens," I said.

"Hmm. I'll let him know." Her frown deepened as she pushed through the exit.

"That was a neat little trick," I whispered to my door. It floated across the room until it hovered over the chair beside me right at head level so I could almost pretend there was someone sitting there, like there was a body beneath my door that I couldn't see with little door arms crossed over its little door chest. I smiled because the door was beautiful and because it came to me when I spoke to it and because it didn't know anything about Julie or Carver or Granny or hunger or worry. It only knew me, and I was all it wanted to know.

I let my hand hover just beneath the streaks of amethyst light swirling at its edges. I swear I didn't know I was going to touch the door until I did.

Just the barest tip of my index finger disappeared inside the whirl of soft colors. My skin warmed, vibrated. It felt like water, just like I'd imagined. The colors pulsed around my skin like a fast-moving stream until they shifted, swirling and eddying around my finger, adjusting to my intrusion. The door seemed to grow brighter where I touched it until I had to squint to bear the light. My skin grew warmer, then hot, until it began to burn.

Something like dust shed from my finger and fell through the air. I jerked my hand away and popped my finger into my mouth without thinking, like a child after touching a hot stove. My door pulsed as it returned to its former shape, sealing up the rift my touch had left behind. Whatever had fallen from my finger landed on the chair beside me. It felt thin and grainy, like sand, when I pressed the tip of my damp finger against it. I held my finger to the light to examine it. Part of me wanted to taste it, but I wasn't sure if it was part of me or part of the little door. I rubbed the grains between my fingers until they disappeared.

Above me, the little door shifted, floated farther away. It seemed bigger than it was before.

"Ms. Walker?"

I jumped. Dr. Owens stood by the double doors, looking

around the waiting room. I watched my door float over to the narrow windows behind me before I turned back to him. Owens was a thin man in a starched white lab coat. His hair was brown and neatly trimmed with a shock of white near his left temple. He was probably about my mom's age if she were still here, though he looked younger. He was the head doctor at the hospital, and almost every patient who came through the doors would see him eventually. There used to be more doctors here, but the hospital funding kept getting cut, people were leaving for better jobs, and the services were dwindling, disappearing. Yet Owens remained. There were rumors about him all the time—how he'd had three heart attacks over the past year because his client load was too much, how he moved here after an incident at his last hospital, how he had a bank safe in his basement filled with money.

I stood and walked toward him. "I'm Ms. Walker."

He glanced down at the clipboard in his hand and nodded. "Your grandmother is doing fine. Pneumonia at her age is risky, so we'll keep her a night or two just to be safe. We're taking some blood now, but she'll be in a room in a few minutes."

"All right," I said and turned back toward my chair.

"We should discuss her memory."

I closed my eyes. "What do you mean?"

"I've been seeing your grandmother for years now. I've noticed some…changes. I tried to speak to you about it at her last checkup, but…"

His voice trailed off so I finished the sentence for him. "But I wouldn't let you talk. Doesn't seem like your luck will be much better this time."

"This is serious, Ms. Walker."

"I know."

"I believe your grandmother is in the early stages of dementia. This isn't something that gets better with time."

"I know."

"Good. Then what are your plans for her care? Are you able to be with her throughout the day? Do you have someone who can?"

"I work."

"Then an at-home worker—"

"Isn't something I can afford." I did my best to keep my voice even, but I could feel it getting louder with every word. "Granny's insurance only covers part of the cost, and not for a full-time worker, either. Just a couple days a week."

"Sometimes people will pay a family member to—"

"I tried that, too," I said. "Granny won't stand for anyone hovering over her, especially family."

Dr. Owens sighed. "I understand that these arrangements can be difficult, but your grandmother's condition *will* deteriorate. It varies from case to case how severe and sudden the changes are, but they *are* inevitable."

"I understand that."

"Then you understand that your grandmother's life is in your hands. It's something you have to take seriously."

"Does it look like I'm not?" My hands were already knotted into fists, so I squeezed them harder. I wanted to hit him very badly. To knock that little strand of white right off his head. Bloody knuckles were a much easier problem to solve, but I held myself very, very still. "I am doing the best I can. I am always doing the best I can, but it's never…it's still never enough."

"I can't speak to your…situation…but I know what your

grandmother needs. Residential homes are another option. There's one here in town that's—"

"No. I'm not putting Granny in a home."

Dr. Owens pursed his lips. "We have counselors who might be able to help, then, but only if you're willing to be helped. Whatever it takes, I suggest you find a way to care for her. And soon. If you'll excuse me."

He dipped his head, turned on his heel, and walked back through the double doors. A woman's voice came on the PA system overhead, but her words were garbled, indistinct. I felt like I was scattered miles apart, like my hands were buried a mile to the north, my legs a mile to the south, my arms and torso split east and west, and my heart was there in the middle calling them home. And I couldn't move—I couldn't move—until they made the long, bloody journey back to me. So I waited where the doctor left me, shaking a little, tears welling up in my eyes.

chapter seven

When she was still here, my mother used to ask me a question that started out the same way but always ended differently. What would it be like…

…if we lived on the moon?

…if your daddy was an alien?

…if we moved to Tennessee?

She would ask me as we hurtled down the mountain in her S-10 with the windows rolled down, shouting to be heard over the roar of the busted exhaust, the wind whipping her hair into a cyclone, the long, brown strands fading to blond at the tips where she'd bleached it herself in the kitchen sink a month before. She would ask me in the grocery store as I sat in the buggy with my legs folded, a book open on my lap, as she eyed two packs of discounted meat, trying to decide which would last longer. She would ask me as we sat on the porch at the end of a long day, both of us freshly showered, hair damp and dripping down our backs, making us shiver.

And it was my job to come up with an answer—something elaborate and strange and beautiful. A kind of story we told ourselves about the lives we'd never lead.

"That's right," she would say once I answered, hitching me up to sit on the rickety porch railing, my legs dangling over the edge. She would press her chest to my back and spread my arms out at my sides like I was flying through the inky dark. The only light visible from our single-wide trailer was Granny's porch light across the road, which she always kept on. "We can do anything, you and me."

After Mom took her door, I kept playing the question game on my own, except I played it with the fog in my chest. The questions got meaner and harder to answer. The day Granny was admitted to the hospital, I went home for a change of clothes and sat in the driveway listening to the questions my fog asked. What would it be like…

…if you hadn't messed up school?

…if you hadn't let Granny get sick?

…if you gave up and took your door?

The last question lingered. The door had ridden in the back seat on the way home, hovering by the rear window so it distorted everything behind me. As soon as I stopped the car and rolled down the windows, my door had floated outside. It was definitely bigger than it had been before. My finger still thrummed from where I'd touched it, but it didn't look like the door had taken anything from me—no missing skin, no blood, no scar. Still, I wondered what I'd done to help it grow as it hovered over Granny's flower beds by the front steps.

I adjusted the rearview mirror and looked across the road behind me at the place where I'd lived with my mother for the first nine years of my life. The trailer was slowly returning to the earth. The front porch—made of concrete and cinder blocks—slumped to one side like a bird with a broken wing. Some brave weed had punched a hole through the last remaining pane of glass in the living room window and thrust its head into the night. The front door was locked, though the only thing of value in the house had been taken long ago.

You're not doing much good here, my fog whispered. *Everybody might be better off without you around. Wherever that door goes can't be worse than here.*

I grabbed my phone and opened my texts. Carver had never responded that morning—not the first time I texted him or the second or the third. My last message to him was just: ???? My stomach churned at the sight. I felt foolish for asking for help, for sending so many messages in a row.

You need too much, my fog said. *Need less. Need nothing.*

I deleted the thread of text messages, then erased Carver's contact. It didn't mean much, really, but it made me feel better in the moment, like I could forget him as easily as he'd forgotten me.

I still hadn't eaten. When I'd stood up to leave the hospital, the waiting room had spun a little and bile had crept into the back of my throat. My mouth still tasted sour and my hands had that shaky feeling in them, a kind of weakness I thought I'd grown accustomed to at work. I closed my eyes and took a few deep breaths, listening to the thud of my heartbeat in my ears. I told myself that I would go inside and I would eat and I would watch a whole episode of *The Golden Girls* before I had to leave again. I said that over and over until, when I finally opened my eyes, I felt steady again.

Inside, the house looked clean and bright and warm. Julie stood by the stove, singing to herself. I listened for a few beats before I recognized the tune from Bible School and joined in, my voice warbling through the air, trying to reach Julie's high notes, but it never quite could. Julie turned, smiling, and opened her arms to me.

We sang, "Who's the king of the jungle? Who's the king of the sea? Who's the king of the universe, and who's the king of me? His name is J-E-S-U-S, yes!"

We laughed when we finished and I leaned into Julie's shoulder. "Why in God's name are you singing that song?"

"I don't know. Sometimes I get church songs in my head when I'm cooking." Julie shrugged. "I feel like the preacher would be real sad that the only thing I remember are the songs we sang at Bible School."

"They're the only things worth remembering," I said and sat down at the table.

Julie put a plate together for me and slid it across the worn tablecloth—soup beans with sausage and a chunk of corn bread still steaming. I could have cried it was so beautiful. I tore into the food without another word and let Julie do the talking, telling me about her day at work and whether or not she'd look good with bangs and how the Reverend had been in a car accident the week before and hadn't been acting like herself since. Then she finally sighed and pointed to my puffy eyes and said, "Since you're not going to tell me on your own, I'm going to ask. Who made you cry and where can I find them?"

I shook my head. "Do I have to talk about this?"

"Do you *have* to tell your best friend your problems? Do you *have* to unburden yourself? Do you *have* to suffer my compassion and gentle pats on the arm and world-class advice? Is that what you're asking?"

I rolled my eyes and told Julie what Dr. Owens said before I left the hospital. At first, she sat listening, but the longer I spoke, the more agitated she got until she was pacing the kitchen. Her long purple skirt swished over the floor as she walked, her little bare toes revealing themselves every other step. By the time I finished my story, I had a headache.

"You got any Tylenol?" I asked.

"In my purse." Julie pointed toward the living room.

As she paced, Julie named all the things she'd like to do to Dr. Owens, his property, and his various cars. Even as she said it, she reached for her wrist, then looked down at her hand, confused, before she went back to pacing. All through high school she had worn a rubber band around her wrist. It had been part of some therapy she was trying. Every time she had a negative thought—about hurting herself or wanting to die—she would snap the rubber band. It was supposed to deter her somehow, though it never really worked. One week she used the band so much that her wrist was bruised and bloody. I took it from her and put it on my own wrist and told her to tell me anytime she had those kinds of thoughts. I would take her punishment. It only lasted a couple hours. Seeing me hurt myself was too much for Julie, and she stopped using the band altogether. Eventually the Reverend stopped making her see the therapist who had suggested it. But Julie still reached for it sometimes when she was thinking bad thoughts, like about hurting Dr. Owens.

"He don't deserve what it would cost you to do all that," I said.

She said, "I know, I know. It's just things like this happen all the time. It feels like somebody is always trying to make things harder when they're already hard enough. I hate feeling like there's nothing I can do back, you know? I'd like to be the one doing the hurting for once."

She kept pacing as I dug through the contents of her bag, the same one she'd carried since high school, fake brown leather with a bright-yellow lining. She said she liked it because it was like carrying around her own personal sunshine. I pushed past her makeup, emergency tampons, a little notebook with daily affirmations written in Julie's thin, neat letters—*I am capable. I am more than my mistakes.*

I embrace possibility with an open heart—to a pair of sunglasses she'd broken two months ago but never had the heart to throw out and a book of crossword puzzles that was mostly finished, but I stopped when I found three small pill bottles. It didn't even occur to me that I should feel bad as I checked the labels. Julie's business was my business; it had always been that way. The prescriptions had been filled a month ago but the bottles still looked completely full. Julie hadn't been taking her meds.

A tangle of feelings knotted in my chest as I looked up at Julie—anger, frustration, sadness, confusion, but fear was the strongest of them all. Fear like a vise around my throat. Julie had attempted suicide in high school. She'd been placed in a care facility once and sent away for more camps and weekend retreats than I could count. It felt like she had one foot in the darkness all the time and I could never be sure when it would take her, or worse, when she would choose to step into it on her own. Who would I sing Bible School songs with if Julie wasn't here? Who would see a rock on the ground and pick it up and think of me? Who would think of me at all? The fear crested into something else inside me, and I wanted to throw the pills across the room and scream at Julie. I wanted to scare her into staying or chase her into leaving so I could give up this other feeling—this not knowing, this being afraid, this waiting, always waiting, for the worst thing to happen.

My little door floated around the corner of the room until it stopped between us. It distorted Julie, blurred her in places, replaced pieces of her with pieces of stars and faint purple light, made her half herself and half something else. Something bigger and smaller all at once. It wouldn't help to yell at her. I'd tried that before. I didn't want to hurt her. I didn't want to scare her or chase her away. I wanted to help and I knew yelling wouldn't help. I took a deep breath and put the bottles back in her purse and grabbed the Tylenol instead.

"Let's recap then." Julie stood in the middle of the kitchen with a ladle in her hand like a conductor's wand. My chest twinged again just looking at her. "The problem we have is that Granny needs someone who can be here to take care of her, but it can't be you because you work all the time."

"And it can't be anybody in the family," I said. "She'll refuse it."

"And we can't afford to hire anybody."

"Nope."

Julie tapped the ladle against her chin. "So what can we do?"

We lapsed into quiet for a while. Julie traded her ladle for a dishrag as she started cleaning up after dinner. She put away the leftover food in the butter containers we used as Tupperware as I rinsed my plate in the sink. I didn't even notice she had stopped until she came up behind me and held out the two bottles of pain pills I'd picked up from the pharmacy on the way home.

"Sell them," she said.

"What?"

Julie shook the bottles as though that would somehow make her point. "You need money to take care of Granny, right? What else do we have that's valuable? There ain't any other jobs in Sterns. The only good jobs are an hour away, and your car won't make it that far five days a week. Even if it did, you'd waste any extra money on gas. Sell Granny's pills."

I bit back a response about Julie taking her own medicine before she tried selling Granny's. I turned off the faucet and leaned against the sink. I felt so thin, like if someone held me up to the light they would see all the holes in me, all the places I didn't have time to mend.

"I can't do that," I said.

"I know it wouldn't be easy, but Carver could help. He got into some…stuff…in Cincinnati. He knows a lot of people around here who buy, and he could go with you. Make sure it was safe."

"It can't ever be safe when it's *illegal*. It won't matter how much money I could make if I get caught and wind up in jail. Or get Carver in trouble."

"People do it all the time!"

"I ain't 'people,'" I said. "You know how I am. The first time Granny looked sideways at me I'd end up confessing everything."

"Then don't look at her."

I rolled my eyes. "How are *you* the one suggesting I sell pills? You can't really think this is a good idea."

"What else are you going to do? If you can come up with some other way, I'll help. You know I will. But you could make enough to hire somebody to watch Granny and, and! Even enough to pay off your debt and get back in school. Then you can make *real money*. The kind that would let you take care of Granny forever."

I chewed on the inside of my lip until it hurt. I'd left college over a year ago when Granny had a small stroke. She hadn't lost any function permanently, but there were a few months where I had to be with her all the time, and we'd driven back and forth to Lexington every month for checkups. I'd lived off the grant money I got from the school and the only credit card I had. I failed all my classes that semester, and all that money I'd taken to survive had to be paid back to the school before I could take another class.

All together, the debt was less than five thousand dollars, but between my paycheck and Granny's disability check, I would spend the rest of my life trying to pay it off.

Julie led me to the kitchen table and sat me down. She put the bottles in front of me. "You wouldn't have to do it forever. Just long enough to get everything squared away, then you quit. Half the people on this mountain sell and the other half buy. It wouldn't be hard to get started."

I was halfway to believing it might work when I thought of the people on the mountain. The ones I knew were on medication just like Granny, most on a lot more.

"Yeah," I said, "a bunch of people who almost killed themselves working in mines and factories their whole life hoping for something better just so they could spend their old age on disability in a town that's dying faster than them and...it's not right. It's not right."

Julie sighed. She wrapped her arms around my shoulders and leaned her cheek against the top of my head and said, "Then we'll figure something else out. We will."

My little door floated into view from behind her, glittering and strange. It hovered above the bottles, casting its pretty shadows over them as though it was reminding me of all the choices I had, even if I didn't want them.

chapter eight

Granny wasn't alone when I returned to the hospital that night. Uncle Tim leaned against the ledge by the windows with a knot of chew distorting his jawline, a soda can in his hand for spit. His twins—Cody and Cameron—shared a chair and a video game between them, looking like a many-limbed deity in the faint blue glow of their screen. My cousin Cheryl sat at the foot of Granny's bed showing her a scarf that she was knitting that looked like a crime had been committed against the yarn. Granny tried to take it from her hands but something fell off the scarf and they both stared, horrified, at the knotted pile of fabric.

I smiled as I watched Cheryl, Granny, and Tim try to untangle the scarf together, each of them making it worse in their turn. My little door moved from my side to hover over Granny's bed. It cast my family's faces in faint shades of blue and pink, turned them into a little galaxy, each of them a planet in their own right. They were cosmic—star-kissed and moon-touched. I couldn't help but wonder how Mom would have looked among them, sitting on her knees just a little too close to the edge of the bed, Granny telling her to scoot in before she fell and broke her neck, Mom's head thrown back in a laugh as Cheryl's yarn became more and more tangled. I wanted to say all this aloud, to share Mom with everyone, but I couldn't. Mentioning Mom's name was one sure way to drain the joy from any room. Everyone suddenly looking to Granny or to the door, remembering appointments they hadn't remembered before, mumbling excuses. Mom had left us all, but she'd been one of us first. I couldn't understand why everyone only seemed to remember the leaving.

Too soon, a voice came over the PA and said visiting hours were over. Everyone lined up to give Granny a kiss on the forehead before they filed into the hallway.

When they were gone, my little door floated over to the window and stared at its own shifting reflection. Without all the distraction, Granny looked small inside the hospital bed. The sheets were a snowdrift, and she was the only person brave enough to face the cold. The harsh lighting made the veins on her arms and hands stand out like narrow rivers. Bruises formed around the IV line in her arm. Her hair, normally pin-curled, drifted into a hazy cloud behind her ears. Without the glimmer of my little door, she looked like what she was—a sick seventy-three-year-old woman.

I said, "You're quite the celebrity tonight."

She shrugged one thin-boned shoulder. "I'm a charming woman."

"I always thought of you as a bit sour myself."

"I'll give you something to think about." She patted my knee as I sat down on the bed beside her. "Did you bring what I asked?"

I pulled my backpack onto my lap and dug through it until I found what Granny had wanted me to bring: a plastic bag filled with prayer cloths and other supplies. She'd brought it home from church after I convinced her to go. We made a small assembly line on the hospital bed. Granny held each cloth in her hand, closed her eyes, and prayed a blessing into the fibers, transferring a little of herself into the thin cloth, every frayed edge carrying some echo of her faith. Then she handed the cloth to me and I pinned it to a little flyer with information on all the churches in the area. Normally, she would deliver them herself, dropping me off at work and then heading off on her own route to deposit prayer cloths in mailboxes all over the county. She'd always preferred community outreach to prayer meetings or even church services. God didn't live in the church, she said. He lived in the world, and so would she.

"How'd you manage to score a room all by yourself? You didn't bribe the head nurse, did you?"

"Of course not."

"You threatened her then?"

Granny rolled her eyes. "They had me in a room with a girl about your age at first. She was detoxing. Moaning all over the place asking for pain medicine. I told them I couldn't stand to be in there watching all that so they moved me."

"Oh."

She didn't say the girl reminded her too much of my mother, or some imagined future she'd feared for me since the moment I came to live with her, but I knew it all the same. I'd tried to ask Granny about Mom's drinking once after she took her door, but Granny had stopped short right there in the Save A Lot produce aisle and said, "It don't matter why she drank. None of that matters. That door might have given her a way out but she left us years ago." She hadn't spoken the whole rest of the trip and hadn't offered to take us by Dairy Queen for a dipped cone, either. She didn't laugh at my jokes or hang up the drawing I made for her, and I was so panicked, so scared she would send me to live with Uncle Tim or one of my cousins that I vowed never to ask her about Mom's drinking again.

And I vowed never to drink myself, never to do anything like Mom had done. I'd held that promise, mostly. And the few times

I did drink in high school had been awful. I was seventeen the first time I tasted Smirnoff Ice, and I was so mangled with guilt that I made myself throw up in the Ace Hardware parking lot while Julie distracted the boys we were with.

Now here I was, considering selling Granny's own pain medicine for money. Maybe I was more like that girl in the hospital room than I thought. I was certainly more like my mother.

Granny waved a prayer cloth in front of my face and whistled. "You all right, little britches?"

"Fine as frog hair," I said and took the cloth from her hand. "What did you tell Tim and them about how you got sick?" I tried to keep my voice even as I spoke. Granny didn't like to lie to anyone, especially her children, and she liked talking about her lies even less.

Granny sniffed. "I told them I got started cleaning out the shed and lost track of time. That I forgot my coat and caught a cold that caught hold of me."

She handed me a prayer cloth and I pinned it to the paper. I said, "You ever think about telling them the truth?"

"I don't want them to worry."

"They're your babies. They're supposed to worry."

"Well, if worrying is all they'd do, then it wouldn't be so bad." She jerked another cloth from the bag. "I've seen what happens to people like me. The family starts out trying to help and then they take over. It happens so slow that you don't even notice at first, but all of sudden they're making all your decisions without even asking if that's what you want."

"I wouldn't let that happen."

"You would try," Granny said. "But you'd want what's best for me. And somewhere along the way you'll all start believing that I don't know what's best. I'm not letting anybody run my life. Especially not at the very end."

She dropped the cloth into my lap, and I stared down at it for a moment. I wanted to fight with her, to tell her she was wrong, but I wasn't sure she was. I picked up the cloth and clucked my tongue. "You didn't even pray over this one."

"I can pray and argue at the same time. Now pin that and quit back-talking me. I'm sick." She feigned a cough.

I shook my head and pinned the cloth to a flyer.

"I am, though," Granny said.

"You're what? Ornery?"

"Sick," she said. "But ornery, too."

"We have to do something about it," I said. "If you won't tell the others, then we have to figure something out on our own."

"I know that. That's why I talked to Dr. Owens."

"I don't like that man."

"I know, but he's the best we've got. And I need my memories. I wonder sometimes, why couldn't the Lord take something else? Why'd he see fit to take my mother's face? Or the day that you called me Granny for the first time? What does he need with my memories?"

"I'll remember for you," I said. "You just have to ask me. And if I don't remember, I'll just make it up. It'll be entertaining even if it ain't true."

Granny closed her hand around mine. Her touch was cold and soft. I wanted to cry but I didn't want to make Granny sad, so I gritted my teeth and pushed down until my jaw ached.

"I know you would," Granny said. "I know you'd go out and hunt my memories down if you could. Bring them back like a deer slung over your shoulders. I wish it worked that way, baby. But there's some things we can do. Dr. Owens said I should have a routine. Stay active."

I nodded. "That sounds all right."

"My friend Betty is down at the Rose Garden and she said—"

"I'm not putting you in a home, Granny."

Granny held up her hand and I fell quiet. "*Listen.* I ain't got much breath and I can't use it telling you to hush. I'm just going there to *visit.* They're putting on a talent show and Betty asked me to sing with her, like we used to back at church. I told her I'd come and I might sing. I ain't made my mind up about that yet."

"But not to stay."

"No, not to stay." Granny took a deep breath. "I don't want to end my life that way."

"You won't."

"I want to die in my own home even if I can't remember an inch of it."

"Granny."

Granny closed her eyes. "Let's not borrow any worries from tomorrow, all right? I ain't willing to tell my stubborn children but I'm willing to try some other things. And you'll help me keep this life of mine, small as it is?"

"Of course, Granny. I'll do everything I can."

"I know you will." She covered my hand with hers and squeezed. "All right, I'm done. Take all this away and put some *Matlock* on the television. I want to have good dreams tonight."

I did as she said, then made myself an awkward little bed in the stiff, floral-printed chair my cousins had shared earlier. I curled into myself as much as I could and watched Granny's breathing, waiting for it to become slow and regular, and though she slept, her breath still moved nervously through her body, sometimes shallow enough to barely move the covers, sometimes deep and gasping, her hand fluttering against the blanket, wingless.

I owed her everything.

My grandfather had died less than a year before my mom took her door. Granny had lost her husband and child in a single breath and inherited a granddaughter to raise. She'd been a housewife and farmer her whole life but had gone out the week I moved in with her and gotten a job at the button factory in the next county. Forty hours a week on her feet, hunched over a line. She'd come home with her joints swollen and back aching, and we still couldn't afford a vacation or to send me on field trips at school. But she'd always found a way to keep us fed and safe. She'd needed me to do the same for her for only two years and I was already fumbling, on the verge of failure.

I looked at my little door floating above me and wished I could send Granny through it instead. There were stories of people who had tried. A seventeen-year-old boy who carried his newborn son in his arms and stepped through his door hoping they would both be together on the other side. They'd found the baby lying in the backyard a few hours later, crying, his little bear onesie soaked through with rain.

Granny said she'd never gotten a door of her own. I wondered if she wished for one now. I wondered what she would say if I told her mine had come. I knew what she would think—that I'd leave her just like Mom did. I'd become just one more name no one mentioned, and without me, Granny would be shuffled off to the Rose Garden where she would grow smaller and smaller every day, until she became a name no one mentioned, either.

"Can you go over there instead?" I whispered to my door, pointing to the air above Granny's bed.

For a moment, nothing happened, and I wondered, all over again, if it was really there for me, if it was real at all.

Then my door slipped through the dim room and hovered above Granny.

"Thank you," I whispered.

I watched the door's light drift over her face like clouds over water.

Nurses came and went, checking the monitors, asking if I needed another blanket, and I gave the same answers and they scribbled the same notes on their charts. I slept fitfully, if at all, until there was a knock on the door. My phone was dead when I reached to check the time. I untangled myself from the chair and fumbled across the room, desperate to keep the noise from waking Granny. I opened the door and immediately went to shut it again.

"Wait, wait, wait!" Carver grabbed the door and eased it back open.

"Keep your voice down. Granny's asleep."

"Sorry."

I stepped into the hallway, squinting against the fluorescent lights. Carver stood with his head down. The collar of his shirt had been pulled out until the seams had torn, revealing an inch of collarbone on one side. He was always tugging at his collar. Said it felt like his shirts were choking him, like he couldn't get enough good air. He held out a paper bag dotted with grease.

"I brought you some food," he said. "I got you chicken strips and a burger because I wasn't sure what you'd want."

"I already ate."

He held the bag out again. "Well, you might get hungry later."

"You can hold it out there until your arm breaks off but I ain't going to take it."

"Come on, Maren, I just got your texts an hour ago. My fool phone died on me and I didn't have a charger."

"Where've you been?"

"Out with Rowdy and them," he mumbled.

I rolled my eyes. "Out drunk with the boy who used to kick your ass for fun?"

"We was kids then. He didn't know what he was doing and neither did I. He ain't so bad now. He gave me a job. I start at the garage on Monday."

"He's a jackass and you know it."

"Yeah, well, he's my boss's son now, too. And I need this job. When Rowdy asked me to go out with them last night, I went. I didn't know he meant going all the way to Lexington."

"Right. And it ain't got nothing to do with how you used to follow after them and how they treated you like shit all through middle school. When are you going to stop chasing after people who don't care nothing about you?"

A nurse walked by and eyed us up and down, the kind of look that said she'd be happy to call the security guard if we got too loud. Carver waited until she passed to say, "I'm sorry. I am. I wish I'd come when you first texted me—"

"But you didn't," I said. "So much for being somebody who makes things better instead of worse."

I felt awful the minute I said it. Felt worse when Carver turned and walked a few steps down the hallway still clutching the bag of food in his hand. He stood with his back to me, staring at the floor. Part of me wanted to apologize, but my tongue felt locked in place. He hadn't been there when I needed him and the fact of my needing him was too much for me to bear. I wanted to hurt him for hurting me. I wanted to board over the feelings between us, brick them up, seal them away so tight that I would never be tempted to reach for him again.

"Look, we both know that this thing between us would have only ended one way," I said. "So let's quit now and save us all some trouble, all right?"

Carver walked back and leaned against the wall on the other side of Granny's door. Her heart monitor beeped rhythmically from inside, filling the silence until Carver said, "Is that what you want?"

I looked away. That question always brought something to my throat, something small and clawed, slick with its own blood. Something desperate.

My fog whispered, *It doesn't matter what you want.*

So I said, "Granny needs your help."

"That's not an answer to my question."

"No. It's not."

Carver shook his head. "Well, Granny knows I'd do anything for her. What does she need?"

I sighed. "How much do you know about selling pills?"

chapter nine

I spent most of the next day at work trying not to think about what I would be doing that night. Carver was supposed to text me the details once he worked everything out. All I had to do was bring the pills and my car, and he would take care of the rest. I hadn't let him leave the hospital without saying *If you remember to text, that is* at least five times, but after the first couple times even I could hear how sad I sounded.

But instead of thinking of nursing homes or Carver's forlorn expression or the pill bottles at the bottom of my purse or anything else that made my blood pressure spike, I thought of my door.

I knew it wasn't a pet, but part of me had begun to think of it that way. Granny never let me have a dog no matter how much I begged. She said she didn't believe in pets, like pets were fairies or love at first sight, so I spent my whole childhood longing for a companion. Now I finally had one.

From the first night I'd found it, the door had followed me wherever I went. It walked beside me through the house, never falling more than a room behind. It came when I called and seemed to understand most of what I said. And since it never spoke, the door was an excellent listener, if a bit judgmental. It rode in the back seat of my car and sat with me in the hospital and followed me into my bedroom at night and hovered over me as I slept, the faint heat of it warming my cheeks and shoulders until I kicked off the covers and slept only under its glow. It was easy to see its constant presence as a kind of loyalty. Easy to forget what it was: a doorway to some other world.

And doorways were meant to be used.

There were stories of people who had kept their doors for months, even years, without taking them. Ida Ross, for instance. She was from one of the few Black families in town. Worked in the library stocking books, married to a coal miner, mother to three children. Her door began as a hole in the wall of her bedroom no bigger than a pin. She only noticed it because it was aligned perfectly to allow a beam of sunlight to shine directly onto her eye as she slept in her bed on the other side of the room. She ignored it at first, not fully believing what it was until she realized the sun it reflected didn't match our sun. The light came from some other source, rising and falling according to some other place's day, twinkling with some other world's starlight.

Some people claim she kept the door a year, others claim two. Ida herself never spoke of it again after she sent it away. Her sister, Catherine, told the story though, often with Ida sitting right beside her in church, fanning herself with a tithing envelope.

According to Catherine, it hadn't been the fact that the hole slowly got bigger and bigger until it was almost the size of the wall itself that made Ida send it away. It had been the heat. The hole emanated a soft, damp heat that grew stronger with every passing day until she couldn't sleep for it, until her lips cracked and her skin chafed. Until she stood up, sweat soaking through her nightgown, and told her door that she couldn't go where it led.

For a moment, nothing happened. Ida had covered her face with her hands, distraught, almost delirious with the heat her husband couldn't feel. He'd brought her a bag of frozen half-runner beans wrapped in a towel to help keep her cool but they'd thawed within an hour, leaving a damp circle on the sheets. When Ida looked back up, the hole was gone, and so was the heat.

There were other stories, too.

Some said they'd started having nightmares after too long. Or hearing a song no one else could hear, murmured words from a chorus they didn't recognize, a harmony made by no tongue they'd ever known. A whistling sound, a rash that started on their hands and slowly worked its way up their body. The doors never came with the same cost but they always had a price when kept too long. Of course, like so many things about the doors, no one was sure how long "too long" was, and the doors gave no easy answer.

My little door hovered in the middle of the last aisle of the grocery store/gas station where I worked. On one side of the aisle were overpriced motor oil and air filters, on the other side overpriced tampons and deodorant. My door seemed particularly interested in a gallon of electric-blue antifreeze.

It was hard to believe it could ever do anything to hurt me or try to drive me toward a decision. All it did was spin and look pretty and keep me warm at night.

But it was a door all the same, and all doors changed. I couldn't know yet what it would do to drive me toward a decision, but it would, in time. It would.

I walked to the back of the store where a tiny closet served as the manager's office, though the manager rarely came in these days. I pulled out my cell phone and checked my messages again, checked to make sure I had service. Carver hadn't texted yet, but neither had Uncle Tim. He was bringing Granny home from the hospital and promised to call as soon as she was settled in. I gripped the phone tight inside my hand like I might intimidate it into giving me what I wanted, but it was silent.

It was just past seven in the morning and the store was empty but for Ms. Pack, a retired school lunch lady who wandered the aisles in her motorized scooter. She had a twin brother who had gotten a door when they were seventeen. He'd taken it. Everyone in town said something changed afterward, like a light had gone off inside Ms. Pack and never shone again. It didn't seem entirely fair to think of her that way, but I suppose there were plenty of people who thought of *me* that way, too. Ms. Pack rumbled past me and lifted a small silver key ring with a single key attached.

"Found this in the corner. Somebody must have lost it," she said.

My little door floated over like it wanted to inspect the key itself. I hadn't touched my door since that afternoon in the doctor's office a week before, but I'd been tempted to. I should have put the key ring in the lost-and-found box and waited for someone to come claim it, but it was early and I was tired and I wanted to know if my door could touch something that wasn't me. I was the only person in the world the door was real for, and it seemed only fair the reverse would be true, too. That everything was just shadow and silhouette to the door and I was the only source of light, the one glowing, solid thing it could see, and that's why it followed me. That's why it stayed so close. Without me, it would be lost.

Besides, feeding the door was the only thing I'd found that I could give to it. I wasn't used to anything staying in my life for no reason. I had to have something to offer to the door, some gift, or else it would leave eventually.

I held the key up to my door like I might unlock it, expecting it to respond like it had to my finger—a slow, gentle parting, a feeling of warmth creeping, building.

Instead, a beam of light burst from my door like a firework exploding. I flinched and pulled away, ducking my head into the closet. I dropped the key but didn't hear it clatter to the floor. The heat from the door intensified for a moment. It warmed the back of my neck like August sunshine. When I looked back, the key was gone and my door was spinning as slowly as ever.

It was just a little bigger than before.

Ms. Pack wheeled down the aisle beside me, frowning at my pale, sweaty face. She didn't seem to have noticed a thing. "You see a ghost?"

"Just you."

Ms. Pack held up her middle finger at me as she rolled past the antifreeze, my little door painting her back in a wash of pastel colors. I laughed, but it was a strangled sound. I looked down at my hand, searching for some mark, some burn, but there was nothing. The key was gone and my door stretched a little wider than before, its light bright enough now that everything it passed cast a shadow. It followed Ms. Pack down the far aisle as the front door of the store swung open and the little bell overhead jingled. Julie walked inside wearing a Carhartt coat two sizes too big and a woman followed close behind. The sight of them together made my stomach sink.

Rachel had grown her hair out since she got out of jail for possession, but she looked more or less the same as she always had. She and Julie had dated on and off since high school. They were the kind of couple who thought their love was part of some epic story while everyone else around them saw it as a tragedy. I would call them fire and gasoline, but that doesn't quite capture how truly terrible they were together. It was more like a hungry bear stumbling onto a Girl Scout campout.

Just as they got inside, Ms. Pack made it to the only checkout counter and began to tap the little bell we kept there. She looked right at me as she tapped it, her pale hand like a jackhammer pounding the bell over and over and over.

I jogged behind the counter with a big smile on my face, took the bell from under Ms. Pack's hand, and dropped it in the trash can beside me. "It's a shame the bell broke like that, but I sure appreciate you testing it for us."

"I like to perform my civic duties when I can." Ms. Pack plucked a pair of thin-framed glasses on a chain from her purse and placed them delicately across her nose.

"You're an example for us all," I said and then leaned forward to look at Julie and Rachel. They were huddled against the glass counter where the manager kept his baseball card collection. He said the cards were priced to sell, but we all knew no one would ever buy them. He really just wanted a place to put them and brag about something no one else cared about. "You know, Jules," I said, "you could have hopped on over here and checked Ms. Pack out."

Julie glanced over her shoulder. "I would, hun, but I haven't clocked in yet."

I said, "Well, maybe you ought to do that, hun."

Ms. Pack snorted as she handed me a wrinkled twenty. "You two ain't changed a bit. She used to distract me while you took extra cookies out of the lunch line. The two of you was always into something." Ms. Pack waved her hand in the air as I opened the door for her. "Tell your granny I said hello."

With her gone, I turned to Rachel and Julie, who leaned against the glass display case, Rachel's fingers toying with the buttons on Julie's coat. I said, "You buying something? Because this store is for customers only."

Rachel smiled at me. She had a tattoo of a rose behind her right ear, and I thought about smacking it and claiming I'd mistaken it for a bug but I held back. She said, "I was just making sure Jules got to work safe."

"You dropped her off?"

Julie took a step back. "Carver was still asleep by the time I got up. Rachel was going this way anyhow and offered to take me."

"I was happy to do it," Rachel said, finally turning toward the door. "I'll call you tonight, okay?"

"I'll answer," Julie said, giggling.

"And I'll vomit right here on the floor," I said, watching as Rachel sauntered back out to her truck. "God, I hate that woman."

Julie rolled her eyes but didn't say anything as she walked around the counter to clock in. I stood in the empty aisle with my arms crossed, waiting.

"I'm waiting," I said.

Julie looked up. "For what?"

"An explanation."

"You ain't my parole officer. I don't have to tell you where I am or who I'm with."

"No, but I thought I was your friend, which might warrant telling me that you were thinking of going back to that disaster. Did you not get burned enough the last three times y'all tried this?"

"People change."

"That's your defense? People change?"

"I ain't defending myself. And if you keep yelling, I won't talk to you at all."

I should have stopped right there. I knew it then, in that moment when I looked at Julie's pursed lips, her hair already slipping free of the bun she'd wrestled it into. There were dark circles under her eyes like she hadn't been sleeping well. I knew I was bringing too much to this fight, more than belonged to just Julie, but I wasn't finished yet. There was still so much anger and frustration pressing against my throat, and I had to get it out somehow. I could never figure out exactly what I was fighting so I could never strike against it. It was like trying to tear down the sky. I could never reach it, never hold it, never hurt it. But Julie was there or Carver or anybody else near and breathing, and I could hurt them when I couldn't hurt anything else, and sometimes that felt like enough.

So I said, "Are these the kind of choices you make when you stop taking your medication?"

Julie went very still. The silence stretched out between us. I could hear every car that passed by on the road beside the store, horns honking, doors opening and closing, but no one else walked in. It was just me and Julie, alone with what I'd said.

Julie pointed her finger at me and then dropped it. "You went through my purse. You…you went through my things. Didn't you? That's the only way you could know."

"Apparently that's the only way I can find out anything about you anymore since you won't tell me a damn thing yourself."

"I don't owe you every detail of my life, Maren Walker! That's not the way friendship works. Are you trying to say that you tell me everything? Are you the only person in this world allowed to keep secrets?"

I almost turned to look at my little door as it hovered by the dog food aisle like a child eavesdropping on its parents' fight, but I resisted. Julie shook her head and looked almost sad.

She said, "If I haven't told you something, it's only because I don't want to add any more to your plate than you already have."

"Well, it's on my plate anyway, ain't it? Why did you stop? You know it never goes well when you stop."

"I'm not talking to you about this."

"You have to talk to somebody."

"I don't *have* to do anything. I'm grown."

I snorted. "You sure ain't acting grown right now."

"Should I be acting more like you then? Running around like it's my job to solve everybody's problems whether they've asked me to or not? Trying to make everybody do just as I say. I never thought I'd see the day you turned into the Reverend."

That pulled me up short. Even Julie looked surprised that the words had come out of her mouth.

I took my jacket off the peg by the door and slipped into it. "Well, I never thought I'd see the day I understood the Reverend, but here we are. I'm taking my break."

I walked outside and wished it were colder. Wished the world wasn't thawing out from winter—little buds of green unfurling on the trees, the hills shaking off their hibernation. I needed a hard wind to blow sharp and strike me, bite me, some kind of feedback that would whittle the world down to something I could take. Anything other than the dread and shame and guilt and hurt that swirled around inside my chest. My fog whispered almost too quick and quiet to hear, *It's no wonder Nell left you. There's nothing good in you worth staying for.*

I held my fist up to the brick wall and thought briefly of driving my hand against it, knowing how much it would hurt, knowing I couldn't afford the doctor bill that would follow. That's when my little door slipped between me and the wall, glowing and spinning just a few inches away from my fist like it was stopping me from making a bad decision.

Or like it was giving me a second choice—come inside and leave all of this behind.

I unclenched my fingers and let my hand fall to my side. It wasn't wrong, my door. I had another choice now. A new way out. If things went badly while I was selling pills, if everything fell to pieces, I wouldn't have to be here to pick them up myself. For once, I could be the one leaving.

My phone buzzed in my pocket and I fumbled for it, my fingers shaking over the keys until a text from Carver appeared.

It read: got everything worked out for our date ;) i'll come by after i get off work at 7. bring me a root beer plz.

I sighed. Carver had come through in finding someone interested in buying some of Granny's pain medicine. At least one thing might go right that day.

chapter ten

When I think back, I remember many things about the night Carver and I made that first deal, but there's at least one important thing that I don't.

I remember waiting on the porch for ten minutes, then twenty, then forty-five until Carver finally pulled into the driveway, rattling off excuses for why he was late. I remember shaking the can of root beer I'd bought him, the only retaliation I could afford because I needed his help, and the fact of that need burned in me until I thought I might turn to ash. I remember going over the pill prices with him—$10 for Lorcet, $15 for Percocet, not a penny less—and then doing a different math in my head over and over. I had two months' worth of each pill, which meant if I sold them for that price, I could make $3,000. That was over half of my debt, the equivalent of more than two months of work at the store, and all because of something I could fit in the pocket of my purse.

I remember the radio forecast calling for scattered showers and thinking maybe we should go home because this didn't seem like the kind of thing someone should do in the rain and because I was terrified of making that kind of money, of what it might mean, of what it might change, of how it would feel to lose all that money before I'd ever even held it. The only comfort I could give myself was to repeat over and over inside my head, *This is for Granny, this is for Granny.*

What I don't remember is when I started to cry.

Carver tells me it wasn't until we got to the top of Burnt Ridge and turned off the car and everything was quiet that I broke down. But I don't remember it like that. I remember the Christmas lights strung along the front porch of the house we pulled up to and how my little door stayed outside with those lights the whole time, like it recognized itself in them, like it was grateful for the company of some other shining thing. I remember talking to the men in the house, the ones who wanted to buy Granny's pills. I remember their names: Timothy and Ryan Napier, cousins, not brothers. We talked until we found our point of overlap—that they'd convinced my mother to bring them a fifth of Tvarscki when she was working at the liquor store over the county line.

"I think I was half in love with her back then," Timothy said.

"Hell, you was fifteen," Ryan said. "You were half in love with the telephone pole after you drank most of that fifth."

They didn't talk about how it was less than a year after she bought them cheap vodka that she took her little door. They didn't remember her leaving, only her being—how our mothers partied together most weekends, and the way Nell danced in doorways; how loudly she laughed when she beat someone at poker; and how no one could convince her to stay past ten o'clock because she had to get home to me, had to read me a story like she'd promised.

I didn't tell them that she rarely read me stories, but she would pick me up on nights like those, her breath smelling sweet and sour, and twirl me, sleepy and soft, around the yard, the unmown grass tickling the soles of my bare feet as Granny watched us from her front porch.

I remember Carver's hand coming to rest on the small of my back as Timothy shook his head and said, "She was a good one, that Nell," and we all dwindled into quiet. I remember selling the pills in that quiet, just a few exchanges of hands. I remember that the bills I shoved into the back pocket of my jeans were a little damp.

I remember walking back out to my car and taking one of the prayer cloths Granny and I had put together from my glove box. I slipped it into their mailbox without really knowing why, just that it seemed like the right thing to do at the time. I remember thinking about Mom and how nice it was to talk about her without feeling worried about how someone might react. To say her name where it didn't sound like a curse word, to smile in her memory. I hadn't thought of how selling pills would bring me closer to the people that loved Mom best, but I was glad for it then.

I tried to explain all this to Carver but I kept fumbling over my words, and I think I was crying before the blue lights flashed behind us. I was crying before John Edward got out of his cruiser, crying as I watched him walk toward us, his body distorted by my little door, which floated in the back seat, its shifting, swirling colors making John Edward look like some kind of archangel descending on us in the dark. I remember, most of all, wiping my eyes dry and calming myself as I rolled my window down.

"Well, Maren Walker, it's not like you to be driving this fast," John Edward said as he leaned one arm along the hood of my car. "You got a door you need to take?"

Carver snorted. I hadn't been speeding. Both of us remember that. But I laughed a little too loudly and said, "I guess it's been a long day. How fast was I going?"

"License and registration."

I nudged Carver's thigh and he started digging through the glove box. The bag of prayer cloths dropped onto the floor and I picked them up, fished one out, and handed it to John Edward alongside my license. I said, "I heard your mom's back in cancer treatment. Give her one of these from Granny."

John Edward took the cloth from my hands and rubbed it between his fingers. "I'll do that. How we doing on that registration?"

"Still looking," Carver said.

John Edward leaned down a little more until his face was almost level with mine. "When'd you get back into town, Greene?"

"Couple weeks ago," Carver said.

"Big city too much for you?" John Edward winked at me like we were sharing some inside joke. I smiled.

"Something like that," Carver said. He pulled out a wrinkled-looking piece of paper and held it out to John Edward.

"I'll take it from her," he said.

I snatched the paper from Carver's fingers before he could speak and handed it out the window. John Edward barely glanced down at it, but he didn't give it back, either. I stared at my license and registration as he talked to Carver, not really listening, just wanting to take back what was mine so I could leave, but John Edward curled his hand toward his chest.

"What's got y'all on the other side of the county this late?" he asked.

"Dropping off these cloths for Granny," I said. "I told her they could wait until morning but she wasn't having it."

John Edward leaned back as a car approached, waved two stiff fingers as it passed. "Been a lot of activity up that way lately."

He said *activity* as though it were italicized. I nodded. "That so?"

"You've heard about the new task force, haven't you? I'm heading it up with a couple boys from the state police. They normally don't give things like that to a town as small as this but I fought for it. Impressed upon them the need that's here."

"Sounds like a lot of work," I said.

"It is. It is. But I can handle it. We're going to be cleaning up this town. Got a lot of big things planned now that the headquarters are finished."

"You mean that single-wide trailer sitting in the parking lot behind the Rite Aid?" Carver asked.

My fingers clenched into a fist.

"Was that supposed to be funny?" John Edward said, dipping his head into the open window until he hovered over my cheek. "You ought to have a little more respect for the people who keep you safe."

"I respect my family plenty," Carver said.

A slow smile tugged at one corner of John Edward's mouth. "You know there's a lot of drugs out this way. You ain't been using tonight, have you, Greene?"

Carver grinned and I saw the whole night exploding in that smile—saw us sitting by the side of the road as John Edward searched the car, saw the moment he found Granny's pill bottles in my purse. I could see the look of heartache on Granny's face when she found out, how Uncle Tim would shake his head, how half the town would feign remorse that I'd ended up being so much like Mom after all.

I couldn't have that. I couldn't be undone right at the beginning.

So I said, "Carver's just angry because we broke up."

John Edward looked down at me. His face was far too close. I wanted to tip my seat back but I was afraid to move.

"Do what?" he said.

"I dumped him," I said. "Just before you pulled us over. Maybe that's what made me speed. I found out he's been watching porn. Real weird stuff."

Carver made a strangled sound beside me.

I said, "I'm just trying to get him home so I can be done with him."

John Edward grinned. "That true, Greene?"

Carver's mouth was open but he didn't say a word.

"Well," John Edward said, "I can't say I'm surprised." He looked over my license one more time before he handed everything back inside. I tucked them under my thigh and smiled.

"I'll just give you a warning this time," he said. "But be careful. And let me know if you have any more problems, all right? You're one of the bright spots in this county. I'd hate to see you lose that shine. Greene, I'm sure I'll be seeing you."

John Edward tipped the prayer cloth at me before he walked back to his cruiser. I was shaking as I turned my car back on and eased onto the road. We didn't speak as John Edward followed us. It seemed like he might never break away, like he intended to see us home and make sure Carver left, but he finally turned onto the highway headed back toward Sterns.

"Fucking prick," Carver said. "Are you all right? Maren? Turn right here."

I listened without asking why. My breath heaved through my chest and came out as a gasp, then another. I sounded like I was drowning. I felt like it, too. Everything that had happened that night and the night before and every night of my life felt like it was pouring down on me in waves.

Carver shifted in his seat until he faced me. He put one hand along the bottom of the wheel to help guide me, and he told me every turn to take until we pulled into an empty field atop Burnt Ridge and he turned off the car.

chapter eleven

I was shaking by then. Sobbing. Babbling.

I don't remember most of what I said, but I know that whatever I thought came out of my mouth. It was like there was finally no more room inside me. No place for anything to hide.

I know I told Carver how everything was my fault. How Granny being sick was because of me and the fact that I couldn't protect her or help her or give her the care she needed. How Julie was angry because I couldn't be quiet when I needed to be quiet and how my mother had left because I wasn't reason enough to stay, and if all this went wrong, if we were caught or someone got hurt, then it would all be on me, too, and I didn't know if I could carry one more thing.

"I don't have enough hands," I said. "I can't hold it all."

Carver sat beside me without saying a word. He just listened and nodded and looked impossibly sad.

After a while I stopped talking. The only sound left was my ragged breathing, and it reminded me of Granny. The way her breath caught in her lungs like there wasn't enough room in her, either. I didn't want her to die suffocating. I didn't want her to die not remembering who she was. Who I was. There were so many things in the world I didn't want that I was running out of ways to run from them. There weren't that many directions left, and every choice I made seemed to narrow them further and further until it felt like there was no place to go that didn't end in pain.

I cried until I couldn't anymore.

Until I hiccuped and coughed and leaned over the steering wheel completely spent. Carver rested his hand between my shoulder blades. His touch was as light as a sunbeam breaking through the clouds.

After a while he said, "Granny isn't sick because of you. She's probably alive because of you. You talk about failing her, but what about all the ways you've helped her?"

I didn't answer.

"And Julie won't leave you. She might go off for a while but she always comes back."

I shrugged.

"And Nell didn't leave because of you, either," Carver said. "I'll never understand her reasons but I know it wasn't you. She loved you, Maren. In her own messy way."

I leaned back and swiped at my eyes. I said, "That just leaves you then."

"What about me?"

"You left, too. Up and moved from Blackdamp. You were gone for three years, Carver. Three. And you keep leaving every time you don't show up or don't answer my texts or don't do what you say you're going to do. You're always leaving me and I've been left enough."

He was quiet for a moment, then said, "You think I left because of you?"

"Is it supposed to be a coincidence that you left right after I kissed you?"

I stared straight ahead at the place where the ridge gave way to nothing. Tall, yellowed grass, then emptiness. My little door hovered there, shining faintly, like an invitation. I imagined walking up to the ridge and tipping over slowly, my head leading my body, and a feeling like cold water as I slipped through my little door. I'd break through a lake on the other side of a different world with a purpled sky above me, the trees like bruises, fruit fallen on the ground, split open, rotting, and sweet.

For most of my life there was a part of me that believed I didn't belong here—in Blackdamp, in Granny's house, in this world. And that part of me ached at the sight of my door, at the thought of home. I wanted so badly to feel like I belonged, and it seemed so much easier to believe that my belonging waited on the other side of my door in some place I'd never seen than to believe that it was here, somewhere around me, waiting for me to find it. To make it so.

Carver stared at the dashboard with a stern expression. He didn't look at me as he said, "You're right. Not about why I left—you're completely wrong about that—but I should have told you why I was leaving. I'm sorry that I didn't. I'm sorry I didn't call. Really."

I hadn't expected him to apologize, and the moment he did, my anger faltered, deflated. All I could think to say was, "Thank you."

"I hope you believe me when I say it didn't have anything to do with you. You've always been one of the best things about this place, but I was so..." He shook his head. "I was so messed up when I left."

I looked over at him. "Why?"

"You know, I'd hoped I'd never have to talk about this. I don't know why it's so hard, but I guess it's time. All right." He took a deep breath. "You remember me talking about Rowdy and me getting something started before I left?"

I shook my head. "I remember thinking it was a dumb idea to work with Rowdy. I stand by that now."

Carver half smiled. "Well, he was trying to start his own garage. Wanted to get out from under his daddy's thumb and do something of his own. He had just about everything lined up but he needed a partner. Somebody to put the money down with him. He asked me."

"Oh. Why didn't you do it?"

"I didn't have the money. I've never been good at saving. So Rowdy convinced me to ask for it. He had me all hyped up thinking it was this great plan. So I went to Pap and asked for a loan. I thought he'd be proud that I wanted to start my own business like he did. But he had all these questions about interest rates and how long I'd take to pay the loan back and what our business plan was, and I had no answers. Looking back, I should have been able to tell him, but at the time it felt like, I don't know. Like he didn't trust me. Like he *should* trust me. He and the Reverend discussed it and she said no. Well, no would have been nice. What she actually said was that she might as well burn the money to stay warm. They'd get more use of it that way than by lending it to me."

I could hear the Reverend saying those words in my head, knew just the way her mouth would turn at the end, like the Great Book of Judgment had been closed and your worth had been weighed and there was no undoing it. Just the thought of it made me feel small and angry and useless. I didn't say anything as Carver curled his knees into his chest until he was all sharp edges, his elbows jutting out to his sides, the brim of his cap pulled low.

He said, "So I had to tell Rowdy, and you know how he is. The things he can say. And it didn't matter to him anyway. He could just go to work for his dad and make as much money as he wanted. So when Jesse Lee said he was moving to Cincinnati and had a spare room for rent, I jumped on it. I thought I could go up there and make some money. That's all Jesse talked about, how he had this job lined up with his cousin and he could get me on real easy. I was going to go and make the money that Pap wouldn't give me and come back and start my own garage. I was going to show everybody just how wrong they were."

"What happened?"

"There was no job. Not for me or Jesse. Everything fell apart the week we got there, and I took a job washing dishes and another delivering pizzas and I still barely made rent. Then another of Jesse's cousins—"

"How many cousins does the man have?" I blurted.

Carver smiled. "Enough to cause trouble. This one was dealing. Selling uppers to college kids, mostly. He let us deal for him and it was decent money, especially compared to what I'd been making. But Jesse Lee was hooked on the shit within a month, and most of the money he made went straight back into it. I never liked pills. I'd rather drown my problems, personally. But everything just kept getting worse. I don't know if you've ever lived with an addict before, well, I guess your mom, but what I mean is—" He stopped and took a long breath. "I had to be drunk most of the time just to stand being there. It was getting worse and worse, then they started getting into fentanyl, and I'd seen what that could do back home so I moved out of Jesse's place and in with this girl I'd been seeing. She was nice. Getting her business degree. She crocheted these little bears for her nieces and nephews and watched those reality television shows every night. I think I was her pet project."

I nodded when he looked at me. The thought of someone being

there for Carver when I wasn't made me prickle with jealousy. I knew I should have been grateful he'd had somewhere else to go, and I was, but I still wished it had been me. I pulled my knees up, folding myself together until I looked just like Carver, both of us curled tight into ourselves.

"Then what?" I asked.

"I drifted a little. Tried to find another job, but it was hard. I think I was depressed or something. I didn't want to get out of bed. Didn't want to shower. I used to turn the water on and lie down on the bathroom floor and just stare up at the ceiling until my girlfriend came and knocked on the door and asked if I was okay. I think part of me wanted to die."

"Carver."

"It's true. I've never much liked myself but I hated myself then. And with your mom and everything I thought you'd never forgive me for selling pills and being drunk all the time. That's why I couldn't tell Julie or you. I couldn't stand the thought of you hating me, too."

"I don't hate you."

He looked at me then. Tentative. The kind of look that had to try three or four times before he finally met my eyes. "Seriously?"

I shook my head. "I hate Jesse and his cousins though. There's a family tree that would be better as a table."

Carver turned his head, and he didn't know it but he was looking straight at my door as it wandered lazily along the edge of the ridge. Then the door started to drift back toward us like it was drawn to him, like it wanted to see his face better in the dark.

Carver said, "I wanted to come back with something to show for myself. Something good. I kept thinking I'd come back all changed and you'd see me for who I could really be and I'd take you out on a real date to a sit-down restaurant and…" His voice trailed off and he leaned his chin against his knee, staring through the windshield that was slowly growing foggy around its edges.

"And what?" I asked.

"I don't know. We'd get married and have a farm with a little place for Granny to stay and another little place for Julie to stay. Maybe a pond. Some goats."

"I always wanted a goat."

"I know."

I smiled. "That don't sound too terrible."

"I want to make a life like that. But sometimes it scares me," he said.

"Why?"

"I don't know. It's like if I'm responsible once, does that mean I have to be responsible all the time?"

I snorted. "Yes! That's how life works!"

Carver shook his head. "I don't know if I can do that though. I want to. Really. More than almost anything. But what if I mess up?"

"Then you apologize."

"But what if the person you apologize to won't forgive you? What if she can't let you have even one mistake?"

I frowned. "You mean if I forgive you once I have to keep forgiving you?"

"Yes!" Carver laughed, and the sound loosened my shoulders and unclenched my fists, so I tensed my body up again in retaliation. I hated the way he made me feel. I hated thinking I might not have to hold on so tight to everything if I had someone else to hold on to, someone to share it with, someone to trust. I hated wanting to reach out for him and rest my head on his shoulder, and I hated knowing he would never close his arms to me, never turn me away.

I held out my hand and splayed my fingers. Carver looked at me for a moment before he eased his hand onto mine. He trailed the tips of his fingers over my palm, and the feeling was so light and tender that I had to clench my jaw to keep from smiling. He slotted his fingers between mine and squeezed gently.

I said, "I don't want to be so hard all the time. I want to forgive people. It's just... Sometimes it feels like if I let up even a little on myself or anybody else that everything is going to fall apart. I have to keep it together and this is the only way I know that works."

"I know."

"You don't though. I wish you did, but I'm glad you don't. You've always had the Reverend to bail you out if you needed it. She's threatened to cut you off a hundred times, but has she ever? Really?"

Carver shook his head.

"You've always had a way out if you needed it. Granny would kill to be able to solve my problems that way but she can't afford to. Which means I can't afford to mess up. Not ever."

"I know."

I sighed. "So, yeah, I want to be easier on you. But I want you to be more reliable, too."

"I want that, too. Both of them."

"If this is what you want, then I need you to be here. Really be here."

"I'm here."

"Well."

"Well," Carver said. "Does that mean you're my girlfriend?"

"What? No! You can't just jump right into that. Just go right to being somebody's girlfriend."

"People do all the time."

"Not this people. There's…protocols."

Carver grinned. "All right, Ms. Protocol. But we'll try, at least? I'll be true to my word, and you'll forgive me when I mess up."

"I'll *try*."

"I'll try, too."

"Fine," I said. "Can we talk about something else now?"

"All right. You want to look at me, at least?"

I did, but not all the way. I squinted one eye at him until he laughed, and it was when he was laughing that I opened my eyes and looked at him. I felt lighter. John Edward and the pills in my purse and Granny's forgetting and Julie's anger seemed like faraway things that couldn't hurt me then. All I had to do was stay in the car on top of Burnt Ridge for the rest of my days and everything would be all right.

Carver turned toward me. "I'd really like to kiss you now. Would you like that?"

"Yeah," I said. "I'd like that."

And after he stopped smiling, Carver leaned over the console and kissed me softly on the forehead and then even more softly on the tip of my nose. He drifted his lips over my right cheek and then my left, and then he leaned back and looked at me. My whole chest felt like it might collapse from want—not just wanting to kiss him but wanting to get it right. Wanting to be the kind of person who could be soft and sweet, someone who forgave, someone who believed they could have what they wanted. And just before he leaned forward I saw a glimmer from the corner of my eye. A faint blue light that made everything it touched look like it was swimming, and I knew that if I wanted to do things right, then there was something I needed to say even though it pained me to say it.

I put my hand on Carver's chest to stop him. His eyelashes fluttered just inches away from me and a frown creased the corners of his mouth.

"Wait," I said. "There's something I should tell you first."

"What is it?"

I let my hand shift until I was cupping the side of his neck. I could feel his pulse pounding against my fingers as I said, "I have a little door."

chapter twelve

Carver was quiet the whole drive home. He held my hand but he kept his face turned toward the window, watching the black night sweep by punctuated by lone sodium lamps glowing gold-orange in the dark. He followed me up to the front porch when I got home. The living room light was on and I could see Granny's house slippers sitting by the recliner, which meant she was waiting for me to come home. I didn't know what to say so I waited for Carver to speak. We stood there—my arms crossed over my chest, his hands in his pockets, both of us staring at the ground. My chest felt too tight. Uncomfortable.

"I should go," he said at last.

I was hoping for something more along the lines of *I don't hate you, let's make out,* so I just nodded and felt useless.

He turned to leave, then turned back. "Will you at least tell me before you take it? You'll say goodbye?"

"I told you I don't plan on taking it," I whispered, nodding toward the window so Carver would lower his voice.

Instead, he stepped closer to me, so close that I could feel his breath on my cheek. He leaned his temple against mine and rested one hand on my hip. His thumb rubbed at the narrow strip of skin that showed between my T-shirt and my jeans, and I shivered. It was hard to concentrate on anything but that feeling, but strange at the same time that Carver of all people could make my heart pound like this, make me feel so desperate for touch. The same person who used to whisper "dammit" in my ear during church service just to make me giggle, who helped me clean up my mess when I wet the bed at the Reverend's house one night after my mom took her door, who tried to give himself a tattoo with a needle and some pen ink when he was thirteen and then cried in my bedroom after his hepatitis shot.

I thought of Carver as a friend, of course, and I thought of Carver as annoying, often. Carver as sweet and frustrating, Carver as constant. But I had not thought of the softness of Carver's mouth or of knotting my fingers in his dark hair or wondered what he would sound like when he was between my legs. I swallowed hard. Those thoughts were new, but now that they were there, I found I could think of little else. And it was so much nicer to think of this than the other things happening in my life. To have some hope of pleasure and goodness.

I nudged his hand away from my hip. "You really have to stop doing that."

"Is that what you want?" he asked as he pulled his hand away.

"No."

In an instant his thumb was back to tracing the line of my hip. I could feel his smile against my cheek.

"I thought you were mad at me," I said.

"I am mad at you, but I still want to touch you."

I huffed out a laugh and wrapped my arms slowly under his, slid my hands under his T-shirt so I could touch his skin. I didn't realize my fingers were cold until I touched him. I leaned my forehead against his neck, nuzzled into the familiar smell of him. I ran my fingers over his skin, tracing the edge of his shoulder blades, until I touched a little knot of skin.

"Scar," he said.

"From wrecking that dirt bike, I know."

"I left half my back on that stretch of road."

"Half your good sense, too."

He laughed and pressed a kiss into my hair. "You should tell Julie, you know. About your door."

"It's hard to do that when she won't talk to me."

"She wasn't home when I stopped by after work. Half her closet was empty. She left a phone number on the fridge in case I needed her."

"Rachel's?"

"Yep."

"Dammit." I gritted my teeth. "She stopped taking her meds again."

Carver sighed. "I knew something was going on. We'll take care of her, at least for as long as you're here."

"Carver, so help me—"

He leaned back and kissed me gently on the forehead. "How would you feel if the doors were reversed, so to speak?"

"You mean if you had a door and I didn't?"

He nodded and I found I couldn't speak for the gulf of sadness that opened in me. I pressed my head harder into his shoulder and let that be my answer.

He said, "Where is it anyway? Your little friend?"

I leaned back and found my door floating over the flower beds. It was bigger than it had been when I first found it and brighter, too. The side of Carver's face was lit pale blue as he turned in the same direction. I wanted to tell him that he looked beautiful this way but I didn't think he would see it as a compliment. He squinted into the night, lifted his arm, and held up his middle finger at my door. I adjusted his hand so the door might actually see it, if it was a thing that looked and saw.

"Listen, you interdimensional piece of shit," he said. "You don't get to keep her." He thrust his middle finger out for emphasis. Then he kissed me again, this time on the cheek, before he pulled away and walked to the front steps, not knowing that his shoulder brushed the edge of my little door on his way or that he sent the stars floating into the air over his head, shining faintly, until they were pulled back toward my door.

"Good night, Maren," he said.

"Good night."

I walked inside just as he revved his Tempest to life, my body backlit by his headlights. I slipped off my shoes and almost set my purse down by the door but thought better of it. It wouldn't be long before Granny noticed something suspicious and started looking for answers, so I would have to make the answers harder to find. Granny sat in her recliner with a notebook in her hand. She glanced up as I walked in and squinted at me, assessing.

She said, "What was you doing out there for so long?"

"Saying good night to Carver."

She raised her bushy eyebrows until they disappeared under her hair.

"Don't look at me like that," I said.

"You know he's been in love with you since you was in middle school."

I rolled my eyes, but part of me was pleased. "Who ain't in love with me?"

"You talk awful big for somebody who ain't been on a date in a year."

"Granny."

"Am I lying?"

"You're one to talk. The closest thing you've had to a date is that time Elmer Day sat on the porch for three hours talking about his hernia surgery."

"He died, you know."

"Did he really?"

"No." Granny tossed her head back and barked out a little laugh. "Quit distracting me. You and Carver was gone an awful long time now. What was you doing?" She wiggled her bushy eyebrows up and down.

"Oh, quit now, you old pervert. We just went to see a couple buddies of his." It was close enough to true that I could have stopped, could have shrouded myself in a half lie, but something made me open my mouth again. I don't know if it was the guilt or my nerves or the fact that I'd told Carver the truth about my little door and the truth was a catching thing, but something shoved the words out of my mouth before I could shove them down. "They knew Mom. Or used to."

The shift in Granny was immediate. Her shoulders stiffened. Her mouth drew into a thin line. It was like watching someone be petrified from the inside, every bit of softness in her being turned to stone. "Oh."

"Yeah," I said. "One of them was Margot's boy. Said they used to hang out together on the weekends. I think I remember them."

"Uh-huh."

"I'd forgot how many friends Mom had."

"*Friends.*" Granny snorted. "Those people weren't her friends. And I ain't sure I like you being around people who *were* friends with your mother anyhow. The whole lot of them together wasn't worth a dime."

"These boys weren't so bad."

"Then what did Carver want with them?"

"He didn't want nothing with them. Just to talk. Sit a while." I did my best not to shift again, though part of me wanted to move from under Granny's gaze.

"Carver's not gotten into something he can't handle, has he?"

"Well, he can barely handle me, if that's what you mean."

"That's not what I mean and you know it. I don't want you speaking to the same people and walking the same roads that she did. That only leads one direction. You hear me?"

"I hear you, but…"

"But what?"

I stared at my little door as it hovered by the window like it was looking for Carver, hoping he would come back, or maybe that was just me. Maybe I was mixing us up already, maybe I always had. Tears tightened my throat and I took shallow breaths through my nose until my vision cleared. It had been so nice to talk about Mom that night. Even with everything else that had gone wrong or almost wrong, she had been a bright spot for me, and I wanted to bring her home. I was tired of tucking her into corners of my memory where no one else might see. But the worst part was that at the same time, I felt compelled to agree with Granny, to say, *Yes, Mom had been terrible, Mom had been wrong*, to say anything as long as Granny would stop looking at me like that, making me feel nine years old again, like she could still walk out any minute just like everyone else had. I felt split between them, split between myself.

I shook my head. "Nothing. It's nothing."

"All right," she said. "Come sit here and look at this with me."

I walked across the room, feeling rotten and grateful at the same time that the conversation had ended without a fight. I leaned against the arm of Granny's recliner. She handed me the notebook she'd been holding since I walked in. Granny had made a schedule with times written on one side and events on the other. Wake up at 8:00 a.m., eat breakfast at 8:30, go for a walk with Cheryl and the kids at 9:00. I frowned at her name. I hadn't forgotten how Cheryl had neglected to check on Granny the night she wandered off again, the night I found my little door.

"You sure you want to go walking with Cheryl and her bowlegged children?"

"Hush now."

"You're not planning to tell her, are you? About your…health?"

"No," Granny said.

"So we're still just pretending everything is all right then?"

Granny didn't answer so I turned the page and there was another schedule—a whole week's worth—and every evening at seven thirty the same thing had been written: talk to Maren before bed. I looked at the clock and frowned. It was already past nine. My throat tightened again. The schedule had me dropping her off at the Rose Garden most days and picking her up again, but I had work to contend with, and now I had my extra *activity* on the side selling pills with Carver. I didn't know how I could manage everything at once. My fog pulled close and whispered, *It's only the first day and you're already messing up.*

"We're a little behind," I said.

"Well, it can't be perfect," Granny said. "But Dr. Owens said that keeping a schedule was important. I need a routine."

"Right."

"What do you think?"

I couldn't tell her that I wanted to rip up the pages and burn them or feed the whole notebook to my little door. I didn't want our days to be like this, didn't want her to be sick, didn't want any of it, not any of it. My door shifted from the window and hovered above us, casting the paper in cotton-candy pink. I said, "I think it's a good idea. We'll do our best to stick by it."

"Good." Granny sighed. Her hand shook a little as she took the notebook back from me. "I figured I could make a copy for you, too. That way we can both have one."

"I'd like that." I ran my fingers over the top of her hair. The curls had gone flat in the back from lying in the hospital bed and guilt pressed on me like a vise, threatened to collapse me into nothing. "Maybe we can curl your hair in the morning. Get you looking fresh before you go practice singing with Betty tomorrow. Send them men at the Rose Garden scrambling for their nitroglycerin."

Granny swatted me away, but I could see the smile on her face. "As long as you curl it right this time."

"I know you'll tell me if I don't."

Granny took my hand and patted it softly with her own. "You're a good girl. Now go on to bed and let me read my Bible."

"You'll holler if you need anything?"

"You'll be the first to know."

I kissed the top of her head. "I love you, old woman."

"I know it."

chapter thirteen

Flowers grew inside my bedroom. I don't know how else to say it. One morning there was nothing; the next morning there was. I wasn't sure if the flowers were a product of my door, but I suspected as much. It liked to work that way, in bursts. Suddenly appearing out of thin air, suddenly growing, suddenly showing me all the strange things it could do. It had a flair for the dramatic, my door.

The flowers appeared a few days after I broke down on Burnt Ridge. I stepped out of bed one morning and something soft tickled my feet. I jerked back at first, as though all my childhood fears of creatures living under my bed might be true. My bedroom had been a porch once but had been boarded up to make a bedroom after Mom took her door. Before that I'd always slept in the room Mom used to share with her sisters, but after she took her door Granny insisted that I have a room that was just mine. The walls were boarded up, the floor sealed, though not very well, because little cracks still showed between the boards where the cold, dank earth waited below. We'd painted the walls purple because that's what I said I wanted, and then I'd cried that night because I hated purple and I couldn't explain why I'd told Granny that it was my favorite color, couldn't tell her that it had been Mom's favorite.

Granny had sat beside me on the bed and told me it was okay to be all mixed up. That she was all mixed up, too. Aunt Forest came over the next morning and we'd painted each wall a different color—green, yellow, blue, pink—so I'd have a wall for whatever mood I was in. I kept it that way until I was in middle school when I stole some paint from the supply closet with Carver and covered the walls with black. I guess I had a flair for the dramatic, too.

Now the walls were an odd color I'd bought on discount from the local hardware store—something between silver and blue. But the paint was cracking with age, showing all the layers underneath. Little pieces of pink and blue and black peeked out here and there, reminding me of all the people I'd been inside this room.

And I was someone else again. Someone who had a thin, pale-green stalk rising up between the cracks in her floor. The leaves were thin, too, and delicate, though an even lighter shade of green, somehow ghostly. Another stalk sprouted a few boards away, and another, and another. Each stem ended in a long, skinny spike that looked almost like lavender before it blooms, but bigger, heavier. It seemed impossible that the stem could hold such weight. Maybe that's why the stems swayed the way they did, each of the flowers bending to the side and back as if my room was rocked by a gentle wind. As I watched them, I found myself moving, too, rocking slowly, side to side until the mattress squeaked beneath me. It felt so peaceful. So calm.

My fog curled into my chest, and I wondered if that's what it would be like on the other side of my door. Was this what was waiting for me? Flowers that could lull me to sleep? Then why was I waiting? I ran my finger over one of the leaves closest to me and a half memory stirred in the back of my mind, some kind of déjà vu, like I'd touched that leaf before but just couldn't remember where or when or why it mattered.

I looked up at my little door spinning above me. It was just a few inches shy of touching either side of my bedroom walls, and this morning it was laced with bright veins of purple that streaked like lightning from its black core all the way to its edges.

"Did you do this?" I asked, but the door didn't answer.

I'd been feeding it more often, something new almost every day for the last few days. It was random at first—stray blades of grass I picked from the cracks in the driveway or three pennies I'd found in the pocket of my jeans. But then I started to wonder where those things ended up when the door took them away and if there was anyone on the other side who might find them. Like maybe my door led to a little house in the woods, someplace with lots of windows that faced a spring-fed pond. There would be a fireplace that reached from floor to ceiling and dark wooden floors with pale scratches from years of use. And the person who lived there didn't even know they were waiting for me, but they started to find strange things. A key ring with a single silver key on the pillow next to theirs, three pennies in their coffee cup, a few blades of grass tucked like a bookmark into the book they were reading. And maybe they began to wonder if something else was coming. Something better.

So I started to be more thoughtful about the things I gave away— like an old picture of me and Mom at my seventh birthday party, me smiling with three missing teeth, her holding a plastic crown atop my head; a cold can of Peach Nehi like we used to drink in the summer; a letter I'd written to her when I was ten that started *Dear Mama* but then I'd crossed out *Mama* and written *Nell* but then crossed that out and wrote *Mother* because I had never been very good at being angry with Mom.

It was foolish, I know, and more than a little sad.

My mother wasn't on the other side of my door. I told myself
that again and again. But still, I gave her a blanket that I had slept
with when I was a girl and one of Granny's homemade biscuits that
I took after breakfast one morning because I knew Mom would miss
the taste and a rude drawing that I made on a napkin at work of my
coworker Eileen and her sisters. It was like I finally had a place to put
all the love I had for Mom over the years since she left. I could never
share these things with Granny or my family. I couldn't share them
with Julie and Carver, who remembered even less of my mother than
I did and who always ended up feeling sorry for me every time I
brought her up.

Now I could give all those feelings to my door. My door never
judged, never pitied me. It just took what I had to offer and kept
me warm at night. And I could pretend that somewhere my mother
received all my little offerings even if she didn't send anything back.

Not that I waited for that, either.

I felt guilty, though, because I knew the door hurt Carver. Every
night since I'd told him the truth, he had texted me the same question: you promise you'll wait until tomorrow?

I told myself that I had been telling the truth when I said I had no
intention of taking my door. I told myself that I was saying goodbye
to Mom. That's all it was. A way to let her go, finally, forever, and
when I was ready, I would send the door away.

Most days I believed it.

I stretched my feet out and let them graze the tops of the flowers.
The leaves seemed to turn toward me even before I touched them,
twisting slightly, like I was their sunlight. When I finally set my
feet down, the leaves brushed against my ankles so softly that I had
to smile. Part of me wanted to lie down and spread my arms out

between them, to feel their silky coldness on the bare skin of my back. Part of me knew, somehow, that they would fold into the crease of my spine, the space between my fingers, would fill all the gaps in me if I would only let them.

Then Granny called me from the kitchen and I jolted like I was coming awake. My skin felt tacky, too warm from the heat of my little door, and I hurried to get dressed in my favorite pair of overalls.

Granny was at the kitchen table nursing her second cup of coffee by the time I left my room. She said she'd lost her dentures, so I helped her look for them. We shuffled around the house half-asleep, opening and closing the same drawers, frowning at the house as though it were deliberately hiding the dentures from us. The dentures were not in their usual spot by her bed or their other usual spot by her recliner, nor were they on any of the tables or cabinets in the kitchen or bathroom. But I found other things in their place: notes. Just like the ones written neatly on the picture frames. There was a note on the small table beside Granny's recliner with a list of her favorite television shows and their channels. A reminder on the coffee maker that the start button was finicky and had to be held for at least five seconds before it would actually turn on. *Cream, no sugar* was scrawled onto the bottom of my favorite mug. The address and phone number of the grocery store where I worked was taped to the fridge on a neon-green sticky note.

There was something about seeing our lives written out in such neat, simple ways that made my chest hurt. It made it all seem so small. So easy to lose. I didn't talk to Granny about the notes. Couldn't. Maybe I didn't want to draw attention to the important things. Didn't want the great eye of God or the Universe or whoever to fall upon them. My quiet was protecting. Hiding. The fog rose in my mind and whispered all the ways that I had failed, made my heart hammer in my chest, until I gave up finding the dentures and opened the fridge to start making breakfast. I saw Granny's teeth sitting between a gallon of milk and a carton of eggs.

"There!" I said.

Granny tapped the teeth with one small finger when I handed them to her, the sound like someone knocking on a real little door. "They're too cold to put in now. They'll hurt my gums."

"You reckon we could microwave them?"

Granny scowled at me.

"Not ready to joke about it, I see." I looked around the room for an answer and settled for setting the dentures in their open cup on the sill of the kitchen window where the sun pooled bright and warm. "There. That ought to do it."

Afterward, I helped Granny into the shower. She was quiet, stern. I kept trying to make jokes, but she wouldn't even smile at me so eventually I gave up. She'd been losing things more often lately— three pairs of glasses in the past year, her favorite pair of pantyhose, the pocket Bible I'd given her as a gift after my first Vacation Bible School. I knew it was part of what was happening to her, but I felt so helpless against it. I couldn't fight what was inside her, couldn't hold it between my hands. We could only do what Dr. Owens said, so Granny clung to the schedule she made, tapping the paper every hour and announcing what came next, and we did our best to follow it.

I sat on the lid of the toilet and talked to Granny as she bathed. We talked about work and Eileen and when Aunt Forest was going to come visit and how the roses were going to do this year, and my door listened intently from the hallway, casting its shifting light against the bathroom floor.

When Granny got quiet, I listened for her breathing under the roar of the water and panicked when I couldn't find it. My heart rate picked up even as I told myself that she was fine, she was right there, she was talking to me for God's sake, but I still felt worried until the water was off and I helped her into a towel.

"You know I get my flat butt from you," I said.

"You need to ask the Lord's forgiveness for looking at your granny's butt, that's what I know."

I smiled. "Was it always like that or did it get smaller with age? If mine gets any smaller, it'll be concave. They'll do medical studies on me."

"They ought to do them now."

I led her to her bedroom and she eased onto the edge of the bed. I opened her closet while she caught her breath. I held out a soft violet housedress for her approval. She shook her head so I tried three more times until she settled for a gray housedress with lace around the collar.

I made sure she had her dentures—now warmed by the sun— and her stack of crossword puzzles and a cold drink before I left her sitting on the porch swing. This was the way we started most of our mornings, but now we had the schedule to follow. Today, at least, we were right on time, and Cheryl should be over soon to pick Granny up to go walking. I paused by my car and looked back at Granny. There was something about the sight of her sitting on the porch swing that steadied me. I could picture her there forever—the mountains shifting through the seasons behind her, from heat to cold, green to brown, the trees withering from age, the mountains worn down inch by inch until the whole county was nothing but a valley baking beneath the relentless sun, and all the names of all the things I'd loved had been lost to time, but still that house would stand, still Granny would squint into the morning light and close her eyes and sigh.

I should have taken a moment longer to enjoy that steady feeling because as I turned toward my car, a familiar engine revved up the hill and the Reverend pulled into my driveway.

Granny laughed at the look on my face and called, "There comes your best friend."

Granny and the Reverend had never cared much for each other, but it tickled Granny that I would have to deal with the Reverend before my second cup of coffee. I threw an ugly look over my shoulder but that only made Granny laugh harder. I had been expecting this visit ever since Julie had started staying with Rachel. It was only a matter of time before the Reverend intervened, and she liked nothing better than recruiting help from me. But seeing the Reverend again after Julie had compared me to her made me feel prickly. I didn't like the comparison to begin with, but I liked even less that Julie wasn't entirely wrong.

"Good morning, Reverend," I said as she rolled down her window. "Hi, Pap."

Pap nodded to me from the driver's seat but otherwise remained silent as he pulled off his glasses and began to clean them with a handkerchief.

"Good morning. I wish I was calling on you in better circumstances," the Reverend said, "but I'm worried about our child."

I frowned. She only referred to Julie as ours in times like this, as though Julie was something we shared between us in uneasy joint custody. I said, "I haven't talked to Julie for days. Not for lack of trying. She really screwed us over at work, too. I don't think Mr. Martin will let her back on this time."

The Reverend pursed her lips. "I'll deal with Martin when the time comes. I haven't spoken to Julie, either. Not since three days ago. She's into something bad this time. Something I'm afraid she won't come back from."

"She's been with Rachel before."

"It's different now." The Reverend stared at some place beyond me, her eyes not quite focused on any single point. "I dreamed about her last night. She was little again. Hair like cotton candy, you remember? She was standing in the middle of a river, and there was a dam about to break. She kept calling for me to come get her because she'd lost her shoe in the mud and she wouldn't leave it. No matter how many times I told her to, she just wouldn't leave it. And I couldn't move, in the dream. I was more stuck than she was."

Pap propped his glasses back on his nose, reached over, and rested his hand on the Reverend's knee. She started at his touch but smiled at him.

"I can't bear to think of her needing me and not being able to help her," the Reverend said. She took off her own glasses and handed them to Pap who began quietly cleaning them as diligently as he had cleaned his own.

I said, "I know the feeling."

"I know you do."

Another long moment passed. My little door moved from the yard and hovered over the Reverend's car, casting dizzying shadows atop the metal roof. I felt mean-hearted for expecting the worst from the Reverend. She had been her worst for many years, but she seemed different now. More fragile somehow. I looked at the soft lines on her face, the wrinkles around her mouth and saw Carver in thirty years. They had the same high cheeks, the same wide eyes. But it was hard

to let people change. Hard not to hold tight to the version of them
you knew because you knew how bad they could hurt you and you
knew you could bear that pain. Giving them room to grow, believing them better, being brought low by the disappointment when
they failed—that was much harder. I was seeing more every day how
selfish it was to believe that no one could change, but I could see no
way out of it, either. No way that didn't hurt. I swallowed and my
throat was tight.

The Reverend said, "I went by that girl's house but no one was there.
Something's wrong, Maren. I know it. I need your help fixing it."

I nodded. "I'll do my best."

"Good." The Reverend leaned forward until she could see Granny
sitting on the porch. She called, "Hello, Iris. I'm praying for you."

I looked back just in time to see the annoyance pass from Granny's
face as she yelled, "Same to you, Tabitha!"

I smiled and waved as Pap pulled carefully back onto the road
and watched the car recede until just before they disappeared around
the curve.

Granny hollered from the porch, "Everything all right?"

I sighed. "It will be."

chapter fourteen

A couple days later, Carver and I headed to a far corner of Blackdamp on roads narrower than my patience, surrounded on all sides by thick trees and rolling hills. We drove through Sterns, which sat like an empty bowl between two mountains—the mountain where I lived on one side and Burnt Ridge on the other. We passed the place where John Edward had pulled us over, and I turned my head to keep the panic from clawing at my chest.

The roads had a soothing, almost hypnotic effect on me. They always had, from the first time Uncle Tim had let me drive his beat-up Geo Tracker when I was twelve years old. Blackdamp didn't have much to offer, but it did have plenty of roads—long and winding roads with curves so steep and smooth you feared that they might never end or that they would loop you around through time itself, spin you back and back until you were standing again in your six-year-old body, staring at a cloud of rising dust that you had made believe was your real father. Roads too narrow for two cars to fit side by side, roads blacktopped and graveled and worn to bare, soft dirt the exact color of my mother's palm.

They were the kind of roads that could make you forget why your heart felt so heavy, like you were carrying the weight of three or four hearts instead of just one, all the lifetimes of all the people you loved crowded in your chest until you thought you might suffocate. Every mile we drove opened up more space inside me, like we weren't driving the road, but driving through me, deeper and deeper.

When the trees began to thin and more houses began to dot the hillside, I turned to Carver and said: "Can we go back and drive it again?"

He eased his foot off the gas so the world slowed and he smiled at me. "Whatever you want," he said, then turned the car around and drove us back the way we came. I leaned my head against the window and stared at everything passing by in reverse, and Carver reached over and cupped his hand on my knee. I rested my hand over his, and for a few minutes more, it was enough just to be there, just to watch, to see.

Halfway back, I straightened up and reached for my purse in the wheel well. I took out the slim bottles of Granny's pills and counted them again like I counted them every day. Carver had set up a deal for us with Thelma Crawford. Her husband still worked in the mines and Carver said she usually liked to buy in bulk, so this was a chance to really put away some money for Granny's care. Thelma had been a clerk at the same grocery store where I worked long ago and she'd known my mother, too. I remembered her in vague flashes, more a presence than a person, but it still made me nervous and excited to see her again. It seemed like I kept finding pieces of Mom inside other people—every pill I sold I also traded for some small story or memory, trying to fill myself up with scraps of a ghost. It didn't make me all that different from the people I sold to, really. We were all trying to find something.

My stomach ached as Carver's Tempest rounded a curve and

rumbled across the pockmarked road. He'd bought the car at a police auction when he was seventeen with money he'd been given by Pap and the Reverend and a few hundred he'd made working part-time at the AutoZone in town. He spent years restoring the car, which meant Julie and I had spent years sitting in the back seat as Carver tinkered under the hood or rolled around on the creeper with the one bad wheel, which had been superglued and duct-taped back into an approximation of a wheel so it always moved with a slight limp. We would give Carver screwdrivers and sips of Diet Coke as we exchanged gossip or took turns reading chapters of schoolwork aloud so Carver could hear.

I'd sat in nearly every position a person could in that car. I'd slung my legs on each side of the passenger headrest and dangled my head into the empty footwell when Carver removed it because it was riddled with rust. I'd stared at him and the world and the Tempest from upside down until Julie tickled my feet and sent me careening toward the pavement. I'd curled fetal position in the back seat with a stomachache after drinking too much on Burnt Ridge, so Carver had given up working that morning and turned the radio on some station low and soft and we'd stayed there together in the cool fall air, not speaking. I'd even sat in the trunk with Julie with the lid propped open, making fun of Carver's new haircut as he changed the bulbs in the taillights.

So the Tempest felt like a familiar thing, something built or born around us. Riding shotgun made me miss Julie fiercely. It had been over a week since our fight in the store and so much had happened since then, so much that Julie didn't know. I was off-balance without her. It took three days of work before I remembered to bring my own coffee because I was so used to her bringing one for me. She should have been there in the back seat of the Tempest telling Carver and me why we really should start meditating or asking us what our favorite kind of leaf was. I had texted her at least once a day and called every night before bed, but she never answered. Carver had stopped talking about her because he knew it ate me alive that she would talk to him but not to me. They'd done that when we were little, too—banded together when I made one of them mad. They always had someone else they could turn to when I wasn't there, and it seemed the most unfair thing in the world to me then. Still did.

Even thinking about it made me start to squirm—crossing and uncrossing my legs, running my finger along the piping on the edge of the seat—so I told Carver about how I'd looked up the course catalog at the community college I'd gone to so I could plan for which classes I could take once I finally paid off my debt. I knew that would get him going, and to my credit, I was right. He almost veered into a ditch.

"That's amazing!" he crowed as the Tempest struggled over the rutted dirt, little clods of grass flying into the air behind us.

"It'll be less amazing if I don't live to finish paying it off. Get back on the road. The *right* side of the road, I swear."

Carver swerved into the left lane and then back into the right lane, grinning the whole time. Despite everything, I still couldn't help but feel hopeful looking at his face. There was something electric about his happiness, or maybe it was just how happy he could allow himself to be. I wasn't sure I would recognize Joy if I saw it in an empty room. We were strangers at best, though most days it felt like we were mortal enemies. I could rely on Doubt and Worry and even Grief. I inhaled Stress and exhaled Obligation. Joy was something different, though. Something strange and feral and bright, and Carver wore it so well.

"Just think," he said, "a few months from now and everything will be different."

"I guess."

"It will! What'll you think you'll do once you got it all paid off and go back to school? Dream with me."

His face was so earnest and his optimism so contagious that I tried. Really, I did. But then I looked through the side mirror and caught the edge of my little door. When Carver had come to pick me up, he'd said the door wasn't welcome in the car—which was fine, because after all my feeding, it couldn't fit into the car anymore. Carver had opened the trunk instead, offering to tote the door like a hostage, but I'd just rolled my eyes. My door had hovered over the car the whole way, nothing but a glimpse of shimmering lemon-lime light from the corner of the side mirror, but now it edged closer, let me see the dark gulf at its middle. And that's what my future felt like—that dark and spinning blackness.

It hadn't always been that way. When I played this kind of game with my mother, I'd found the brightest version of ourselves and put us in the brightest version of the world. I thought I could believe us into something better—away from poverty and bad boyfriends and Mom's restlessness, the way she'd get so agitated sometimes late at night and wander from room to room chain-smoking cigarettes until the smoke hung like a haze around the windows. I'd lost that hope somewhere along the way, or maybe Mom had taken it with her when she'd gone through her little door, all the best parts of me trailing after her, following her when I couldn't. My throat felt tight and I looked away, watched the trees blur and blend. My fog crept around me like kudzu over the mountains, whispering: *You can't imagine something better because you know this is all you'll ever have. It's what you deserve.*

"I don't know," I said when Carver nudged me with his elbow, shaking the words loose. "It's hard to think of something that doesn't go wrong."

Carver took my hand and pressed my knuckles to his lips. "Then I'll think of something for us, all right? Hmm. Well, first thing is you'll register for classes. I'll take you school shopping myself. Get you some fancy pencils."

"What makes a pencil fancy?"

Carver scoffed as though it was an absurd question. "Glitter, of course."

I laughed a little, which only egged him on, his fingers playing across the top of the steering wheel.

"I know you were thinking of being a nurse, but maybe you'll find something else you like. Decide you want to be an orthodontist instead. Or maybe you want to be a teacher of some kind. Or somebody that sits behind a desk and wears glasses."

"You can't just *decide* to wear glasses."

"Oh, Maren," he sighed. "There's so much for you to learn." He took a curve a little too hard and sent me sliding over the leather seats until my hip collided with his and I was crushed against his side. "You'll graduate with a 4.0, obviously. Me and Granny and Ju— Ah. Me and Granny'll be there to see you walk. We'll get you flowers and take you out for a big steak. You won't eat half of it, which means I'll get a steak and a half and everybody will go home happy."

I wrapped my arm under his, hooked our elbows together. "Is that so?"

"It is. And then from there, it's just a straight road to anything."

"Like that farm?"

Carver grinned. "Yeah, like that."

"And the goats."

"Oh, there'll be goats," Carver said. "Little Sid and Sweet Iris."

"You want to name one of our goats after Granny?"

"I think she'd like it."

"I think she'll skin you alive."

"Fine. Gloria then. Sid and Gloria. They'll have a real will-they-won't-they kind of romance. But Sid's patient. He knows she's worth waiting for." Carver lifted his arm over my shoulder and hugged me tight against him. "It's going to be good. You'll see."

"What about you?" I asked, because the thought of all that goodness made me nervous, like some sorry little creature peeking its head out from a cave after too many years down deep in the dark. "What're you going to be doing while I'm out there wearing glasses and feeding goats?"

Carver stiffened a little. "Oh, you know me. I'll find something."

"I guess I got to imagine for you then." I sighed as though it were some great burden. "It seems like the only thing you can do is start that garage."

"We done talked about that."

"No, you talked," I said. "I listened. Very graciously. But what is it that Julie says? That sometimes a loss is really the universe removing obstacles from your path. If Rowdy ain't an obstacle that needed to be removed, then I don't know what is. You deserve your own garage. Do things your way."

"I don't know the first thing about running a business."

"If Rowdy Hacker and his no-neck daddy can run one, then I know for sure that you can."

Carver shook his head. "I wish it was that easy."

"You got to be more like Sid the goat. There's lots of things in the world worth fighting for. Sid's worth it, too."

"Well, shit," Carver said, and I thought I had worn him down, that he was ready to admit the brilliance and necessity of my words, when I turned my head and saw what Carver had already seen. We turned left into the driveway of Thelma's house and I clutched my bag against my stomach and heard the rattle of the pills waiting to be sold as John Edward lifted his head and looked at me through the window of his police cruiser.

chapter fifteen

"What do you think he's doing here?" I asked, grabbing the rearview mirror and tugging it askew as Carver parked. Once, a post office had sat not far from where John Edward was, but all that remained was the concrete pad that had served as a parking lot. And there he sat maybe half a football field away, just enough to obscure whatever expression soured his face.

Carver took the mirror from my hand and gently adjusted it. "This is original to the car, you know. You can't just go yanking her around any old way."

I rolled my eyes.

"And I don't know what he's doing here," Carver said, "other than he got tired of being annoying on one side of the county and wanted to spread some to the other side."

"What do we do? If he sees us together, he'll think I was lying the other night about breaking up with you."

"Or he'll think you couldn't resist my masculine wiles and we got back together."

"Carver."

"Maren," he said and smiled.

"Stop smiling," I said. "This is bad."

He stopped smiling. "All right."

"And stop being so calm. I'm the calm one. I know what to do."

"You can know what to do next time, all right? I'll know this time."
He leaned forward and touched his forehead to mine. "You said you
needed me to be here for you. I'm here. All the way. And all we have
to do is go inside and do what we came to do. If John Edward had a
warrant, he'd already be inside. I guess it's possible that he's here on
some kind of important official business that has nothing at all to do
with Thelma or her house. But he's probably here to intimidate her.
Or to make himself feel like he's worth something. Or he just got lost
and ain't sure how to find his way back up the nearest stater's ass."

I snorted. "Don't be funny when I'm nervous. I don't like this.
At all."

"The record will reflect that."

"And we'll leave in half an hour, right?"

"Whatever you say," he said.

"And you'll buy me an ice cream afterward."

Carver smiled. "I got something right now." He leaned over and
popped the glove compartment open. Inside was a pile of boxed
candy, chips, granola bars, packs of peanuts and cashews—a dragon's
hoard of snacks. "I let you go hungry once. I won't do it again."

It's hard to say what I felt in that moment but I didn't feel alone.
It was like a window opened briefly inside me and let in a soft, cool
breeze. I wish I could say that's all I felt, but there was anger, too.
Some feral part of me that screamed: *I don't need you. I don't need you.*
I didn't trust myself to speak because I wasn't sure which part of me
would do the talking, so I plucked a Kit Kat bar from near the top of
the pile and slipped it into my purse.

We got out of the car, and I followed Carver up the steps and
onto Thelma's porch. It took everything in me not to turn back and
look at John Edward every other step. My little door followed me

onto the steps where it stayed, casting its shifting plum-colored shadows onto the stunted grass below. Thelma sat on the porch with two other women who introduced themselves as Crystal, who was busy tearing a newspaper into long, thin strips and dropping them into a bucket beside her chair, and Amanda, who looked about my age with short-cropped hair, a worn denim jacket draped across her knees, and a blue T-shirt with *No Hate in My Holler* written across the front. We talked for a moment about the hole in the knee of Carver's jeans and when summer was ever going to come and how Thelma's grandchildren were doing before I finally broke down and looked behind me at John Edward's cruiser. I hoped that he might have disappeared like the last sticky threads of a bad dream, but he was still there, and still staring in our direction.

"You see my little shadow over there?" Thelma asked, looking past me at John Edward. She lifted her hand in a wave, and Crystal shook her head and muttered something under her breath.

"Hard to miss him," I said.

"He's been coming by every day since Amanda got into town. She brings supplies to the folks around here. Things to help them stay safe when they're using. Of course John Edward ain't too keen on that," Thelma said.

"It's harm reduction. Clean needles, mostly," Amanda said. "I've got a whole bag of Narcan this time, though."

Thelma nodded. "Don't look too good to have someone out here supporting the people he's trying to arrest. And I suspect I've been on that little list of the sheriff's for a long time. He'd just love to make me the first feather in his cap."

"Do what?" Carver asked. "I didn't know he could count high enough to make a list."

Thelma smiled. "It's for raids. He's been gearing up for it ever since he got that money from the state." She jerked her head toward a police scanner sitting beside her, its volume lowered to just barely a murmur. "We've been keeping a close eye on him. They like to think their channel is private, but there's nothing private in this town."

Amanda shook her head. "It's one thing when it's state boys raiding houses, but when it's one of our own…" Her face twisted into a grimace. "He knows why people sell around here. He knows what they've been through, what they need, but he's still going to make a name for himself off somebody else's life."

Carver rested his hand on the small of my back and said, "Amen."

I looked between all their faces, feeling some strange mixture of guilt and hope, when Crystal grabbed the scanner and held it up to her ear. "Hush now. I heard something."

Thelma rolled her eyes. "Give me that before you hurt yourself." She put the scanner back down and toyed with some of the dials along the front, but the garbled voice still swam through static so thick that I couldn't make out a word it said. Thelma held her ear close to the speaker and closed her eyes so she looked almost like she was praying.

"It's them," Thelma said after a moment. "Same ones we heard about last night. They ain't found them yet. But they're looking for a blue Chevy truck. No plates on it." Thelma's face darkened and she pressed her ear almost straight to the plastic before she cursed and leaned back. "That's all I got."

Crystal whistled from her rocking chair. "Whoever it is, they better hope nobody finds them."

"What happened?" I asked.

Thelma sat up a little straighter and I imagined her as some great keeper of the truth, a freckled prophet who interpreted the whispers of the scanner and passed on what she knew to those who were worthy.

"Well," she said, "apparently somebody tried to break into Dr. Owens's place up on Hospital Hill."

"Allegedly," Crystal added.

Amanda smiled but didn't say a word.

"When?" I asked.

Thelma said, "Late last night. They seemed to be right smart about it. Cut the power and everything, but Owens has got one of those big alarm systems with a backup generator. They said there's video of them escaping—"

"Alleged video," Crystal said.

"Oh hush, you old criminal." Thelma swatted at Crystal with her dishcloth, then turned toward me. "Come in here with me, honey, and we'll make some sweet tea. Carver, why don't you take a look at Amanda's car while you're here? It's been making this funny sound, and I don't trust it to take her all the way out to the Well. That ain't the kind of place I want her getting stuck. Tell Carver about it, Manda, and quit giving me that rotten look. You know I'm right."

I looked back at Carver and raised my eyebrows in a way I hoped communicated *See, I was right. Everybody thinks you're good with cars*, but that felt too subtle, so I called "What a great idea, Thelma; I keep telling him he ought to open his own garage" as I followed her into the house. My door trailed after me, lighting up the lightless room with its pale swirl of colors. We walked through a narrow living room and into a wide, bright kitchen. The table and chairs had been pushed to the far wall, and the floor was littered with drawing paper, crayons, and pencils.

"Don't mind the mess," Thelma said. "My grandbaby was here this morning and he'll be back again tonight. He throws a fit if we don't draw the fireflies together." She walked over to the fridge, opened the freezer, and rustled around inside. When she leaned back, she had a wad of money in her hand, the bills tipped with frost. She dusted it off and said, "Show me what you got."

The whole thing took less than two minutes. Thelma bought nearly everything I had, then secreted the remaining wad of money back in the freezer and whisked the pills out of sight.

For a moment I wasn't sure anything had happened, but the weight of the money in my hand was hard to ignore. I made almost a thousand dollars in those two minutes—which was over a month of work at the store, more money than I'd ever held in my hand at once. A giddy kind of dizziness bubbled up inside me, like drinking too much coffee too soon, and I felt like laughing or jumping or running back outside and punching John Edward in the face. It was the kind of feeling that could make you think you were invincible. I had to take several breaths before I could focus on anything other than the weight of my purse in my hands. I knew it couldn't have actually been heavier than before, but it *felt* heavier, more important, now that it had the money inside.

Thelma leaned against the stove and sighed, seeming not to notice the fits of feeling passing through me. She said, "You know my husband quit school when he was thirteen. He was in the mines not long after that. He was nineteen when we met. Tall and broad-shouldered and covered in coal dust." She smiled. "Now he's got bulging disks and degenerating disks and slipped disks. Every kind of disk but the right kind. He can't quit working. Not when we're supporting our Alicia and her husband and she's pregnant again and my arthritis keeps getting worse. The medicine will about bankrupt you. The pills is the only thing that helps him keep going anymore, and we need him to keep going."

"You don't have to explain anything to me," I said.

"I guess I don't. Still feel like I should, though. I'm always trying to explain myself to somebody."

"I know the feeling."

Thelma swiped at a pale stain on top of the stove. Carver's laughter filtered through the screen door and into the kitchen, and I smiled before I could stop myself. I could feel Thelma watching me before she said, "You know you look just like her."

"Who?" I asked, but I already knew the answer. I'd been hearing it my whole life but some part of me still liked to hear it anyway.

"That mother of yours." Thelma sighed. "You know me and her about burned this county to the ground two or three times."

"So I've been told."

"Me and her and Karen." A little smile played at the sides of Thelma's mouth. "None of us could have guessed how we'd end up. I guess nobody ever can. It's been a while since you've seen Karen, ain't it?"

I was about to answer when a loud noise came from the room beside us. Thelma sighed and took a bottle of Gatorade from the fridge. I expected her to go through the closed door but instead she turned to me.

"Can you take this in there? I wouldn't ask but she's mad at me. She's always mad at me these days," Thelma said, handing me the bottle. "Besides, looking at you is like looking at your mother. That's just who Karen needs to see right now."

chapter sixteen

My little door followed me as I walked into the back room, which was small and stuffy and dark even in the middle of the afternoon. The only window I could see had been covered with cardboard. I let my eyes adjust until I could make out a twin bed in the center of the room surrounded by piles of clothes and half-packed boxes. I stepped further and bumped into a dresser. Something tumbled to the floor.

"Shit," I whispered.

When I bent to search for whatever I'd knocked over, a voice croaked, "Don't worry about it. Nobody can tell the difference."

"Karen?" I asked.

"Who's asking."

"Maren Walker," I said. "Thelma wanted me to bring you a Gatorade."

My eyes adjusted to the dark just in time to see Karen smile. Something flared inside my chest. I hadn't seen her since I was a girl and I felt like a girl again, not quite sure how to act or what to do.

"Hey, Keefer," I said, using my mom's old nickname for her.

Her smile grew wider. "I wondered if you'd remember me."

I shuffled forward, being as careful as I could be of everything on the floor, and sat down on the bed as Karen scooted over. She propped herself up against the wall behind the bed. I handed her the Gatorade and she lifted it to her face first, pressed it against each cheek like a kiss. Her movements were labored, painful. Even breathing seemed to cost her something. From this close I could see a bruise beneath her right eye, a deep blue that turned to mottled green at its edges, and it looked almost like my little door, which settled into the air above us, illuminating Karen for the first time so I could see just how much she'd changed—her face grown soft with wrinkles, her hair brittle and graying.

My stomach twisted with some mixture of longing and remorse and fear. Karen had been like an aunt to me—she'd given me my first chew of tobacco and held my hair back when I puked it all up after swallowing some, and she'd tied our loose tailpipe up with a red ribbon and told me that just because something was busted didn't mean it couldn't be pretty. She'd driven me home from school and passed out drunk on our kitchen floor and gotten into screaming matches with her boyfriends on our telephone until deep in the night. She was there until the very end. She'd come by Granny's house a few days after Mom had taken her door and asked to see me, but Granny refused. I'd watched them from the window, screaming at each other in the driveway until Karen peeled away in her old Cavalier, leaving nothing but a cloud of dust hanging in the air. I never saw her after that day, though I heard years later that she'd moved to Nashville with her boyfriend to become a country singer.

Karen gagged a little on the Gatorade, which turned into a cough, and I turned my head to give her some privacy. I stared at the cardboard covering the windows until I noticed the little holes poked into it so the light from outside could shine through. The pattern was thoughtful, even pretty. The longer I looked, the more I saw that a city had been made—the shape of houses and buildings and trees.

"Me and my grandbaby did that," Karen said. "I promised her I'd take her to Lexington and show her all the tall buildings. That was before my daughter decided I couldn't see her anymore."

"Why?"

"I wrecked her car," Karen said. "Again."

I turned back toward Karen and raised my eyebrows.

"And I may have neglected to mention that I was taking her car in the first place."

I smiled. "Just slipped your mind, huh?"

"In my defense, a lot of things slip your mind when you're high as a kite."

"I suppose they do."

We were quiet for a moment. Karen took slow sips of her drink, and I stared down at my hands and tried not to look too long at Karen's face. I listened for Carver's laugh again but there were only the crickets stirring outside as the sun set. The room grew even darker.

"You know what made me want to quit?" Karen asked after a while.

I shook my head.

"My *husband* told me I should use my grandbaby's birthday money to score us some meth. And I was going to do it. I was driving my happy ass down the road thinking it didn't matter anyway because it's not like I was going to get to see her anytime soon or ever again, and why not be high? Why not? And I just started crying. It was like somebody tore down some dam inside of me and everything came pouring out. I had to pull off the side of the road, I was sobbing so hard. I just couldn't hold it all in anymore. Couldn't keep on like I was. When I came back home without anything, my husband didn't take too well to that. He liked it even less when I told him I wanted to straighten myself up. He decided to punch some sense into me."

I winced and Karen waved her hand in the air like she could dispel the image. "It wouldn't the first time, honey, but it'll sure be the last."

"I'm sorry."

"Don't be. I've been detoxing for three days now. Amanda came in all the way from Knoxville to look over me. She's been through this kind of thing with folks before."

"I'm glad she did. I've heard it can be rough."

"I think I've died at least three times...and wanted to plenty more than that. It's not just details that slip your mind when you're high. Memories leave, too. Regrets. Guilt. It all kind of...floats away." She lifted her hand so a few pinpricks of light fell through the cardboard and onto her skin, dotting her wrist like stars. "But then they come back. Your mama always told me that. Karen, you can't outrun your own head. You'll still be the same person when you come down. Don't you think you're worth getting to know? She was a real pain in the ass, your mother."

I smiled. "So I've been told."

"You look like her. Even sound like her. And you're here selling pills so you must be a lot more like her than I thought. I figured your granny would have baptized all the Nell out of you by now." Karen shook her head. "Anything else I'm missing?"

"I got a door like her, too."

I didn't know I was going to say it until just before I did. I didn't regret it, though. Not even a little. Somehow I knew that Karen wouldn't panic or judge me or demand anything from me. She whistled low and soft and sat up a little higher in the bed.

"Since when?"

I looked up at my door spinning above us and Karen looked up, too. "Few weeks now."

"Will you take it?"

I shrugged. "I change my mind about every day. Every minute, sometimes."

Karen nodded. "You know, back when I was little, they used to celebrate the doors. People would throw big parties anytime some-one got a door. Everybody would go over and see the person, ask them about it. Treat them like royalty for a while. Of course we never knew for sure if the person had a door or not—some people just liked an excuse to throw a party and get some attention—but I never really minded as long as I got to eat somebody else's food and dance in the grass."

"It sure ain't like that anymore."

"No, people treat it more like a funeral now."

"Was it that way with my mom?"

Karen sighed. "I reckon you can find out for yourself."

"What do you mean?"

Karen dragged a purse from the darkness beside her and rustled around inside. My little door moved a bit closer to us like it was curi-ous, and the heat emanating from it made me shiver. Karen handed me a small notebook with a dark-red cover, then leaned back against the wall, exhausted. I listened to the wheeze of her breath and felt a pang of guilt at the thought of Granny at home and what she would think to see me sitting here in the dark with Karen. I wondered, for the hundredth time, if she would understand that I was doing all this to help her. My fog tried its best to whisper dark nothings into my ear as I tilted the notebook back and forth until I could make out the name written on the front in flourishing letters. When I did finally manage to read it, the name chased every other thought out of my mind.

Donna Nell.

"Mom," I whispered.

"I found it after she took her door. There was a note for me inside with strict instructions. I was to give it to you after your mom was gone. I tried, but your granny wouldn't have it." Karen sighed. "She said if Nell wanted to be gone, then she would be gone, through and through. She told me she'd call the sheriff on me if I came back on her land. So I left. I may've said a few choice words before I did, but I left."

I turned the notebook over in my hands but I couldn't bring myself to open it. "Why didn't Granny take it?"

"Honey, I don't know. That woman used to be like my own mother. She fed me and nursed me after I lost my first baby and called me every holiday right up until the very end. Your mom... She was struggling a lot before she took her door and leaving you with your granny more and more and... I don't know. I think your granny saw it coming and she wanted somebody to blame. It was easier to blame me and Thelma and your mom's drinking, I guess. A lot easier than taking her own part in it. Does she know what you're doing? Your granny?"

I shook my head. "She'd never forgive me if she did."

"You know, it's not easy to be a mother in this place. It's hard and it's lonely and sometimes your babies are the only thing you got. So you start expecting things from them that ain't always fair. I wished somebody had told me this when I was your age so I'm going to tell you now. At some point, you have to ask what you owe yourself, not just what you owe the people who raised you. You hear me?"

"I hear you."

Karen settled down into the bed, propping herself up against a mound of pillows. When I went to leave, her hand shot out in the dark and grabbed my wrist. Her touch was hot and clammy. She said, "Would you stay a while? I keep having these dreams. Sometimes it helps me if I know I'm not alone, you know, when I fall asleep."

I scooted back onto the bed until I touched her legs under the covers. Karen tossed fitfully for a while before finally easing into something like rest. And all the while I held my mother's journal in my hands. I couldn't put it down but I couldn't open it, either. I'd wanted my mother to answer for what she'd done for so long. Wanted some explanation, some reason that would make her leaving make sense. It was like some part of me was caught in the moment I realized she was gone and never coming back. The rest of me grew up and changed, but that part of me was stuck living that moment over and over, never growing older, never understanding. Some tender, bruised part that I couldn't find no matter how hard I searched, and that part of me would answer to no voice but my mother's. The only person in all the world who could let me go, and she was already gone.

Until now.

I held what was left of her in my hands, my fingers clenched so tight that my knuckles went white.

I didn't move until I heard Carver calling my name through the house, the sound of him getting louder and louder, like he was being born there in the dark, and the first thing he did in his new life was come to find me.

chapter seventeen

We were halfway home when Carver's phone lit up. He cursed under his breath, softly at first, then louder before he turned the screen toward me. Julie's text message was short but it made the hairs on the back of my neck stand up: need help, come quick.

Carver did a U-turn through a field of wildflowers so tall that their brightly colored heads whipped inside my window. I reached out just in time to snatch a handful before we were on the road again. I rolled the wildflowers between my fingers until the petals grew damp and dark, until little holes appeared in them and they began to disintegrate, leaving nothing but a bright-green scent against my fingertips. I clenched my fist around what was left and held my hand out the open window. The wind buffeted my arm as I fed the withered flowers to my door, thinking of my mother sitting by some dying fire in some strange world, her face upturned as dead flowers fell from the sky.

I felt so far away from myself. Like that night I came home and found the house all lit up and Granny gone. I felt like I was floating in some dark, deep water, and everything that happened to me happened above the surface so it could never really reach me. All I saw were dim shadows and vague impressions… Somewhere, the car skidded onto a gravel driveway and Carver opened my door and reached out his hand and some version of me reached back and followed him inside Rachel's trailer and all the lights were on there, too.

Rachel lay on the floor with one arm slung over her eyes, groaning in pain. Julie grabbed Carver as soon as he walked in the door and started sobbing.

"It's all right," he said again and again. "We're here. Everything's all right."

I stood on the porch with my little door at my shoulder. Julie murmured something to Carver, and Carver mumbled back. When we were little, I used to feel left out of the space between them. No matter how close Julie and I became, she and Carver still shared things I had no part in—a family, a home. I felt it again, that old twang of jealousy and sadness, and my fog curled around that loneliness like it was the sweetest feeling in all the world, the only feeling we could trust.

Julie was freshly showered and wore her favorite sweatshirt, the one with the holes sewn into the sleeves so she could stick her thumbs through, but Rachel looked like she'd been lying on the floor all day. She wore dark jeans and a black T-shirt. I stepped a little further inside, and my foot hit a backpack slumped against the wall. I toed it open and saw a single flashlight and a hint of silver—a screwdriver, maybe, or some other tool. I don't know what made me turn and look outside to see if Rachel's truck was in the driveway. I could claim it was some brilliance in me, but that doesn't feel exactly true. It was more like the part of me that always suspects the worst is about to happen. The part always waiting for some dark disaster to fall from the sky so it can sit back and nod its head and say *I saw this coming* as everything falls to pieces because sometimes knowing is the only comfort you're given. That part urged me across the porch and around the yard to the back where I found Rachel's truck sitting in the grass, covered with an old tarp. A blue Chevy with the plates torn off.

When I walked back inside the trailer, Julie was kneeling beside Rachel. Carver was in the kitchen with his cell phone pressed to his ear. Outside, the crickets were screaming at the dark and I wished I could scream with them. But I kept my voice level as I said, "It was you then. Y'all tried to break into Dr. Owens's house."

"What?" Carver said. He held his phone at arm's length as he looked between me and Julie. "What did you say?"

"Was it?" I asked.

Julie looked down at Rachel without answering.

I shook my head. "Julie…" I didn't know what else to say so I just rubbed my hands over my face.

Julie clutched her elbows in her palms. "The alarms weren't supposed to go off that way. We did everything right—*everything.*"

"Are you serious?" Carver asked. He looked down at the phone in his hand as someone picked up the other line. "I'll call you back," he said, then pocketed the phone. He took three steps into the living room before he turned back. He jerked one direction, then the other, unspeaking for at least a minute. It was like his body was trying to process the information for him, but even it struggled to make sense of what Julie and Rachel had done.

"Did anybody see you?" Carver asked.

"No!" Julie said, indignant, but her cheeks were already turning red. She always cried when she was angry, which only made her angrier, which only made her cry more. Already her hands were balled into little fists. "No, nobody saw us. We left as soon as the lights came on."

"There were cameras," I said. "There's footage."

"Shit," Carver said. "Thelma's police scanner. Hell, Julie, half the county already knows what happened. Rachel's probably already on their list. There can't be that many blue Chevys in Blackdamp."

"It's in her daddy's name!" Julie shouted.

"How does that make any bit of difference?" Carver looked at me as though I could answer the question, but I just shook my head.

Julie pressed the heels of her hands against her eyes. "But we cut the power. They couldn't have recorded us when we were up close, not where they could see our faces. And they couldn't have gotten video of her truck, either. The best they could have done is seen us jumping over the brick wall at the back of his property. That's when Rachel slipped."

"I didn't slip," Rachel croaked. "Something caught the edge of my jacket, and it threw me off. I was going to land on my feet until I didn't."

"We took the back roads home," Julie said. "We were careful."

"You can't be careful when you're doing something wrong," I said.

"Oh, you're one to talk," Julie said. "Selling pills to anybody who has a dollar to give you. Ain't that wrong?"

"You're the one who told me to sell them in the first place!"

Julie laughed. "When did you start listening to me? I'm not even an adult, according to you. Can't even take care of myself. I'm just some little girl with a fucked-up head who only makes bad choices."

"I never said that!"

"You've always acted that way. Always hovering over me like I'm going to spin out and do something terrible any minute of the day. You've never trusted me."

"You're the only person I've trusted!" I shouted. "You and Granny are all I've had, Julie. You know that."

"Well," Carver said, but grew quiet when I rounded on him. He held up his hands and slowly walked toward me until he was standing between me and Julie. I was breathing hard, every muscle in my body tensed. I wanted to grab hold of something and tear it apart, wanted something I could sink my teeth into, but there was nothing I could hurt that I didn't love, and it made me feel so helpless, so worthless, that all the energy started to drain out of me until I felt small enough to slip through the cracks in the floor and fall away into the dark. It would have been nice, really. To disappear. To be gone.

Tears welled in my eyes as Carver looked at me. "Hey," he whispered so softly that I could barely hear him. He put his hand on my hip to anchor me. "Everything's okay. All right? We're here. Julie's here. The cops aren't. We have some time, at least. A little time. That's all we need, you and me. We'll figure things out. We've always been the brains of this operation. I mean, more me than you, but you always helped out where you could."

I let out a heavy breath as Carver smiled. I never could figure out how he did that. Made me want to laugh when laughter felt like the furthest thing in the world from me. He pushed his hand against my hip to jostle me a little, shake me loose from whatever held me in place.

He said, "Why don't you step outside a minute? Go sit in the grass a while. Write me a poem or something. I'll take care of this and come get you when things are a little less ridiculous, all right?"

I nodded but didn't move until he wrapped an arm around my waist and turned me toward the door. He followed me across the porch and down the steps and he hovered over me as I sat down in the grass under the front porch. He was backlit by the glow of my little door as he leaned down and pressed a kiss to my forehead.

"I'll be back," he said.

I don't know how long I sat there. I don't remember if it was warm that night or cool or if the ground was dry or if the dew soaked into my jeans and made me shiver. I just remember sitting there and staring out into the dark. There were a few other trailers nearby, their windows lit dim and golden. The road was empty but for the occasional car passing by, its headlights illuminating the trees overhead, their branches flashing ghostly white, then gone. I pulled the grass beside me absentmindedly. Yanked up weeds, roots and all, and fed everything to my little door. It sank lower and lower, like holding up its own weight had become too much a chore, until it was finally eye level with me. I'd never seen it that close to the ground before. I tossed bits of gravel and a single rusted nail into its swirling surface like I was skipping rocks across a pond. I watched the sparks of light that each thing made as my door swallowed them whole, the light so bright it left deep trails cut into my vision that took a while to fade. My door was wider than Carver's Tempest now, bigger than the porch above me. It had to be eight feet across, at least, where once it could have fit inside the circle of my arms. I guess that's what happened when you fed things. They got bigger. Soon my door wouldn't be able to fit anywhere.

"Little door, little door," I whispered. "You ain't so little anymore."

I closed my eyes and let the warmth of my door wash over me. I imagined my mother still sitting by that fire, now with a cup of coffee steaming in her hand as little flecks of mud and grass rained from the sky. I liked the idea of making a mess she'd have to clean up. It felt right, somehow, that I would be nothing but dirt in that other world, something so small. My fog rose up in me, deep as the sky, and said, *You're nothing here, too.*

I think I was crying when Carver came back outside. I remember the feeling of his fingers on my skin, wiping a tear away, and the solemn look on his face. My door drifted back up into the air until it hovered over Carver like some great shining halo.

"You're awful pretty," I said.

He smiled a sad smile. "Try to remember that when I ask you this next question, all right?"

I nodded.

"Julie said that Rachel pulled something in her back. She doesn't want to go to a hospital because she's afraid it will look suspicious, Rachel being hurt and all. They're trying to lay low right now." Carver sighed. "She wants you to give Rachel some of the pills we've been selling to tide her over."

I closed my eyes. Carver traced the line of my jaw as I thought, his touch gentle, barely there. I knew I couldn't do it. Part of it was spite—I never liked Rachel and I didn't want to help her. But helping her was helping Julie, which is why I paused there, waiting for some answer to come to me. Helping Julie might make it easier for her to stay with Rachel, which I knew, in the end, would hurt Julie, too. And it felt different, somehow, to sell pills to strangers. I got to leave before I saw what happened. I skimmed the surface of their life and I could tell myself that I was helping them somehow—helping them stop hurting, helping them get up and go to work in the morning, helping them make their life a little more bearable. But with Julie and Rachel, I knew too much. I couldn't get more involved than I already was, couldn't have something else to blame myself for when it all went wrong.

I shook my head. "I can't do that."

"You're sure?" Carver asked.

"No, but…" I rubbed my fingers against my eyes. "No." Carver pulled back, but I reached out and grabbed the hem of his shirt. "I can tell her myself."

Carver pushed my shoulder gently, holding me in place.

"I'm not a child," I said. "I can clean up my own messes."

"I know you could, but you don't have to do it on your own. I'm here, Maren. Besides, she'll take it easier from me." He slipped the keys to the Tempest in my hand. "Go sit in the car and turn the heat on. I'll be out in a minute."

He kissed me again, gently on top of the head, and walked back inside alone. I didn't want to hear what followed so I got into the car and locked all the doors and watched my little door paint starlight onto the hood of Carver's car.

chapter eighteen

Back home, I sat down on the porch swing and let my weight carry me backward. The sound of the chains creaking melded with the crickets whirring in the grass and the frogs bellowing somewhere damp until it felt like the whole world was singing, or maybe screaming. Summer was waiting somewhere in all that noise. Maybe the noise is what brought it. Maybe I was sitting in the middle of some great conjuring, all things small and scaled and slick crying out to break the hold of winter, and my only hope of ever feeling warm again was depending on something I could crush in the palm of my hand.

I watched my little door hover at the foot of the steps, casting its ghostly glow over the tips of the dead flowers. I wished I could cry. It would have felt nice right then to let go of something, even if it was just tears. But nothing came.

I tossed Mom's journal onto a rocking chair a few feet away and imagined her sitting there with a cigarette between her teeth, grinning at me. Carver walked onto the porch, went inside the house, and came back with two bottles—a beer for him, a pop for me—all without looking at me. We hadn't talked the whole drive home. I just knew he was angry for what happened with Julie, how I'd said no and left him standing there alone with nothing to give his only sister. He would blame me, and he might be right. My fog assured me that

I was right. It was inevitable that he and Julie would band together the way they always did and I would be left outside of them, alone.

Carver sat down on the swing beside me. He said Granny was sleeping with her hand tucked under her chin and we both smiled. We clinked our bottles together and drank without looking at each other.

After a while Carver said, "I sure could use a hug."

I huffed out a breath and lifted the arm nearest him. Carver shifted his weight, tipping the swing from side to side as he set his beer down, then wrapped one arm around my waist. He tucked his head against my neck and kissed the lobe of my ear, the tender skin beneath it, and then my neck. I shivered against him and I knew he was smiling.

"You reckon I could build a house here?" He tapped the edge of my collarbone. His finger was cold from holding the beer and I suppressed another shiver.

"I don't think it's zoned residential," I said.

"I know a guy down at city hall who could smooth things over."

I smiled, but my stomach felt nervous. So did my hands, my arms, all my joints. I said, "I didn't think you'd want to live near me after what I did."

"What do you mean?"

"Telling Julie no," I said. "Not giving Rachel what she needed."

"Oh. I thought you did the right thing. Well, at least you did what I would do, and I'm usually right about most things."

I closed my eyes and something like laughter bubbled up in my chest.

"What?" he asked.

"I thought you'd be mad at me."

WHERE I CAN'T FOLLOW

"Why?"

"I don't know."

Carver shrugged. "It wasn't an easy choice, Maren. You did the best you could."

"Julie won't think so. She'll hate me."

"She's hated you before."

"When?"

"Most of seventh grade after you tried to dye her hair red and it came out orange."

"I deserved it then."

"Maybe." Carver smiled. "But if she can forgive you for making her look like a neon carrot on Picture Day, then I think she'll forgive you for this. We've all come through worse before. We'll come through it again."

"Maybe. It just seems like something worse is bound to happen. I keep waiting for a meteor to come flying out of Jack's Fork and carry me on to Hell."

He laughed. "Well, if Hell is anywhere on this earth, it's Jack's Fork."

We clinked our bottles together and drank to Hell until they were empty. I lay my head against Carver's shoulder and listened to the scuff of our bare feet over the worn wooden boards of the porch. It reminded me of when Uncle Tim brought the twins home from the hospital. He used to carry them both at once, one pressed to each shoulder, making the same sound over and over, a huffy little *chh-chh-chh*.

It felt like someone was lulling me off to sleep, too, when Carver cleared his throat and said, "You going to read that journal or not?"

I sighed. The little book sitting on Granny's rocking chair seemed harmless there in the dark, but the sight of it made me feel stubborn, mulish, like when Mom refused me something as a child, which wasn't often and always came as a surprise. I'd waited so long for some glimpse of Mom, and now that she was here, I wanted to refuse her. I wanted to be the one to turn away and pretend like the book meant nothing to me. Like I could wait for days, weeks even, before I cracked its spine.

"It can wait," I said.

Carver snorted. "It's Nell's name on the cover, ain't it? Your mom's journal? Sitting right over there."

"Mm-hmm."

"And you're not even a little curious?"

"I'm tired," I said. "More tired than anything else."

"Hmm. Well, what does your door think?"

"It don't think. It don't have to. That's why I'm jealous of it."

"What does it do then?"

"Floats. Spins." I shrugged. "Sometimes I…"

"Sometimes you what?"

I swallowed. "Sometimes I feed it things."

"It's got a *mouth*?"

"No." I smiled. "Not exactly. It's like one of those black holes you see on the Science Channel."

Carver followed my eyes to where my little door floated in the yard. He frowned and it deepened the narrow line between his eyes, making him look so much like Julie that I almost laughed, or cried.

"I can show you," I said.

He didn't respond so I took his silence as permission. I grabbed his empty beer bottle and walked barefoot over the porch. I teetered on the top step for a moment. The edge of the door was just a few inches away. Its pale-pink light danced over my arms and chest, but Carver wouldn't see that. He would only see me standing there in the darkness, backlit by the windows, staring off into nothing. He wouldn't see that the nothing stared back.

I held the bottle up and slowly fed it into my door. No matter how many times it happened, I still felt a little thrill in my belly as the bottle began to disintegrate, eaten into specks the size of dust, then turned into its own swirling trail of light. My door grew brighter and brighter until I had to close my eyes and look away.

The imprint of it was still seared on my vision when I looked up again. The world eaten down to its simplest shapes. The bottle was gone and Carver was standing right beside me. The look on his face scared me—somewhere between angry and confused and a little afraid. He reached out and swept his hand through the air where my little door floated, and though he couldn't see, the door shifted around his touch, broke apart, and then re-formed as soon as his hand had moved away.

"Are you all right?" I asked.

He didn't answer.

"Carver. Hey, it's okay."

He wrapped his hand around my elbow and pulled me away from my door like it might be hungry for something more.

"Hey," I said. "It's all right. I've done it before. Nothing ever happens. Well, nothing bad happens."

"It's there," he said, looking at the place where my door floated.

"Yeah. I told you."

"I know, but...I think I didn't really..." He looked at me and frowned. There was something so hurt in his expression that my heart broke a little.

"I'm sorry," I said. "I didn't mean..."

"Can I kiss you?" he asked. "I really want to kiss you."

"Yes," I said, and before I could even grin, Carver bent down and kissed me firmly on the mouth. It was not the kind of soft and gentle kisses he'd given me before, and not like that first kiss, either, all those years ago, sloppy and a little surprised. It was the kind of kiss that meant to be a kiss. The kind that grew roots and spread all through me until I felt it in the tips of my fingers, a tingling kind of spasm that made me grab hold of Carver's chest for balance. He wrapped his arms around my back and pulled me close to him as he trailed his tongue over my lips until I opened my mouth. I had never been this close to him before. The feeling of it overwhelmed me, short-circuited every other thought or feeling in my brain until there was only the warmth of him, his mouth.

He pushed us toward the house, opened the front door with one hand, and led us inside. He broke away from me to lock the front door and the fact that he was still thoughtful even now, still wanted to make sure we were safe, made my chest feel warm and tight. I would have laughed if he hadn't been looking at me the way he was. He stared at me the whole time like he was holding on to that moment between us, refusing to let it break. I was breathing so hard that the sound embarrassed me a little. It must have been so obvious how badly I needed him to kiss me again, but I was too tired to try to hide it. When he stepped toward me, I held out my arms for him and I hoped he felt wanted because he was.

This time I pressed Carver close to me, my hand slipping under his shirt and snaking up his skin until I found that little knotted scar on his shoulder, something familiar to ground me in him. We stumbled from doorway to doorway. He pressed me against the kitchen table and then the hallway wall beneath the pictures of my family as he undid my bra.

Finally, we fumbled backward into my room. My feet brushed against something soft and a little cool, and I almost cried out in alarm as I tipped onto my mattress. Carver shut the door softly behind him, careful not to wake Granny. He pulled his shirt over his head, knocking his baseball cap off in the process. My bedside lamp wasn't on, but the curtains on both my windows were pulled back, revealing the underside of my little door where it floated just outside. The light that danced along it was bloodred deepening to purple, and it cast my whole room in a rosy glow. Shadows shivered under Carver's eyes and along his shoulders. I've said before that Carver was beautiful but I think it bears repeating. There is a softness to him that is misleading—something in the easiness of his smile and those curls around his ears and the way he wraps his arms around his chest when he laughs real hard. Something that says he is sweet through and through. But there was such a sharpness in the way he looked at me that night, a feral kind of concentration that made me feel warm all over.

My breath hitched at the sight of him, and I wish it had been only him that made my chest ache that way.

But there was something else, too.

All around him were the same deep-green stalks I'd seen that morning. But instead of just a few creeping up through the cracks between my floorboards, there were dozens. Maybe hundreds. It was impossible to count them when they were knit so close together. And they had grown taller, too, and thicker. The green of them was deeper than before, striated with thin veins of a paler green that appeared almost blue in the dim light of my room. Most of the stalks were

knee-high, though some were higher, stretching their tips toward the
fine down of hair along Carver's belly. He didn't feel them brushing
against the skin above his belt, but I saw them, and felt a twinge of
jealousy, though I couldn't have said right then if I was jealous of
Carver for being touched or the flowers for touching him.

"What is it?" Carver asked.

He placed one knee between my thighs and I scooted further
onto the bed. He followed and settled himself between my legs, held
aloft above me with his dark hair falling into his eyes. I reached out
beside the bed until I felt a stalk against the back of my knuckles. It
seemed almost to respond to my touch, curling between my fingers
until I held it loosely in my palm. I ran my fingers along the little
nubs where flowers would soon bloom, packed hard and tight, waiting to burst.

"Are you okay?" he asked.

"Yeah," I said, but my voice was a little hoarse.

"We don't have to do anything."

"No, no, that's not it. I promise."

Carver nodded and settled a little lower against me, the weight of
him pressing into my hips in a pleasant way. "Is this what you want?"

I nodded.

"You have to tell me," he said. "All right? You have to say it."

My gaze roamed around the room, following the rise and fall
of the flowers. They writhed as though they were moved by some
anxious wind. The stalks bent and shivered and swayed and I know
it must have looked to Carver like I was considering his offer, like I
was thinking about what it all meant, and I suppose that, in a way,
I was. I felt torn again, the way I'd felt in the hospital after talking
to Dr. Owens, split into a dozen different pieces—part of me was

stuck with Mom, part of me was here, part of me wondering when the flowers would bloom, when my door would stop growing. Now and then and next all swirling around inside me. I wanted to tell Carver all this. I wanted him to know that we were in a field of some other world's making and that flowers that could never grow here were growing here anyway and that soon they would bloom a blue so bright that it would ache your eyes to see it, like your eyes knew, somehow, that they were never made to look at something so lovely, but they wanted to anyway. And that's how I felt right then. Hungry. Needy. Like I was reaching out to hold a newborn star and I didn't care if it burned my hands to ash as long as I got to feel that first moment of warmth. Some things were worth that much. Sometimes just one touch of something you couldn't keep could keep you going your whole life.

So I said, "I want you to kiss me."

And he did.

chapter nineteen

I woke up alone. It was cold in my room without Carver and without the heat of my little door. I looked out the nearest window and saw my door there, floating, spinning, looking almost lazy in the weak morning light. I pulled the covers up to my chin, which sent the flowers beside me shivering. They reacted as though they were a single thing, passing the disturbance from one stem to the next like dominoes falling until the whole room was filled with their quiet chattering. I guess I wasn't entirely alone then. The flowers were still there, still waiting to bloom, and I wondered if a flower was a flower when it didn't have petals or color. I didn't have a word for something that was waiting to be, but I thought it might be my name. A Maren. A waiting.

I reached for my phone on my bedside table and felt the rock Julie had given me instead. I ran my fingers over the smooth side and then the rough—the two halves of me—and hoped she would still see the good in me when this was all over. I pushed the rock out of sight and rolled over, not wanting to think about her or the flowers or any of my problems. Carver's hat was lying on the empty side of the bed. This was his way of telling me that he was still here, because I knew he would never leave without that hat. I ran my hand around the worn bill, traced along the letters on the front, which were worn almost to the point of disappearing. I picked it up to hold it to my face—knowing, already, that it would smell like his dandruff shampoo and sweat and a little bit of motor oil—but still pleased when I was proven right.

I slipped out of bed and changed, still reluctant to be awake just yet. There were even more flowers than the night before, crowded so thick that I couldn't take a step without touching one, and the floor felt slick with moisture, chilling me even more. I knew this must be it—the pressure from my little door. It had been with me for weeks now and it would start changing my world a little more every day, just like the heat from Ida Ross's door slowly burning her from the inside out. Of all the ways the door could have pushed me toward an answer, flowers seemed an awfully gentle nudge. They were beautiful now, even before they bloomed, and even as they reminded me of my mother and her journal, which was tucked under my bed where the flowers hadn't yet started growing. I knew I would have to choose.

But it was hard. There was so much promise in a door left shut. As long as you never opened it, you could never be disappointed by what you didn't find. And you could make it anything you needed it to be on any day you needed it. If you wanted to, you could spend your whole life thinking about some other world and never really be present in the world you were given. Half in and half out. It was easier, in ways. Things hurt a little less, the sting already numbed by the time it reached you. But it dulled other things, too. Joy, hope, the tingle of Carver's skin brushing over my own.

I picked his hat off the bed and settled it over my hair, pulled low just the way he wore it, before I walked down the hallway and into the kitchen. Granny was standing by the stove stirring what looked like sausage gravy in her big cast-iron skillet. Steam rose from the top and twisted through the early morning light like a ghost. The room was warm from the oven, and there were covered plates sitting on the table beside me. Carver was at the fridge, bent double, and the whole picture seemed perfect, at first, until I saw how many plates were on the table. And how much food was piled high, waiting to be eaten— more than the three of us could ever manage.

Then Carver turned and saw me. His face lit up at first, his eyes falling on his hat, and then my face. But his smile was short-lived, replaced too quickly with that solemn expression he wore more and more often. He hurried over and nudged me back into the hall, far enough that Granny couldn't see us from the stove.

"You look cute in my hat," he said and gave me a quick, warm kiss. "Can we pretend for a second that's all I need to say to you? Just for a second?"

Fear curled tight in my belly but I nodded anyway. Carver closed his eyes and took a few slow breaths before he opened them again, looking somehow even sadder than before. He said, "Did you have an uncle David?"

"Yeah, he was the oldest of Granny's kids. He died before I was born, though."

"Well," Carver said. "Granny thinks that I'm David."

I felt for a moment that I might sink right into the ground, but I stayed standing with Carver's hand firmly on my hip. "Okay."

"And it's my birthday, I guess. David's birthday. And she thinks everybody is coming over to eat breakfast together. She already had everything going by the time I got up so I called Cheryl and asked her to come over and bring the kids. She said she would call Tim."

I shook my head. "They don't know."

"Know what?"

"That Granny is... That there's..." I waved my hands in the air.

"This. That this happens sometimes. They don't know. None of them do."

"Ah, shit."

"We can't tell them," I said. "Granny would never forgive me."

"Well, they'll be here any minute."

"Right." I closed my eyes. "Maybe I can bring Granny around before they get here?"

"Maybe," Carver said. "But what's so bad about them knowing? Wouldn't it give you a little more help?"

I shook my head. "Granny doesn't want everyone treating her different."

"I don't know if you have much choice in this. We could at least tell Cheryl, huh? It'll be better if she knows. If she comes in acting normal, then it might make things worse. And what about the kids?"

I covered my ears with my hands and closed my eyes. It was too much. Part of me wanted to blame Carver. I wanted to shove him out the front door and turn the lock and go back to a place where I made all the decisions and managed all the crises, a place where I could control the damage or, at the very least, *choose* the damage I knew I could take. My fog curled tight around me and spurred me on. These decisions didn't hurt Carver the way they hurt me; it wasn't his granny lost in the past and dependent on him for her future. He wouldn't have to look her in the eye after Cheryl learned the truth. He didn't carry what I did or know how it felt. *There's only you*, my fog said. *You're the only person you can trust.*

But I'd asked him to be here and he was here. I wanted him here. Even if that meant letting go a little.

"Okay," I said. "Okay, tell Cheryl. Have her keep the kids outside for now."

Carver turned to leave but turned back and grabbed my hand, squeezing it gently. "We're going to get through this, all right?"

He kissed me on the cheek, then turned and headed through the living room. I heard him shouting hello before the door even shut and knew Cheryl must be in the yard with the kids. I took a deep breath, put on a smile, and walked into the kitchen. Granny had poured the gravy into a bowl and dropped a dishcloth on top to keep the steam from escaping. She hummed to herself as she poured flour into a bowl, and when she looked up and saw me, she smiled.

"Forest," she said. "When'd you get here?"

I cleared my throat. "Just a minute ago. You need some help?"

"No, but you can keep me company."

I nodded and moved to Granny's side. She thought I was Aunt Forest then, my aunt who lived a few hours away now. I wondered where I was in this version of Granny's world. If I existed in Granny's mind yet or if I had been erased completely. I took slow, even breaths though my throat felt narrow as a straw. Granny's schedule was taped to the side of the fridge. Most of the items had been crossed off but our seven o'clock evening talk remained. I'd come home late most nights and found her already in bed. I'd forgotten to pick her up from the Rose Garden once. How many things had I missed? Outside the windows, my little door shivered into place, spinning slow circles over the stunted trees still clinging to the side of the mountain.

"I almost forgot the biscuits," Granny said. "Can you believe that? Everything done and not a biscuit to be seen."

"There'd be a riot," I said.

Granny smiled. "Is Nell here yet?"

"No. Is she coming?"

"Of course she's coming." Granny smoothed out a little well in the flour, making space for the Crisco and milk. "Has she…told you anything lately?"

"About what?"

Granny looked at me from the corner of her eye. "I can't tell if you're playing coy with me, but I can't hold it in any longer. Has she told you about the baby?"

I didn't trust myself to speak so I just nodded.

Granny smiled. "I figured she'd tell you. You'll midwife for her, won't you? She'll need somebody there with her. The first is always the hardest." Granny opened the cabinet, frowned, and closed it again. "I hope this will straighten her up. Get her away from them people she calls friends. There's nothing like a child to make you grow up yourself."

I was alive then, in Granny's mind. Just a little wisp of a thing tucked away in my mother's belly.

"I know everybody thinks their babies are special," Granny said, "but I have a good feeling about this one. This baby is going to be just what we need."

"I hope so," I whispered.

Carver announced his presence by coughing loudly. Cheryl stood behind him trying to smile, but it was too wide and showed too many teeth and she looked more like a hostage.

"We brought some orange juice," Cheryl said and then held up an empty hand. She stared at it, surprised, until Carver held up the juice.

"Got it right here," he said.

"Right. Right." Cheryl tugged at the low ponytail that bound her hair. "We'll just be over here. All this food sure smells good."

Granny smiled at her but didn't say anything so I turned my back to them and tried to breathe like normal, but I'd forgotten what normal felt like. My whole body felt disjointed, jagged, and every breath I drew seemed too loud or too long or not nearly enough. Granny's hands hovered over the bowl before her. She looked down at her fingers, dusted with flour, and then up at the cabinets. Her eyes flickered from place to place until they settled back on her hands. "What comes next?"

"What?" I asked.

"First the flour and then..." Her voice trailed off. It took me a moment to realize she'd forgotten how to make biscuits. I felt, briefly, like I was falling, or at least like something inside me was falling. I knew I would cry if I kept looking at the expression on her face, like she'd just woken up deep in the woods and had no idea which way was home.

"Here," I said. "Let me help."

I nudged her to the side and she went willingly enough, her hands still held out in front of her, dusted white all the way to the third knuckle. She looked like she was turning into a ghost. Just the tips of her fingers, just the wrist, but part of me thought it might spread, swallow her up a little at a time. I wiped a tear from my eye with my shoulder and hoped she didn't notice. I reached for the milk and then turned to her.

I said, "Next is milk, right?"

"Milk?" Her eyes had a glassy, faraway look.

"For the biscuits," I said.

"The biscuits."

"Granny?"

She blinked a few times and then looked down at her hands again.

She rubbed her fingers together until the flour flaked away, revealing pale skin beneath. When she looked up at me, she seemed different somehow. Closer.

"Maren?" she said.

"Yeah, Granny." I felt a tear slip down my cheek but I had no way to hide it this time. "It's me."

"What're we doing?"

"You're showing me how to make biscuits. I never can remember how." I pointed at the bowl on the counter. "First you make a well with the flour. Then you put in your Crisco."

"Then milk," she said, reaching for the little half gallon between us.

"Then milk," I said and smiled.

She poured the milk into the bowl.

"Now exactly how much milk is that?" I asked.

"Enough."

I snorted. "Is that what I should write on the recipe? Add enough milk?"

"Recipe." She shook her head. "You don't need a recipe to cook. You feel it."

"Where exactly do you feel it because all I feel when I cook is annoyed."

She smiled at me, but the look faded too quickly. She leaned to the side and glanced over my shoulder where Carver and Cheryl were sitting at the kitchen table. Outside, a truck door slammed and Carver got up to intercept Tim before he walked into the house. For a moment I worried that Granny might be slipping, fading back to the hazy place she'd been before, but then she looked at me and I could see her there, my granny.

"Maren?" she said.

"Yeah?"

Her voice dropped to a whisper and she looked a little affronted as she asked, "What's Cheryl doing here?"

I smiled. "I invited her over. Tim too."

"Oh," she said. "Why?"

"Just thought it might be nice."

"Oh. I guess it is."

"Why don't you sit down and keep Cheryl company while I finish these?"

I caught Cheryl's eye as Granny turned and tried to tell her without telling her that she was back and everything was okay. Cheryl seemed profoundly confused so I said loudly, "You and Granny thinking about running any marathons? Y'all been walking so much I figure you must be ready for something bigger."

Cheryl's face brightened. "That's not a bad idea, you know. What do you think, Granny?"

"I'd be glad to cheer you on from the sidelines," Granny said.

Uncle Tim walked into the kitchen doorway. He looked at Granny and smiled. "I hope you cooked enough for me."

"I never could cook enough for you," she said. "You've got two hollow legs."

Tim grinned and held out his arm. Granny walked over to him and wrapped her arms around his waist. The top of her head barely reached Tim's shoulder and he looked at me over the cloud of her hair and I knew that Carver had told him, too, and that the truth was there between us, heavy as the air before a storm.

I mouthed *She's okay* and Tim nodded. He said, "Cheryl tells me you've been playing rummy with the women down at the old folks' home. You ain't been cheating them, have you?" He led Granny over to the table and pulled out her favorite chair. I watched them all sitting together as Carver walked into the kitchen and joined me.

He wrapped an arm around my waist and jostled me a little, but it didn't feel like there was anything left in me to shake out. "You okay?"

I shrugged.

"That's fair," he said. "I told Tim the truth. Don't hate me."

"I don't."

"You sure? I was ready to bribe you and everything."

"What kind of bribe?"

"A variety of baked goods, mostly."

"Doughnuts?"

"Powdered and plain."

I smiled. "Let's see how Tim and them react to all this. You may need to bribe me yet."

He kissed the top of my head. "You going to eat?"

"In a minute," I said.

So he stood with me and watched Granny and Cheryl and Tim sitting at the table talking until the kids ran into the house, streaming through the door like water down a mountain, and filled the room with noise, with laughter.

chapter twenty

I was an hour late for work that day. Eileen was standing by the front door by the time I made it. She was reading a pocket Bible—the kind with the green cover—and she glared at me as I hurried inside, but I didn't have time to feel guilty, at least not about her. I tossed my things into the narrow office in the back, shrugged off my coat, clocked in, and then stepped behind the counter.

The store was empty and silent but for the hum of the coolers along the wall and the little whine that the fluorescent lights always seemed to make. My fog swooped in the very moment I was alone and filled me up with all the ways I'd failed and all the terrible consequences that would follow until my breathing sounded even louder and for a moment I wondered if something was wrong with me, which only set my heart beating faster until it felt like there were wings in my chest, all of them stirring, beating. I reached for the register, meaning to count my drawer and give myself something else to focus on, but something small and yellow caught my eye. I bent down and pulled a sticky note from the floor. A footprint marred one corner but didn't obscure the message written in Julie's neat letters across the top: *You are exactly where you need to be.*

My chest tightened. I imagined Julie writing this to herself. She had written notes like this since we were in high school, maybe even longer, always some reminder that she was okay. But if you had to keep telling yourself that, could it really be true? Sadness tightened my throat and I stared up at my little door, watched the soft pinks and yellows at its edges swirl slowly into the endless black of its center, waiting for the sadness to pass, hoping there must be some kind of limit, some end to feeling, some place you could go where you'd be beyond the reach of yourself.

The bell over the door jingled and I smiled without thinking— the kind of smile that said *No, of course I'm not falling apart. There's nowhere else I'd rather be than selling you this overpriced gallon of milk that's two days shy of going bad*—but the smile turned genuine as Ace walked through the door. Ace raised her eyebrow when she saw me, just a little tick upward and a crinkle around her eyes, but anyone who knew her knew this was the equivalent of wild and raucous delight. We'd gone to high school together, though Ace was a few years ahead of me. She was over six feet tall and broad-shouldered, her dark hair cut close and covered with a knit beanie. Most everyone had a crush on her at some point, but I'd been one of the few people to date her. We'd been on and off again, falling into and out of rhythm with each other for years. She ambled over, pulling up the sleeves of the plaid button-down she wore to reveal the tattoos on both forearms, then leaned across the counter and said, "Why do you always look so sad?"

I smiled. "Life, probably."

"That'll do it." She studied me a moment. "Where's Jules?"

"She quit."

"Again?"

I shrugged.

"You seen her much?"

"Not lately."

"You know what she's into?"

"Whatever Rachel's into, I guess."

Ace frowned and the pale light from my little door cast her face in pastel shadows. "So I'd heard. You been up to the Well lately?"

"Not since high school. Have *you* been to the Well lately?"

Ace laughed. "Not for the reasons I used to go. I'm seeing a girl who does harm reduction. Free Narcan and clean needles, mostly, but her work takes us to some interesting places."

"Like the Well."

Ace nodded. "I saw Julie there a couple nights ago. She didn't look good."

"Is she using?" I asked, wondering if they'd gone to the Well in search of the pills I'd refused to give to Rachel, if I'd somehow sent Julie even further into places she shouldn't go.

Ace toyed with a box of mints on the counter. "Hard to tell. She took one look at me and was gone before I could get halfway across the room. I just thought you ought to know."

I sighed. "Thanks, Ace."

The bell over the door chimed again and John Edward walked into the store. He was out of uniform that morning—no wide-brimmed deputy's hat, no buttons on his lapel shined to the point of blinding anyone who walked past him. He seemed about to walk up to the counter until he spotted Ace and stopped. He tipped his chin to us and turned down the nearest aisle.

Ace frowned. "He's not still creeping around you, is he?"

"Not as bad as he used to."

"I'll wait out in my truck until he leaves, all right? And hey, your number still the same?"

"Yeah, why?"

"Just in case." Ace squeezed my hand, quick and firm. "Hopefully I won't have to use it. Take care of yourself."

"You too."

The store felt somehow smaller once Ace was outside, like all the air rushed in around me, the walls curving closer. I grabbed a bottle of cleaner and pretended to shine the counters as John Edward walked up with three energy drinks. I scanned the drinks as he yawned widely.

"Long night?" I asked.

"Long enough to take my first day off in three years."

I hummed a little as I packed his drinks into a bag. I was about to total the sale when he dropped a pack of gum onto the counter.

"You hear about it on the news this morning?" he asked.

I shook my head. "I was running late and didn't have time to watch."

"Ah. Well, I'm sure they'll rerun it this evening. The biggest bust since the KSP took down the Taggert brothers is the kind of thing that makes the news twice."

My hand slowed as I dropped the gum into his bag, and just like before, John Edward reached down, grabbed a candy bar, and dropped it onto the counter before I could total out his sale. I tried to find my breath again but all I could feel was the tightness in my chest.

John Edward leaned his elbows against the counter. "I knew it was getting rough on that side of the county. But it's always the people you don't suspect that surprise you the most. I knew Thelma Crawford had been buying half the county dry, but those Napier boys seemed to be getting their acts together."

That meant he'd arrested everyone I'd sold to and had made a point of telling me. I tried to keep my voice even as I said, "Thelma's in jail then?"

"Her and five others."

"It sounds like you cleared out Blackdamp pretty good."

"Biggest bust since oh-three," he repeated.

I dropped the candy bar into his bag and totaled the sale before John Edward could add anything else. He pulled his wallet from his pocket with exaggerated slowness. My little door floated closer, hovering just a few inches overhead. The heat of it warmed my shoulders, my cheeks.

"What happens to them now?" I asked.

"A fair trial. Just like we're promised." He wet his fingertips before he leafed through each bill one at a time. "That's all anybody can get at that point. Once the arrest is made…" He shrugged. "That's why it's important not to be around places like that. People see you hanging out with the wrong crowd and begin to wonder if you're not up to something similar."

I glanced toward the door, but all I could see was one side of Ace's truck. There were no other customers coming, no distraction.

He said, "I know people like to talk about me, but I want the same thing as anybody for this county. I want it to be a safe place. A good place. That's why I do what I do. Nobody wants to put a grandmother like Thelma in handcuffs, but that's part of the job, doing what nobody else is willing to do."

John Edward held out a twenty-dollar bill. I grabbed the edge and pulled, but he didn't let go. We both held on, bound together by the thin paper between our fingers.

"You have to be careful about that kind of thing," he said. "I don't want to arrest anybody in this county, but especially some people.

There's some people I'd do just about anything to protect. If they'd let me."

I pulled the twenty from John Edward's hand with a jerk. "Not everybody needs protecting."

"That so?"

"Some of us get by just fine on our own."

The bell chimed over the doorway and I could have cried in relief. I counted John Edward's change as quickly as I could and laid it on the counter to avoid touching his hand. He stared at me as he collected it, but I was already smiling at Darcy Turner and her daughter. Darcy waved and asked how I was doing, and I answered more loudly and sincerely than I ever had before. Her daughter ran by the counter and John Edward watched her until she was around the corner, then caught my eye again.

"Good luck," he said.

I waited until I saw his car pull out of the parking lot and heard Ace's truck roar to life before I sat down on the little stool behind the counter and put my head in my hands.

The flowers bloomed blue. Of course they did. There was no other color they could have been—radiant and too bright, like the edges of the flowers were almost too thin to hold it, like any moment the blue might leak out into the air and set itself free. They made the rest of my room seem more beautiful by comparison. The threadbare quilt on my bed, the secondhand lamps, the cheap curtains—all of it seemed softened by the flowers.

I'm not sure how long I stood in the doorway to my bedroom

that night just staring, my feet throbbing from walking on concrete floors all day, my eyes burning from all they'd seen. It seemed impossible. My room transformed over just a few days, filled to the brim with flowers born from another world. Flowers just like the ones my mother tucked into her hair in the weeks before she took her own door. I couldn't be sure if it meant that she was waiting for me on the other side, or if the door was just giving me something I wanted, plucking random images from my memory like it did for its shape.

The house was quiet around me. Carver had dropped me off half an hour before and we'd spent ten minutes talking on the porch. I ignored a call from Uncle Tim and didn't listen to the voicemail, either. I knew a conversation was coming about Granny and her memory, but I couldn't face it that day. That day I'd faced enough.

I'd checked on Granny three times and three times found her sleeping in her own bed. I'd called Carver to make sure he got home safe and called Julie just to listen to the sound of the phone ringing. The kitchen was clean, all the dishes put away, and all the lights turned off, and there was nothing, nothing left to do but reach under my bed and pull out my mother's journal.

Even after it was in my hands, I still sat there for a while. My little door was outside the windows again, and the room shivered in its soft honeycomb glow—pale-yellow light skimming over the tips of the flowers and the quilt on my bed and my skin, too, when I held out my hand like I was offering my door a good-night kiss.

I thought I had prepared myself for this. I'd let myself be angry at the journal and to ignore it and to think of little else but it. I'd even let myself feel a brief flare of hope at the thought of speaking to my mother again. I could still remember the sound of her voice—a little raspy, like she'd always just gotten over a cold or was about to catch one. She rumbled when she talked and when she laughed, and I swear the vibration of her was still trapped inside me somewhere, wrapped like static around the softest parts of me.

But it was a lot like seeing my door for the first time. No matter how much I thought about it, I still wasn't ready. I took a deep breath and opened the journal. I read the first words and started to cry.

Dear Maren.

chapter twenty-one

Dear Maren,

You're going to be so proud of me. I did something today
that's going to change our lives for the better.

I signed up for GED classes. They teach them at the
old hotel in town. Every Monday, Wednesday, and Friday
evening. I've been meaning to get my GED forever. I
only dropped out once I got pregnant with you. School
just didn't seem important then, but it seems important
now. If I get my GED I'll be able to apply for more jobs.
Maybe even sign up for classes at the community college
someday.

Of course I had to get Mom to drive me because the
wheel bearing on the Corolla is going out again and I
don't trust it to take me down the mountain to the store
let alone all the way to another county. She sat out there
with the door open and ate sunflower seeds and worked
a crossword puzzle while she waited for me. By the time
I got back, there was a whole mountain of seeds on the
parking lot beside her. I expected her to have a bunch of

questions—how are you going to pay for all this and who's going to watch Maren and are you sure you're not going to quit this like you've quit everything else? She's always been hard on us kids. You never got to meet your Papaw Richard but he wasn't an easy man. I think Mom had to be hard to deal with him. You know, I can only remember her hugging me a few times. I don't think she's said "I love you" in years. I guess I expect the same from her now.

But she didn't say anything like that. She said she was proud of me and that she'd watch you during my classes because they're all in the evening.

It feels like maybe this is what I've been supposed to be doing my whole life. And now that I'm doing it right, it seems like the world is helping me out, you know? Like maybe God is opening up the path before me, the way people say He does. It feels nice to have something to look forward to. Other than you, of course. You're the thing I look forward to every day. I haven't told you about all this yet, but I will tomorrow. Tonight Thelma and Karen and a couple of other girls are going up to Burnt Ridge to celebrate me and Karen. She just got an interview at the nursing home in town. There's just so much to be happy for.

Love,
Mom

May 2, 20—

Dear Maren,

I thought I'd have a better story to tell about how I found my little door. My friend Kathy said she got her door the first time she ever learned how to masturbate. She said she'd been lying in bed really giving herself what for and that she'd closed her eyes and orgasmed for the first time and when she opened her eyes again, there it was. A bright-yellow balloon hanging in the air over her bed. She said she knew right away what it was and that she'd have to grab hold of the string in order to take her door, but she never did. She set it free a week later and watched it float off into the sky until it disappeared. I always thought that was the best door story I'd ever heard. I wanted to find mine like that—in a moment of goodness.

But I guess my story will have to be this: I was tipsy on cheap wine and traipsing over Burnt Ridge looking for a tree to pee behind when I saw my door for the first time. There's no way I could have mistaken it for anything else. Ever since they reclaimed the ridge it's been empty of everything but those short little trees and bushes, all stunted looking. Just hills rolling for days. And that's where it was. Right in the middle of one of those hills. One minute there was nothing but tall grass and wildflowers, and then next, my very own door.

It's made of clay. Can you imagine? There's a great, thick mound of it sitting on the ground, but then it thins out and shapes itself into a door. It looks just like the door to Mom's house. It even has the same scratches in the same places and the knuckle prints near the middle from when Tim and Dad got into a fight and Tim punched the door.

But there was no doorknob.

I think I have to make it. Mold it. I have to do that part myself.

I had just enough time to run my fingers down the length of it to see if the clay would give way, and it did. I left four streaks down the center of my door, and it was cool and damp and it made me shiver to touch it. I think I could mold it into any shape that I wanted.

That was about the time Karen came hollering over the hill, singing "Sweet Caroline" at the top of her lungs, and Thelma not far behind telling her that she was going to call every bear in the county down on our heads sounding like a dying animal out in the woods and Karen fell and I'd gone running toward them. The door stayed where it was so it must be the staying kind, like Tonya's door from ninth grade or Mary Anne's from when I was little or Billy Ray Adams's door, which was really a house that sat in Taylor's Woods with no door at all and no windows, either. He eventually took an ax to one of the walls, and the moment he stepped inside, he was gone. That's another good door story.

Now I don't know what I'm supposed to think. I had everything all planned out yesterday. Does this mean I did something wrong? Is it trying to tell me that I'm on the wrong path? Most people say the doors don't tell us anything, they just show up when they show up and we have a chance to stay or to go, but I don't believe that. It has to mean something.

Love,
Mom

———————————

May 5, 20—

Dear Mare-Bear,

Thomas called the dinette this morning. He knows I pull doubles at the first of the month so he knew I'd be there. I told Lynne to tell him I had already taken my ten and couldn't come to the phone without making the manager angry. The phone was ringing the minute I came home, too, and I didn't even have to look to know it was Thomas. It took everything in me not to answer it, but I didn't. He left three messages. All of them was about you—how he'd like to help me get you set up for school this year, how he knows you need a new pair of shoes, and asked whether or not you'd be going out for basketball. He tries to use you against me when he can. He knows I want to give you the stars when all I can afford is a flashlight. But he has a family of his own to buy for. I've spent the last two years waiting for him to make good on his promises and be a part of our family, but there's always some excuse. Well, let him stay where he's wanted now, because he's not wanted here anymore.

I'm done waiting for people to change, especially men. Done hoping for the better in them instead of seeing what they really are. I hope you never depend on a man, Maren. You can only count on yourself in this world. Remember that.

Love,
Mommins

May 10, 20—

Dear Maren,

I went to see my door last night. I told myself that I wouldn't go. That I'd just ignore it, pretend I never even found it, but I was just feeling so nervous about classes starting in a couple weeks. I messed up and told Marjorie Napier what I was doing. She was in line behind me at the Save A Lot and she was talking about the new ring her husband got her and how she'd never have to work a day in her life, and I just couldn't stand the whine of her voice anymore so I told her I was going back to school. And you know what she said to me? Bless your heart. *I almost smacked the Maybelline right off her pointy face.*

I told her about the classes to make myself feel big, but

I ended up feeling smaller and I started to second-guess the whole thing. I called Karen and she came over to stay with you even though you'd been in bed since nine. I told her I just needed some air. She brought a pack of wine coolers and a VHS tape of Gone with the Wind *and I left her laying on the couch mooning over Clark Gable's mustache.*

It was probably close to eleven by the time I made it to Burnt Ridge. My door was easy to find. I didn't even have to look, really. It was like some part of me knew the way, but I still felt a little flutter in my chest when I saw it, like you do when you see someone you love. I think that's my favorite feeling. If I could, I'd fall in love over and over for the rest of my life just to keep it.

I sat down and told my door about my day and about that old stick-ass Marjorie and how I was worried about my classes and if I got the wrong kind of notebook. The place where I'd dragged my fingers through the clay were still there and I traced the edges of them as I talked. The door still looked just like the one to Mom's house, and something about seeing it put my nerves on edge, like she was there with me, watching, judging. I don't know when I started reshaping the clay. I can't remember deciding to touch it. I can remember wanting to. Wondering. And then my hands were breaking it apart, the clay all gummed up between my fingers, and I was molding my door into something new.

There was a party going on in one of the little dips just below the ridge. I could see the fire they had built through the trees and hear their voices, singing and laughing. I listened to them as I worked, and I thought that whatever they thought they had in their life, I still had something better. I had something they'd all die to have.

My whole life I've done without. A whole life of wanting and never really having. And most of the things I got had been someone else's to begin with. Even Thomas. I don't think it's wrong to want something just for yourself and nobody else. The rest of the world seems to get it easily enough, so why couldn't I love my door? Why couldn't I want it back?

I made a mountain out of the clay. I didn't mean to make it, but I did. There were flowers on it that I'd never seen before. Something like lavender, only bigger. The petals felt blue when I touched them even though they were really just the same rusty color as the rest of the clay, but somehow I knew that they were blue, the brightest blue I'd never seen. I made a little figure, too, that didn't have a face because my fingers ain't small enough to do fine work, but if she did have a face, it would have been mine. She was carrying one of those flowers up to the top of the mountain and she wasn't following a path. She was making her own.

I wondered if that mountain was on the other side of my door. If that's who I could be over there. That little figure who didn't have nothing holding her back. Nothing to worry about. She was going to make it to the top of that mountain, I was sure. She could make it anywhere.

When I got home, Mom was sitting on her porch waiting for me. There was no avoiding her so I walked into her yard to take my lecture. She asked if I'd been up to Burnt Ridge again, and when I told her I had, she said, "There

must be something up there worth seeing if you keep going."
And I went stammering on about something, I can't even
remember what, because the whole time I was thinking,
She knows about my door. And even though I knew she
couldn't, some part of me was still afraid that she'd send it
away for me. Make the choice before I ever got the chance.

When I got done talking, she asked me if I had been
drinking again. She said "again" like that was all I ever
did.

So I laid into her. Kicked over a planter full of
marigolds. Honestly, them flowers were ugly anyway so I
was really doing her a favor.

I was halfway across the road, all hopped up on
adrenaline after I threw my little fit, when she hollered
after me: "However you feel about yourself, that little girl
still deserves the best of you."

I told her that you get the best of me. You always do.

"Well, what if that ain't enough?" Mom said.

I'd rather she asked me if I was drinking again. Called
me a junkie or a whore or a thief. Anything besides that.

Karen was asleep on the couch when I walked inside,
or at least she pretended to be asleep. I put a blanket over
her just in case and turned off the movie, and I went and
crawled into bed with you. You're still young enough that
you don't mind things like that. One day you won't want
me to cuddle with you, but right now you don't care. You
just slung your arm over me and asked me if we could
have pancakes for breakfast and you was asleep before you
finished the sentence. I told you about my door then, when

you was halfway to some other dream. I told you about what I thought was on the other side and about those big old flowers blooming on the trees and how I thought we could be happy there, you and me. A fresh start. Something brand new that nobody had screwed up yet. I sure wish that we could go.

Love,
Mom

chapter twenty-two

I took two days off work. I'd never done that before. Eileen called to apologize for being short with me when I was late and to tell me that she'd started a prayer chain because she knew things had to be bad if I was missing work. I stayed in bed until noon the next day. Granny knocked on my door twice to check on me and I begged her away both times. Carver texted, then called, and I ignored it all. I knew a visit would be next but I didn't want to see him. I didn't want to see anyone. Even my door annoyed me, lurking outside my window, casting its pale-orange light onto my hands, reminding me, always, of the choices I had to make. I didn't want to make choices. I didn't want to explain myself. I just wanted to read.

So I did. I read all of May's journal entries twice, then all of June and half of July before I realized the journal was almost finished and I wouldn't have anything left if I kept going.

I couldn't get over how Mom's journal reminded me of me. I didn't have a daughter but I had all the rest—the guilt, the fear, the dead-end job, the trying to fight for something better without really knowing how. And I knew how her story ended even if I hadn't read the end yet. No matter how hard she tried, somehow it wasn't worth staying for, and she'd left. It made me wonder why I kept trying. It made leaving feel inevitable, but leaving had always felt inevitable in Blackdamp. I'd been told my whole life that if I wanted a good job, I couldn't find it here. If I wanted to hold a girl's hand without worrying, I couldn't do that here. Most everything I wanted for myself was somewhere else.

Even now, when I was trying for something better, it was all falling apart. I kept seeing John Edward every time I turned my head—every shadow, every car that passed by, every noise was him coming to take what little I had left because I refused to give him what he wanted. The twelve hundred dollars I'd made from Thelma was sitting in a shoe box in my closet. I'd been afraid to touch it since I found out she'd been arrested. Like somehow the moment my fingers closed on the bills, John Edward would pop out of the dark and drag me away. Even if I stopped selling now and used the money to pay my debt, I'd still owe three thousand dollars to the school. And even if I used the money to hire someone to stay with Granny, it would only be temporary, because the money would run out and I would have nothing else to give. I would have risked everything just to barely put a dent in my problems and I'd be right back at the beginning, empty-handed but even more tired than before.

And there was Carver. Sweet and gentle and needing. He'd done what I asked. He showed up mostly on time, came through for me when I needed, and answered most of his texts. And even though things seemed to be going well, something still felt wrong. Off-balance. The further we went, the more comfortable I got with needing him and the more I got used to having someone to rely on, which meant it would hurt even more when he left—and he had to leave, didn't he? My fog assured me that he would. It was the only thing that made sense, after all. So it would be better to close off now before I forgot how to be on my own.

There was a chance that things might be different this time, but I couldn't count on that. Besides, I wasn't sure I even knew how to change.

It all made me feel like one of Darwin's finches. I'd never forgotten that image from science class, the birds perfectly adapted to fit the environment they were in. So the birds who ate seeds had beaks that were perfect for seeds, and the birds who ate fruit had beaks that were perfect for fruit. All of them changed until they couldn't survive outside their home. That's what it was like to be in Blackdamp, to be me. My whole body shaped by the gravity of the mountains—the bend in my shoulders, the length of my stride, the curl of my mouth—all of it perfectly designed for this place. I felt *right* here in a way that I couldn't feel right anywhere else.

But it was like someone had come in and stolen my seeds. Carted them away with the coal and the jobs until there was nothing left to eat. Everything was changing but me. So it didn't matter, really, if I stayed or if I left. Either way, I'd starve.

chapter twenty-three

When I finally slunk out of my bedroom, the scent of the blue flowers trailed after me like perfume. It was a sweet smell but earthy, too, the kind of smell that felt green somehow. The flowers reminded me of Mom more than ever, and the message in her journal lingered: *You can only count on yourself in this world.* I had decided, at that point, that the only way to go forward was to go back to the way things were before Carver came home. The way I knew, the way I'd been built for—alone, without help, without interference. It felt better that way, even if there was a sadness clinging to me that I couldn't quite shake.

I texted Carver: I need some space. Everything is just too much right now and I need to be alone. I'm sorry. Then I turned off my phone and left it on my bedside table.

Granny was waiting in the living room, dressed in her church clothes, and I had almost forgotten, again, that I was supposed to take her to the Rose Garden. Guilt stabbed between my ribs and I comforted myself by saying it wouldn't happen again. There'd be no more distractions after this, nothing to take my attention from what I needed to do.

The drive to Sterns felt good—the familiar turns, the squeak of my brakes as we held tight to the curves of the mountain. We kept the radio on low until John Edward was introduced to talk about the new Clean County initiative he was leading. The radio host started rattling off arrest statistics, and I turned the knob so fast that I almost broke it. Granny stared at me but I kept my eyes on the road.

I parked in the corner of the Rose Garden's lot under a dogwood tree and kissed Granny on the cheek before she left. My door followed her halfway to the building and then floated back, shedding amber light onto the blacktop until it rested above the windshield where I could watch it spin. I reached into the back and pulled Mom's journal from my bag. I rolled down all four windows to let the breeze inside. The wind was rolling through the trees, flipping up the leaves to reveal their pale bellies until the whole mountain seemed to be shaking off the winter.

The pages of Mom's journal ruffled as I skimmed the last few entries I'd read—Mom had started taking GED classes and she seemed happy, if a little lonely. There was a whole entry just listing the qualities she wanted in a man, and then a second list with the qualities of the men she'd actually dated which was hard to read. There were drawings of me and her, crude sketches with my wild hair and her big sunglasses. I was all over Mom's journal. Every entry, every day, there was something about what I'd said or done, some moment I'd made her smile. I'd spent my whole life thinking I hadn't been enough for her, that it was something I was or something I wasn't that had sent her through her door. I wish I could say that reading the journal made her leaving hurt less, but somehow it made it hurt more.

I turned the page and found the entries near the middle of July. The next time Mom visited her door she wrote: *The flowers I molded on my door were there. Like there, there. Can you believe it? A dozen of them at least. Growing bright and big and blue as you please right beside my door. I shouted when I saw them, looked around for somebody to show, but it was just me and the birds. I knew they were blue, didn't I? I could just feel it somehow. It got me to thinking... If the flowers I made grew, then what else could I make? Mold a new house for me and Maren, mold a car that actually works like it's supposed to, enough money for all our bills and a vacation to Pigeon Forge. But most of that wouldn't look right on my mountain, and now that something had happened, I was afraid to change what I'd made. Maybe the flowers would go away if I did. Of course I wondered if I could make me a man so I added a little figure beside the little me. Taller, of course. Broad-shouldered. I tried to add a bulge in his pants, but there's only so much a girl can do, so I settled for putting his little clay arm around my little clay shoulders. It looked sweet. Like it was supposed to be that way. Maybe next time I'll go back and he'll be there, waiting for me.*

I turned the page. It seemed like Mom's plan to make herself a man had worked. At least that's what Mom thought.

Two entries later she wrote about how she'd gone into town to pay the electric bill, and when she went back to her car, it wouldn't start. And where was she parked? Right in front of the law office where Thomas worked. The minute she lifted the hood, there he was.

Wearing a new suit, of course. Looking sharp as a butcher knife. I tried not to let him notice me noticing him but it didn't work. He did that thing men do where they unbutton their coat and kind of brush it to the side so they can move better, and that's when I thought about my door and the little man I'd made from the clay. I hadn't talked to Thomas in weeks and yet here he was now? Just when I needed somebody the most? I know it might sound foolish, but part of me thought that it might be meant to be. Wouldn't that make a pretty story? Well, we got to talking as he gave me a boost, and he said what I really needed was a new battery

and he could bring one by after work, if I wanted. So I told him I did.
I wanted.

I shook my head. I remembered Thomas, but only vaguely. In my mind he was a tall shape outlined in the headlights of the brand-new truck he'd drove to our house so he could take Mom for a ride. I was wearing my pajamas by then, so it must have been late. Thomas had a bottle in his hand and I know now it was tequila, but back then I just knew it as *mommy's drink* and that I wasn't supposed to touch it or any of the cups she drank from. I remember asking to go on the ride, too, and the pained look on my mother's face and not understanding why she left me with Granny anyway. But then Granny had asked if I wanted to make no-bake cookies and most of the hurt melted away. All that was left was the sting of being left behind.

A car pulled into the parking lot and my heart skipped a little. John Edward's face flashed inside my mind, eating up the memory of Thomas and his truck, and for a moment I felt oddly suspended— caught somewhere between then and now. It took a moment for me to catch up and check the side of the car, but it was no police cruiser behind me. Just an old Monte Carlo with a *Jesus Loves You* bumper sticker barely clinging to the trunk. The man driving it waved to me and I waved back.

I propped the journal against the steering wheel and read on. The next few entries were about school, mostly, though Karen made appearances. She'd given me her phone number when I saw her at Thelma's, and I'd thought of calling her a hundred times but somehow never seemed able to dial the number. In this entry, she'd bought Mom a whiteboard to work out her math problems on and Mom had divided it in two, one side for her and one side for me. I'd mostly made drawings on my half, but Mom said they reminded her of what she was putting herself through all this algebra for. I looked for Thomas's name and only found it near the end. He'd convinced her to go on a date with him. He would take her to Lexington, buy her a new dress, take her out to the best Italian restaurant, the kind with tablecloths. They'd be in public together and nobody would know she was with someone else's husband. But it would have to be on a Wednesday night, which meant she'd have to miss GED class and she hadn't done that yet. I didn't have to read the next entry to know she'd gone. I could feel it in the way she wrote about him, about herself.

I almost put the journal down, tucked it back into my bag beside my cell phone and sour gummy worms and the pills I had left to sell, but I held on to it a little longer. I checked the date on the next page, and two weeks had passed without an entry. It was the longest I'd seen her go without writing something. And the words on the next page were not written in the soft, looping style of the previous entries, the letters so big that they overlapped onto the lines above and below, like there wasn't enough space to contain Mom, not even on the page.

The next entry was written in sharp letters instead. Harsh. She'd actually torn through the page near the middle. My heart hammered in my chest as I ran my finger over the slight tear, wondering if she had done the same thing, if there was any trace of her left on the paper. I felt afraid, suddenly, and remembered feeling that way when I was little and Mom was in one of her dark moods. Slurring words. Stumbling. I remember waiting until she'd fallen asleep on the couch and then drawing pictures for her. I'd leave them on her chest so she'd be sure to see them when she woke up, then I'd fall asleep curled in the recliner beside her, listening for the sound of her breathing to make sure she was still okay.

I tried not to remember those parts. I had gotten so good at not remembering that the memory scared me a little. Filled me with feelings I hadn't felt for over a decade, feelings that prickled my skin, heated my face. My door hovered nearer so it seemed almost to blend with the hood of the car, and I couldn't tell what was door and what was reflection.

The page read: *She won't take her. I don't care what she says. The fact that she would threaten it at all—THREATEN my CHILD! She's never understood me. Never seen me for who I am. She's always tried to change me, make me into somebody more proper, somebody who does what they're told. Well, she won't have me at all after this. Won't have Maren, either. If I had known what Thomas would do, I would have never gone with him. IT WASN'T MY FAULT. I'll leave this mountain before she takes my child. I'll leave this world if I have to.*

The next page was scrawled with black marks like she'd tried to take out all her feelings on the page. The pen must have broken because globs of ink long dried were smeared on one corner like dark clouds. The journal's pages glowed a faint green and yellow from the light of my little door, which seemed to draw closer to the car as if it was trying to read the journal over my shoulder. Its starry light shone above me as I read and reread the entry, but there was too much I didn't understand.

Had Granny threatened to take custody of me? Why?

I tried to cast my memory behind me, but whatever light I shone into that darkness was too weak. Most of my childhood was that way. I remembered moments, fractions. Like stones scattered across a creek, I could skip from one age to the next—there I was at seven forgetting the words to "O Holy Night" during the Christmas play at church, and then I was drinking apple juice out of plastic champagne flutes to celebrate the new year and falling asleep early on Granny's lap while she watched the news, and then a great leap to me at eight watching Mom and Thomas leave in his new truck. But what happened in between? Or worse, all those years before eight? I tried not to think about that, either—how much of myself I'd forgotten. I knew I'd lived those years. The impression of them was still inside me, but the memory of them, the actual living, was gone. If I thought too long about that, I felt afraid, like maybe I wasn't a whole person. Like maybe I'd forgotten something so important that if I ever remembered, it would change everything about me and I would never be the same. And maybe it was whatever happened in those two weeks, whatever Thomas or Mom had done to make Granny threaten to take me away.

A voice called out and I looked up to see Granny in the parking lot turning toward a small woman in a yellow dress. They huddled together for a moment, giving me enough time to close the journal and tuck it back inside my purse. I tried to fix my face but the muscles didn't want to relax. My mouth kept tensing, my eyebrows pulling down so I looked angry or confused, and I was both and neither. I was all of it, everything in between.

Granny slid inside the passenger seat as raindrops smacked against the windshield and exploded, dotting the glass with little beads of my door's shifting light. Granny was talking the moment she sat down about Betty not practicing their song and how they'd bought two different shades of green for the stage's decorations, but I barely heard a word she said.

I reached out to shift the car into reverse and grabbed something soft instead. One of my blue flowers had snaked its way between the base of the gear and whatever lay underneath. I didn't know how it grew there or where its roots were bound. I didn't know what soil it could have found inside the car, or maybe it was beyond that now. Maybe it only needed me to grow.

The flower wrapped itself along the length of the gear, stretching up to meet the light that trickled over the dashboard, and that's where it bloomed pale blue. As I watched, the blue brightened and the stalk thickened and another stem appeared, stretching slowly to meet the first.

Then another. And another.

By the time I shifted the car into reverse, there were four flowers growing there and the scent of them clung to my nose, thickened the air. The stems were cool beneath my fingers and slightly damp, and I kept my hand resting there the whole drive home.

chapter twenty-four

When I left for work the next morning, a piece of notebook paper was tucked into the jamb of the screen door. I opened the note slowly, unfolding it with shaking hands, sure it would contain some threat or warning, but it was only Carver's long, loping letters, scrawled like they were trying to run away from his hand the moment they touched the page. There were only three words, but they were all it took to make tears well in my eyes: *I'm still here.*

I was rereading the note when Uncle Tim pulled into the driveway. I tucked the paper into my purse and headed down the front steps. Fear swirled inside me like blackbirds on a breeze, and they all turned their eyes to Uncle Tim and worried there instead. I knew he'd come to talk about Granny, but I feared him doing exactly what Granny claimed he would, making decisions that weren't his to make. And part of me feared that he knew I had been selling pills and had come to call me down for that as well. But I still plastered a smile on my face as I walked across the yard. My little door followed overhead, casting pumpkin-colored shadows on the hood of Tim's truck.

Tim rolled down his window and said, "You know your muffler is about an inch from the ground."

"I like to live dangerously."

"You must take that after Granny." He leaned out the window

and tugged at a loose strand of my hair. "You know what I came to talk about."

"I don't figure it's my flower beds."

"Not this time." He sighed. "How long has all this been going on with Mom?"

"Year or two, I guess. Not long after her stroke."

His eyes widened. "And you never told us?"

I nodded toward the screen door. "She told me not to worry the rest of y'all."

"That sounds like her." Tim shook his head. "You know Suze's great-aunt had dementia. They tried to take care of it on their own. Did home workers and doctors and had people staying with her around the clock, but it about bankrupted them. The only thing they could do in the end was put her in a home."

My shoulders tensed. "Granny ain't there yet."

Tim said, "I ain't saying it needs to happen now. I just want us to be realistic about all this. I work all the time, so does Suze, and Forest has her head so far in the clouds she don't even know the rest of us is here most of the time. Cheryl's got the business she's running and you're still going to school, aren't you?"

"I'm trying."

"I thought so. I know the director down at the Rose Garden. Good feller. His people used to live down Owl's Nest. Real good folks. It's a good place. Clean. Near enough that we could all visit regular."

My little door sank closer and its heat warmed my shoulders, my neck. Its color deepened around the edges, going from orange to something closer to black. I didn't realize I'd held out hope for something better until then. I'd wanted Granny to be wrong about Tim.

I wanted him to fight for her the way she'd fought for her children their whole lives. The way she'd fought for me. But this wasn't the help we needed. It wasn't really help at all.

I said, "I still don't think it's come to that."

Tim nodded. "I'll take your word for it then. You let us know if you need anything. I'll do what I can."

Then Granny hollered from behind the screen door, "Did my son finally remember where I live and come to see me?"

Tim stepped out of his truck, gave my arm a squeeze, and then headed up the steps, making excuses while Granny stood behind the screen and shook her head. I watched them until Tim disappeared inside the house and there was nothing but the mountains around me, the birds singing the hills awake, the trees sighing in the breeze, the hush of night giving way to a new day. I reached into my purse for my keys, and my fingers brushed against Carver's note. For a moment my heart leapt again toward hope, but my fog was there just as quickly, whispering, *You see what happens when you give people a chance? They disappoint you. You're better off alone.*

Part of me wanted to destroy the note, toss it from my open window as I sped down the mountain toward work so the blue jays could tear it apart and tuck it into their nests, let Carver's words make a shelter for something else, something that could appreciate it. But I couldn't bring myself to tear it apart, so I tucked the note into a pocket, folding it smaller and smaller until I thought it might be safe.

chapter twenty-five

A few days passed without a single text or phone call from Carver. It was what I'd asked for, but it was still hard. For the first time since I started selling pills, I had to do it on my own. I know he would have been there if I asked, but it felt wrong to ask, selfish somehow. So I traded some pills for a refurbished washing machine when ours broke down and made three hundred from the deacon's wife, another fifty from a woman who used to date Tim in high school. I lost a week's worth of money when the power steering went out on my car and I had to take it to the only garage in town where Carver didn't work. I sat in the backyard for an hour after that, crying where Granny couldn't hear me because I'd told myself I wouldn't need to sell pills for long, that it was only a means to an end. But that end seemed to be stretching further and further away.

Then in the last week of the month, things slowed down. No one wanted to buy anything, at least nothing I was selling, and life grew quiet. Without distraction, I had more time to feel my loneliness. I thought it would be better on my own, but this was the first time in my life when I didn't have either Julie or Carver for company, and I found that their absence took up almost as much room as their presence did.

I took to feeding my little door every time I wanted to call one of them. When Eileen was annoying at work and I thought of the perfect insult, I fed my door a handful of pennies from the cup holder of my car instead of texting Julie. When Granny went to bed early and I was too chicken to watch a scary movie by myself, I settled for feeding my door stray pieces of popcorn instead of asking Carver to come over.

By the time another week rolled around, my door was the size of my house. It didn't hover atop it so much as loom, shimmering like the sky itself had cast a shadow and that shadow hung like a storm cloud over the roof.

Then Karen stopped by the store one afternoon when I was working and wrapped me in a big hug. She told the three stray customers that my best friend in first grade was a piece of cardboard with googly eyes glued onto it that I'd named Steven. Before she left, I asked her something that had been on my mind since the last time I'd read Mom's journal—the angry scrawl of her hand across the page, the long gaps in my memory.

"If I ever had questions about my mom…" My throat grew tight around the word and I couldn't finish what I'd meant to say.

Karen squeezed me close. "You can ask me anything. I'll tell you what I remember and make up the rest. You know where I live, baby."

It took another two days for me to draw up the courage to drive by her house after work. The blue flowers had spread from the gearshift to the glove box, crowding between the outdated insurance cards and drive-through napkins and junk mail that I'd piled inside. They squeezed between the trunk and the back row of seats, their heavy blue heads bobbing and swaying as I took the curves a little too fast. I watched them like a mother watching her child in the car seat, my eyes constantly drawn to the rearview mirror, hypnotized by the flowers' gentle movements until a car laid on its horn and I realized I'd drifted into the wrong lane.

Karen's driveway was soggy when I pulled in, and my shoes squelched under me as I hurried toward the porch and banged on the door with my elbow. My little door followed me, hovering just a few inches over my head, but it could offer no protection from the rain. The drops burst straight through, leaving narrow holes in the door's swirling colors that closed back up, then collapsed again as another raindrop fell. I banged on the door again, holding my coat over my head and peering up at my door through a small gap as the rain smattered my cheeks. I could smell something cooking from outside and only recognized the smell as turkey when Karen opened the door with a cigarette dangling from her mouth and yelled, "Hello, stranger!"

She shook my coat off in the kitchen and offered me a towel, which I took and patted at the wet spots on my face and shoulders.

"A woman's liable to drown standing up out there," she said, checking the oven.

"Is that stuffing?" I asked.

"It is! I was sitting here wondering why nobody ever makes turkey except at Thanksgiving and what a rotten oversight that must have been so I decided to treat myself. I've got an apple pie in the freezer, too, and ice cream. You want to eat with me?"

I smiled. "I'd like that."

So I helped Karen peel potatoes over the trash can as she talked about the last fight she'd had with her husband. He'd tried to claim the trailer and the acre of land under it, so Karen had set fire to one of the bedrooms and told him he could keep the ashes.

"You're not serious," I said.

"Open that door if you don't believe me." She pointed her knife at a closed door at the end of a long hallway. "It was only a little fire but it scared him anyway. Barely singed the wallpaper. It's fine, though. I'd rather have to spend money fixing my mess than fixing his anyway."

"That makes a kind of sense."

"I always do."

We ate on paper plates with tall glasses of pop. Karen brought a skinny white candle out from a drawer and put it on the coffee table.

"To set the mood," she said.

We talked about the stack of job applications scattered across the table and what she wanted to do with her life. We talked about Thelma making bail and all the other people who didn't. Somehow the only two Black men in the holler had been held on a higher bond than all the rest and were still waiting in jail.

Karen said, "John Edward claimed they have connections to something that happened up in Louisville but it's all bullshit."

"It always is," I said.

We sat together on her worn couch with the rain pinging on the sides of the trailer and the light of that one thin candle and I felt a kind of peace that I hadn't felt since I pushed Carver away. I didn't have to hide anything from Karen. She knew about the pills, my door. She'd known me before I even really knew myself and I didn't realize how heavy it was to carry all that until I could put it down for a while.

It was almost ten o'clock that night before Karen said, "Wasn't there something you wanted to ask me?"

"Apparently I don't want to," I said. "Not the way I've been avoiding it."

"It's not easy to talk about your mom for me, either."

"You're a lot better at it than me."

She shrugged. "I just have more practice."

I took a deep breath and told her about what I'd found in the journal—the two-week gap, the angry entry, the spilled ink. "I don't remember any of it," I said. "But something had to have happened."

"You're sure you don't remember?" Karen said. She had a pained expression on her face that only grew more pained as I shook my head. "Well, shit. I told you I'd tell you whatever I could. I just kind of hoped you wouldn't ask me about that."

"Was it that bad?"

"Let me get another pop before I do this." She unfolded herself and shuffled into the kitchen. "If I can't have a beer to take the edge off, at least I can have some blessed carbonation. Looks like the pie has cooled, too. You want some? Yeah, you want some. This'll help. Sugar makes everything easier."

She brought the pie in its little silver tin with two forks sticking out of it and placed it between us on the couch.

"All right," she said. "The thing you need to know about Thomas is that he was a piece of shit. Still is. He'd had your mom on the hook for almost over ten years with no intention of ever setting her loose or making it legitimate. At least that's what I thought. Now I ain't sure what happened on his part, but he started spending more time with her there toward the end. He used to always hide her away but he was taking her out more. Trips to Lexington. Public stuff. Then he asked her to go away for a weekend trip with him. First time he'd ever done that."

My phone buzzed but I quickly pushed the button to ignore whoever had the nerve to call me at such a time.

"What about school?" I asked.

Karen shook her head. "Thomas didn't like the idea of her getting a GED. He didn't come right out and say it, but he was always asking her out on Wednesday and Friday nights, knowing damn well she had class. And he would guilt her something awful. Talking about all he'd done for her and all he was risking to be with her." Karen rolled her eyes. "So she'd missed about two weeks straight there at the end and was starting to talk about how maybe she wouldn't need it after all. He always filled her head with dreams and her belly with alcohol. All they ever did together was drink. Anyway, she was all geared up about the weekend trip to Gatlinburg. She had this whole itinerary planned out, but then when she asked your granny if she'd watch you over the weekend, your granny said no."

"She did?"

Karen nodded. "I reckon it was the first time she'd ever done that. So they went back and forth a little and your mom said she'd just have to take you with her and she wasn't sure how long y'all would be gone and your granny caved."

Karen took three bites of pie before she continued. "Your mom was calling me every three hours on the night they left for Tennessee, telling me how he'd bought her all these new outfits and a new set of luggage. But then the phone calls stopped on the second day. And she didn't call on the third, either. Or the fourth, or the fifth."

"I thought it was just a weekend trip."

"So did your mother."

"I don't understand."

Karen sighed. "He wanted them to run off together. This was his big moment. His plan."

"He wanted her to leave me?"

Karen nodded. "He had no problem leaving his wife and children. He'd never really wanted them. And he never really liked you, either, baby. Saw you as more of a threat, I think, on Nell's time. An obstacle to his wild and free life where he could drink anytime he wanted and not have any consequences."

My stomach ached. "And Mom stayed with him?"

"You can't get mad at her, baby."

"I can," I said, though what I felt was much closer to sadness than anger. Tears welled in my eyes and I willed them back down.

"Yeah. Yeah, I guess you can. I can't help but be on her side. It wasn't easy on her. She always wanted more from her life but she never seemed able to get it. And it's so hard to make anything in this place if you're not married. She had this dream of the three of you starting over together. She thought that was what he was going to ask her to do. Finally make a family out of the three of you."

"Why didn't she come home when he told her the truth?"

"She tried, I think. But like I said, he kept her buzzed. Any idea seems possible after a fifth of vodka. I think she didn't really realize what she'd done until she'd come down a little and he was talking about renting an apartment there near Gatlinburg. That's when she called me to come pick her up. So I went. Thomas didn't even put up a fight. He just let her go. Nell cried. Lord, how she cried. I thought she was going to make herself sick on the way home. But by the time we was headed up the mountain, she'd calmed right down and seemed dead set on making her life right. Getting back to what she'd been doing before."

"I feel like there's a but."

"There's always a but in these stories." Karen sighed. "But then we got home that night and I followed her into the trailer. Our plan was to let her get some sleep and then go pick you up from your granny's in the morning. But Nell stopped dead in the doorway. She said something was wrong. It took me a minute to figure it out, but your mom noticed straightaway."

I leaned forward, waiting for Karen to finish. "And that was?"

She sighed. "I keep hoping some of this will jog your memory and I won't have to keep saying it. This was the worst time in your mother's life. I don't think I've made that clear enough. She had never hated herself more than this moment, and I'd seen her at some pretty low lows. But I'd never seen her like this."

"Please, Karen."

My phone buzzed again and I fumbled for the buttons until it went silent.

Karen closed her eyes and took a deep breath. "All your stuff was gone. There wasn't a toy left in the house. Your closet was empty. Your mattress was gone, even the little lamp you and your mom made together with the buttons on it. Nell tore out of that house like a bat out of Hell. I tried to slow her down but there was no stopping her. She busted into your granny's house near midnight, screaming for you to get up and get your things. Granny looked cool as a cucumber when she came out of her room in her housedress. You poked your little head out of her room and started crying. You didn't know what was going on, little thing. You just wanted to see your mom. But your granny sent you back inside and closed the door, and her and Nell *had it out.* I mean, I'd seen them fight before. That's how they loved each other half the time, but this was something else. I tried to help. I did. But there was no helping. Your granny said that Nell was an unfit mother and that she had already started the paperwork to get legal custody of you. I had to pick Nell up off the floor after she said that. She just collapsed. It was like she couldn't hold herself together anymore."

"Oh."

"Yeah. I wish I could forget that." Karen took another bite of pie. "She didn't sleep that whole night. After she stopped crying, she just laid in bed and stared at the wall. It wasn't until the sun was up that she finally drifted off and I cleaned up the house, tried to make things look normal as I could."

"What happened then?"

Karen shrugged. "They came to some kind of agreement. You would stay with your granny through the week and she'd make sure you got to school on time and Nell could come see you in the evenings and on weekends. Your granny had that paperwork over her head so she used it to make Nell act right. Well, right by your granny's standards anyway. It seemed to be going okay. Nell was miserable but she went to work and came home, and she signed back up for GED classes for that winter. Then she took her door. I'd suspected she had one for a while but she never would admit it. I never thought she'd take it, though."

"Why would she take it if things were okay?"

"I don't know. I'd stopped by to see her the day she took the damn thing. She seemed happier than I'd ever seen her. Maybe that should have tipped me off."

"And then she was gone?"

Karen nodded. "And then she was gone."

"Thomas was my father, wasn't he? Is my father?"

"Oh, honey." Karen speared a piece of pie and then dropped it back onto the plate. "There's not enough pie in the world to make up for that. But yeah. You're Thomas's."

I shook my head. "So neither of them wanted me."

"Oh, baby. Oh no." Karen pulled me in to her, smushed my face against her shoulder, and squeezed. "Nell wanted you. She loved you more than anything. And she tried. I swear to you, she tried every day of her life."

I shook my head. "I keep thinking that if I knew what happened, it would make it easier."

Karen smoothed my hair away from my face. "You can lose your whole life that way, searching through the past, worrying about tomorrow. At some point you have to be where you're at. You have to make peace."

We stayed that way for a while. I was too sad to move and Karen was so soft and warm, so much like the mother I needed that I let myself hold on to her for a while. And she didn't seem to mind. She ate pie over my head and talked to me about her plans for the weekend and what kind of flowers she wanted to plant in the backyard until my phone buzzed again and she plucked it from my hand. "If you're not going to answer it, then I am. Hello?"

I reached for my phone but Karen swatted my hand away. "Yeah, hello. No, this is her secretary. Oh. Well, damn. No, I'll tell her. You just drive, baby."

I snatched the phone back and pressed it to my ear. "Hello?"

The line was empty.

"Who was that?" I asked.

"Carver. He's on his way."

"Why?"

"He said Julie's in trouble."

I closed my eyes. "Shit."

Karen tucked a stray hair behind my ear and said the only thing she could in a moment like that. "Let me fix you a plate before you go."

chapter twenty-six

Carver was quiet as we pulled out of Karen's and onto the dark road. He must have come straight from a shower because his hair was damp and clinging to his neck. Dark-brown curls turned black by the water stuck to his cheek and forehead. His shirt contoured to his back and little flowers of water darkened the fabric of his T-shirt. My little door raced through the darkness above us, large enough that I could see its edges from every window in the car. It danced rose-colored light over Carver's cheeks, skimming the surface of his skin like he was too delicate a thing to really touch, or maybe he was just beyond the reach of my door, beyond me. My throat tightened when I looked at him so I looked out the window instead.

I said, "Thanks for calling me."

"You're welcome."

"It was nice of you," I said.

He grunted.

"I really appreciated it."

"Uh-huh."

When I ran out of ways to thank him, I tried something else instead. "I got your note."

"Well," he said.

"That was nice, too. Of you, I mean. Nice of you."

"I meant it."

"I know. And I just… I want you to know that I'm sorry. I know I hurt you when I cut you off like that. I told you I needed you to be there and then I left."

"You noticed that, too, huh?"

"Don't exactly take a detective to see it."

"Guess not." Carver ran a hand over his forehead to push the hair from his eyes, but it just bounced back into place. "Why'd you do it then?"

"I don't know. I'm just…a mess. Everything is a mess. I mean, look at us. On the way to a pill house to rescue Julie. You picked me up from Karen's house where she was telling me a sad story from my sad past. I'm selling my granny's pain pills behind her back. You only came back to Blackdamp to get away from selling pills. This ain't exactly a Hallmark story."

"Why not? Happy endings ain't just for people with money and no criminal record, Maren. It's for us, too."

"Maybe." I sighed. "But I just can't right now. If I keep on the way we were, it's not going to end well. I'll mess it up even bigger. I just need some space."

Carver was quiet for a moment. "Am I supposed to wait on you?"

"No."

"I have things to do, you know."

I smiled a little. "I don't doubt it."

"Me and Pap have been working on something. The Reverend, too, actually. She's been nicer lately. It's kinda weird. I think all this stuff with the car accident and now with Julie really changed something. But they're both helping me."

"I'm really glad to hear that."

"I've been wanting to tell you about it but I couldn't. And I saw

another turtle that looked like Julie and I couldn't even tell anybody
about it. Plus nobody else cares how many bags of hot peanuts I eat
in a day."

"I just don't see how it's healthy. I mean, five bags a day?"

"See? I haven't had you for days and days. You know how bad
that sucks?"

I looked down at my lap. "It's hard for me, too. I just..."

"Need space. I know." He sighed. "If that's what you want, then
I want you to have it."

I took a few slow breaths to calm the trembling in my hands, my
jaw, my lips quaking as I said, "I really am sorry. I never wanted to
hurt you."

"Dammit." Carver punched the flashers on and pulled onto the
side of the road. He opened up his arms, and I all but flung myself
over the seat and into his chest. He held me for a while. How long I
couldn't tell. The car rocked every now and then as someone passed
by too close in the dark.

Eventually Carver kissed the top of my head and said we should
get going. I went back to my side of the car and he pulled back onto
the road, but the space between us didn't feel so wide anymore.

It took another twenty minutes to reach the Well. There were a
lot of stories about this place—what it was, what it used to be. Some
said that the Well had never been raided by the police before because
it technically didn't belong to any of the surrounding counties. That
long ago a woman emancipated herself and eight acres of prime
forest and gave it a name that no one could remember, a land that
everyone forgot. They say she lived there alone, her only company
the strange lights that appeared in the skies every month or so. Some
said the Well was started by a group of Vietnam draft dodgers who

wanted to make art instead of war, which is why there were so many sculptures in the woods around the Well. Bits of twisted metal growing from the trees, long strings of Christmas lights that never seemed to burn out no matter how long they shone. The sculptures were simple enough, mostly squares and circles, most of them broken at some point so the ends never quite met flush. Many of them had been half-covered by kudzu or moss so the mountains seemed to be swallowing them whole or spitting them up like some kind of otherworldly offering. Some people said that the sculptures grew on their own, because that had happened someplace nearby. It wouldn't be the strangest thing that Blackdamp had ever seen.

Whatever the truth was, the Well was just a double-wide trailer sitting in a clearing between some pine trees. My door floated ahead and hovered over the trailer, splashing rhubarb light onto its siding. The ground was covered with a thick layer of dried needles the color of rust, and the scent of pine was so strong that not even the rain could wash it away. Normally I would have taken a deep breath, but my stomach was too full of the wrong season's food and I felt queasy, like an overripe fruit. I wanted to go home and crawl into my bed and think about my mother. I wanted to brood. To take my sour mood and make it worse by listening to sad music on my phone. I wanted to pull my loss around me like a blanket, yank it right up to my chin until I could make sense of it.

But I couldn't because I was following Carver across the wet and muddied ground in front of the Well, hoping Julie was safe inside. I let myself stare at Carver as he walked ahead and I took slow, small steps because at least this way, when he wasn't looking at me, I could pretend that everything was okay.

Inside, the house was crowded. Most of the walls had been torn down, revealing the seams that held the trailer together. Bits of wire and insulation drooped from the ceiling. A few people played rummy at what used to be the kitchen counter, but it had been painted and painted again, cast in vivid circus colors. A few more people crowded around an old tube television, the cracked screen filled with static, and one of them swore that the color was leaking out. He dragged his finger over the broken edge and held it up to the crowd.

It made me feel uneasy to be around so many people who were high. Some old holdover from when Mom was still here—a feeling that at any moment things might turn from laughter to crying, a shaky, unpredictable feeling that made me push ahead, searching until I found Ace standing at the end of a narrow hallway. She'd tried to call me and had called Carver when I hadn't answered.

"She's in here," Ace said.

Carver cupped my elbow in his palm briefly. "I can go in."

I shook my head. "It should be me."

"All right. I'll be here."

I felt a twinge of guilt at those words, but I just nodded to him, then Ace, then slipped through the doorway. There were lamps all over the room, crowded into the corners, stacked onto shelves. Most of them were dark, but enough were lit that the room felt like it was glowing from the inside, like we were all caught in the belly of a lightning bug and it was carrying us away to somewhere only lightning bugs knew.

Julie sat on a wide velvet couch with her eyes closed. She'd shaved her hair at some point—her head covered in a fine blond down. It wasn't the first time. That was in seventh grade when she'd shaved it to the scalp in the girls' bathroom before Picture Day just to spite the Reverend. She'd done it again in high school after her first breakup with

Rachel. Shaving her head had always been a way to reset her life, take herself back to some beginning so she might try again. Amanda was beside her, one hand wrapped around Julie's wrist, checking her pulse.

"You need to drink some water, Julie," Amanda said, but she was looking at me. I nodded and she stood up. "I'll be out in the hallway if you need anything." Amanda squeezed my arm gently. "She's going to be fine. She's almost come down now, but I'm still not sure what she took. If she starts acting funny, go right to the hospital, all right? Tell them someone dosed her drink if you need to."

"Thank you," I whispered.

When Julie and I were alone, I took the place that Amanda had left, sinking into the couch until my knee touched Julie's. She flinched a little but she didn't open her eyes.

"Funny meeting you here," I said.

I looked around at all the shadows on the wall. A stink bug was caught inside one of the shades and it buzzed loudly every time it tried to escape, batting its body against the narrow cone, and its shadow played out its struggle across the walls, magnifying it.

"You remember the last time we came here?" I asked.

Julie didn't make a sound. I leaned over her belly just to make sure she was breathing, and I didn't talk again until I saw her body rise and fall at least three times.

"We must have been about sixteen. I came because some boy was supposed to be here and I was after him. I heard a rumor that he thought I was too straitlaced so I was going to show him the real me." I snorted. "I can't even remember who it was now, but it seemed so damn important at the time."

"Corey Dale," Julie said.

"What?"

"It was Corey Dale you was after."

"I was not."

"You was."

"No," I said with dawning horror.

A smile quirked the corner of Julie's mouth. "You stole some lace panties from Walmart to wear that night."

"I remember that," I said. "Damn things fell apart the first time I washed them."

"You get what you pay for."

I smiled. "I know to God I wasn't after Corey Dale, though. Even I had more sense than that."

Julie shook her head. "You thought he was dangerous."

"He drove a PT Cruiser."

"I know."

"It was orange!"

"I know," Julie said.

"Well, I just lost some respect for myself."

"I'm amazed you have any left."

I almost laughed. "I guess I deserved that."

"You deserve a lot worse than that."

I sighed. "What do you deserve then?"

A tear slipped down Julie's cheek as she shook her head. "This, I guess. Alone in a house full of strangers."

"That's not true."

"It must be. Why else do things keep going so wrong?"

"I don't know, Jules."

"She left me, you know. Rachel. So I guess you were right about that much."

"What happened?"

"I don't know." Julie pressed her hands against her eyes. Outside, someone began to sing a Fleetwood Mac song very poorly. "We were fighting. It was pointless. She walked outside and I thought she was going to get some air but she never came back. She left me here. I was so angry and I felt so foolish. I took something. I don't know what, so don't bother asking. I just wanted everything to go away."

"Did it?"

"Yeah. For a while."

"Was it nice?"

"Yeah," Julie said. "It was."

We listened to someone laughing in the other room, the twang of the guitar floating through from outside, the rumble of so many voices we didn't know. The two windows in the room had no curtains and no glass, were only covered with plastic sheeting, and my door hovered beyond them, casting its strange colors across the plastic like light on water.

"I can't keep going on like this," Julie said. "I've tried everything I can think of. I tried doing it the Reverend's way my whole life. The doctors' ways. I tried it without therapy, without meds. I joined a bunch of online groups. All these people preaching love and light and how you can just manifest money and happiness, but you can't manifest your way out of this. It's bullshit. And I'm just so tired."

I dragged the toe of my boots through the threadbare carpet. "I'll do whatever I can to help you."

"That's part of the problem."

"What?"

"Your *help*," Julie said, sitting up and looking at me for the first time. "It's not helping, Maren. It's taking. It's...it's controlling."

"That's not fair."

"Ain't it? I went along with it for so long because I've been terrified my whole life of becoming my mother. The Reverend, the doctors, everybody acted like it was just a matter of time before I drove myself into oncoming traffic like she did."

I winced. "Jules…"

"It's true. She did. And I thought I would, too. My whole life I haven't trusted myself. I've doubted almost every thought I've ever had. Every feeling, every dream. Do you know what that's like?"

I shook my head. "I only wanted to keep you safe."

"So did the Reverend. But she shut me out of my own life. And it's the only one I'll ever get! Even if I have a messed-up head."

"It's not messed up."

"No," Julie said. "It's not. It's mine. And I can take care of myself. I can make my own choices. Pick my own doctors, my own girl-friends. And every choice I make ain't because of this mental illness, you know. I'm more than just that, and I'm done being under anybody's thumb."

I looked down at the floor and felt incredibly small. "I'm sorry."

Julie reached out and took my hand. She shook it a little until I looked up at her. "I know you are. I just want us to be on the same side. I want us to be equals."

"I want that, too."

"Well, then?"

"Well what?"

"Aren't you going to tell me?" Julie asked.

"About what?"

"Your door."

I dropped my head. "Shit."

"I've known you most of my life, Maren Walker. Did you really think I wouldn't notice how weird you was acting?"

"I hoped it would blend in with my normal weird and nobody could tell the difference."

"I could." Julie pulled her legs under her. "How long have you had it?"

"Since that night I called you to help with Granny."

Julie frowned, remembering. "Shit. That's longer than I thought."

"I wish you could see it."

"Is it pretty?"

I nodded. "Yeah. It is."

"What're you going to do?"

"I don't know."

"If I had a door right now, I think I might take it."

I smiled. "I used to think that, too. It's a lot harder when it's right in front of you, though."

Something hard pinged against the side of the trailer. A door slammed outside and someone shouted, but their voice was too muffled to understand.

"What's happening?" Julie said.

"I don't know."

Carver poked his head in the door. "I hate to interrupt, but the cops are on their way. They're planning another raid."

There was a moment where everything was eerily quiet and it felt like everyone might handle the news calmly, like we might file out of the house and into our cars, tip our hats to one another and be on our way, but that moment was brief and broken by a chorus of curse words from the kitchen, voices raised in shouts, coats and bottles flying through the air, the sound of glass crunching underfoot, and still, amidst it all, someone singing Fleetwood Mac off-key.

"Come on," Ace said, and we followed her through the chaos.

She ushered us through a door that looked like it might fall from its hinges at any moment, down a narrow, dark hallway, and out through a back door. Dozens of people were flooding into the woods behind the Well. Many had parked in the yard, but most had chosen to leave their cars nearby, like Carver and me. Headlights arced through the trees, their crisscrossed beams like pale ghosts floating through the woods. Ace led us to a creek that ran muddy with the recent rain.

"This should take us just by the old fire station," Ace said. "We're about a mile away, maybe less."

Carver hopped down and looked back to me, offered up his arms like he would catch me, and he did when I jumped, guiding me into the mud, whispering, "Careful now," as I landed a little crooked.

"I always knew the two of you would end up together," Ace said, smiling as she turned toward the water.

Carver didn't say anything and neither did I. Julie looked at me—her eyebrows asking a dozen different questions, none of which I had the time or heart to answer, so I just shook my head and helped her down into the creek. The water was higher than normal and it soaked through my church mission boots even as I tried to keep to the edges. I zipped my jacket to my chin and helped Julie do the same when her fingers were shaking too hard to catch the clasp. Carver was behind us and Ace behind him and Amanda lingered near the bank, walking backward with a backpack rustling on her shoulders. I kept looking back, waiting for the glow of blue and red lights, the sound of sirens. I stumbled once and Julie steadied me.

There were a dozen people, maybe more, walking ahead in knots of two or three, their voices cast low. Every now and then someone would slip on the muddied bank and slide down into the water, their fall punctuated by a soft shout. Whoever had been singing back at the Well had finally stopped, and I found that I missed the sound.

I said, "Do you think everybody got out all right?"

"I do," Ace said, crossing ahead of us. She held her hand out until Amanda twined their fingers together. "I think John Edward and them are going to find an empty house, and I can't think of anything they deserve more than absolutely nothing."

My door hovered overhead. Its light turned the muddy water into a swirl of soft colors and made the moment somehow less terrible, even as cold and scared as we were, though I was the only one who knew we were wading through starlight, and the knowing made me so sad I nearly cried. I reached out and took Julie's hand and held on tight. We would all make it home safe that night, and the cops would find nothing but an empty trailer. Then the Well would catch fire a few hours later and the report would claim it was an electrical fire caused by unsafe wiring, and a week later a few people would gather around the ashes and drink to what the place had been. But we didn't know that then. We just knew we had to hurry, so we hurried with the sound of police sirens lifting like prayers through the dark.

chapter twenty-seven

Blackdamp suffocates. Uncle Tim explained it to me once when I was little, how our county got its name from something that could kill you. How old mining shafts were poorly ventilated and often closed up once the vein was empty or when the company went out of business. Then a new mining operation would come and dig new shafts, but they'd have to be careful not to open up the old wounded places in the earth because that's where the blackdamp lived. It was a chemistry I didn't quite understand, but I knew it was a kind of gas that ate up the oxygen, made it so no one or nothing could survive inside. If an old shaft was opened by accident, it was impossible to know the blackdamp was there—there was no smell, no warning. Just a slow, creeping dizziness, a drowsy kind of clumsiness you could mistake for fatigue, just being too tired on your feet after hours of mining. But all the while you were dying.

When I look back on the days after the Well, that's how I feel. A slow and creeping dread, a tightening of my throat, a closing up. I thought things were going to get better, for a while, but that's because I couldn't see what was coming.

I wish I could tell some other part of this story. Any other part, really. I wish you could see me right now, writing this, where I am and how far I've come, but I haven't made it there yet, not here. No, I am here again.

I can't remember if it happened four days after we took Julie from the Well or five. I know it had rained every day in between until the field where I'd first found Granny had filled to the brim with water and finally turned itself into a pond. It was still raining on the night I don't want to remember. A fine, misting rain that clung to my hair and my eyelashes and made me feel like I was drowning when I got out of the car. I didn't notice anything at first, but every step I took toward the porch seemed to show me something new that was wrong. My little door hovered over me, shining pale-peachy light onto everything I noticed like it was trying to help me understand, trying to help me see what was right in front of me.

Like that the front door was open despite the chill of the rain.

But then I got closer and realized the door wasn't open, but broken.

The hinge on the top had been pulled loose and the door just kind of tilted there, like it was drunk and stumbling into the house.

Or like the tire tracks across the grass.

The front yard was already soft from the rain, but the tracks had turned it into mud, dug through the front, and crushed the little Hello Spring flag that Granny had brought home from the Dollar Tree just a few days before because she was so sick of the gray skies and the rain and she wanted to believe that spring would come after all.

Like Uncle Tim standing in the doorway with his arms crossed.

I'm not sure how long he watched me standing there at the bottom of the steps, but he was the one who finally took my arm and led me inside.

Later on I would hear that it was Rachel who rolled on me. She was picked up the night she abandoned Julie at the Well, for driving

on the wrong side of the road through town, high as a kite. When
they took her in, she gave the name of every person she'd bought
drugs from in her life, including people who had died years before,
including me, who had never sold or given her anything other
than a bad attitude, but a lead was all John Edward needed. She'd
taken all the blame for the break-in at Dr. Owens's house and never
mentioned Julie's name, but she traded everyone else she knew, so
they let her go.

But Rachel was the furthest thing from my mind when I stepped
inside the house. Someone had tried to mop the floors to get rid
of all the muddy footprints but they'd only succeeded in smearing
the mud around until the whole floor looked brown. So instead of
seeing the path that John Edward and his team had taken, it looked
like they had touched everything, and every place they'd touched was
touched by my flowers, too. All the cabinets were open in the kitch-
en—a box of macaroni fallen to the floor and spilled, and from the
box snaked a thin green stem with a thinner stream of blue flowers
bursting from its top. The flowers grew through the burners on the
stove, twisting through the grates until they could stand up straight
enough, their bright-blue heads bobbing gently from side to side.
The kitchen table had been pulled away from the corner, and there
was a deep gouge in the linoleum from where it had been dragged
and the flowers grew through the gouge. There were bubbles in the
walls, rising like blisters on burned skin, and I knew that if I chipped
away the paint and the drywall, there would be flowers underneath,
searching for the sun.

The only thing that seemed the same were the pictures of Granny's
roses hanging on the wall. I remembered hanging them back up on
the last night she disappeared. So much had changed since then. So

much had gone wrong. The cracks were still spider-webbed over the photo of Mom's hand and I wished she was there with me, wished I had someone else to share this with, to help me make it right.

I didn't even feel it when Tim sat down beside me. His weight tipped me toward him and he was warm and smelled like Old Spice and there was something about the smell of him that made me want to cry.

But there were no tears. Just that familiar emptiness. That feathery, faraway feeling under my skin. I was grateful for the distance when Tim said, "I think it's best if Granny stays with me for a while."

I shook my head without thinking, my body disagreeing for me, but Tim pressed on.

He said, "I don't know what you've gotten mixed up in. I know that Nell… Well. That don't matter. The only thing that matters is that this isn't good for Mom and we have to do what's best for her."

"A few days ago you thought what was best for her was putting her in a home," I snapped.

Tim leaned back. "Now I've been kind to you, Maren, because you're one of my own, but there's a limit to that kindness. I'm going to take Mom home tonight. The boys are going to bunk together for a while so she'll have her own room and her own bathroom. She'll have everything she needs. She's got that thing down at the Rose Garden in a few days. We could all use a little time to calm down. You can come see her then. And when you do, I'll know that whatever it is that caused the deputy to come here is over. If you're involved in anything now, you won't be involved in it anymore. That clear?"

I closed my eyes. I felt just like a little girl being scolded for not cleaning my room. Like this was all caused by my poor choices, my selfishness. Like all the reasons I'd done what I'd done and all the sleepless nights and all the days I'd fought through on an empty stomach and all the worry didn't seem to matter. I'd done something bad and now it had to end and it was as simple as that.

Except it wasn't.

And being told now, of all times, what I had to do, by someone who hadn't been there, hadn't tried the way I had… It was almost too much to bear.

I wanted to yell at Tim. To ask him where he'd been all those weeks I'd struggled. He knew how much money we made, how hard it had to be for us to get by, and yet as long as I was quiet in my struggle, nobody had to get involved. But the minute I faltered, the minute I fumbled, he was here to tell me how to do what I'd been doing on my own for most of my life.

Granny had been right. So had Julie. People didn't know how to help, really. They just knew how to take over.

I said, "Where's Granny? I want to see her first."

"In her room." Tim rose from the couch and took a slow look around the house. "I can have Suze come by tomorrow and help you put things back together."

"I can handle it," I said.

He nodded and walked toward the door, which was still open, still hanging from a broken hinge. "Just send her outside whenever she'd ready. My truck's parked at Cheryl's."

I waited until I couldn't hear his footsteps before I walked down the narrow hallway and stood by Granny's door. The pale-yellow light of her bedside lamp leaked onto the floor. Her bed was made, her closet door open. I could see that most of the clothes were gone and she was dressed as though for church in one of her dark dresses and the shoes I'd bought her last Christmas. She didn't say anything as I walked in or when I sat on the edge of her bed. She didn't respond when I asked if she was all right.

"Are you going to talk to me?" I asked.

"I don't know what to say."

"Neither do I."

Granny toyed with the curtains. Behind her, through the glass, my door appeared. I could only make out the thinnest edge where the colors shifted from green to gray and back again as she said, "I never thought I'd have to worry about you and drugs. I thought seeing what happened to your mother would be enough to chase you away from something like that. I should have been more careful."

"It ain't up to you to make my choices, Granny. And I'm not taking the pills. I'm selling them."

"What's the difference?" She let the curtains fall back into place. "It might be worse what you're doing. You're helping people ruin their lives, just like Nell ruined hers."

"That's not fair."

"I'll tell you what isn't fair. Living to be this old just to be took out of your own house, made to sleep in somebody else's bed. They'll have me in the Rose Garden before the year is out, just you watch. All I wanted was to see my life through on my own terms, and I can't even get that."

I closed my eyes. My fog tightened around my throat and chanted *She's right, she's right, you failed* until guilt threatened to swallow me whole.

"That's what I was trying to do," I said. "I was trying to help."

"How has this helped?"

"I don't know. It all made sense when I started. You said you didn't want to be in a home and you didn't want Tim and them to know you were sick so I tried to make more money so I could get you a home health worker. That's what the pills was for."

"I didn't ask for that."

I threw my hands in the air. "No, you asked me to help, and I was trying to help. I never meant for things to happen like this, but I was on my own and trying to make it work."

"I didn't know I was such a burden."

"That's not what I'm saying and you know it."

"I suppose you think they're right to cart me off like this."

"It's what you did to Mom," I said without really meaning to and without really knowing why. I covered my face with my hands.

"What did you say?"

"I read Mom's journal," I said. "I know you took me from her after that trip with Thomas. I know you threatened to take me away for good. Is that why she took her door?"

There was a long silence as Granny stared down at the floor and I stared at her. I felt like I might collapse, sinking in on myself until there was nothing left, or maybe the other direction, every little part of me getting further and further from the other parts, drifting and drifting until I couldn't find myself in the dark.

"All I know is I always did what I had to do to keep you safe. That's all I've ever done." Granny's voice trembled as she spoke. Her hands were curled into fists, and I looked down to see my own hands tightened the same way. "I wish I could say you'd done the same for me."

She left then. The last thing I heard was the slam of Tim's truck door and the slow grind of the engine and then nothing. Just silence.

chapter twenty-eight

I almost took my door that night.

I did my best to put the house back together—the front door back on its hinges, the food back in the cabinets, the furniture back in its place, piecing together, one more time, what had been taken apart. I answered a text from Julie without telling her what had happened. The Reverend had taken her six hours away to Nashville to celebrate the fact that Julie was still alive, and I didn't want to ruin her newfound happiness. I texted Carver, too, and told him I was all right when he said he'd heard the police had been headed up the mountain.

I told myself to lie down and sleep the day off. To sleep until I could wake up and see a way out of this, but I'd rarely slept alone in this house since I moved in with Granny. She had always been there, predictable as the sun, moody as the moon. The house didn't feel right without her in it and it seemed disrespectful to pretend everything was normal, so I took the pillow from my bed and went to the couch instead.

All the way through the dark house, the flowers' silky leaves stroked my calves and tickled the backs of my knees. They whispered to me in words too quiet and strange to understand. I turned on the television to drown out their sound but the news only made me feel worse. There were hollers flooding all over the county. Smaller creeks overrunning their banks and creeping under houses, sinking cars into the mud. The forecast warned it would only get worse so I turned off the television and went onto the porch, dragging my pillow with me.

The blue flowers had spread outside. They poked their weary blue heads up through the spaces between the boards and between the front steps, too. They trailed down the yard to the end of the drive-way, almost like they'd followed Granny as far as they could and stopped short where Tim's truck had been parked. They spread as I watched, pushing up through the soggy earth along the road and blooming in fast-forward.

I climbed onto the porch rail, tossed my pillow up, and then followed it. I wasn't as quick or as limber as I used to be, but I could still reach the toehold I'd discovered as a girl on top of the nearest window and haul myself onto the roof with only a scraped knee. I wobbled to the very center, past the place where Uncle Tim and I had patched the roof the year before, dropped my pillow and lay down. From there, all I had to do was turn my head to see Mom's old trailer across the road, the place where I'd spent the first years of my life. The blue flowers had spread there, too—growing atop the moss that had grown over the roof, fighting for space among the weeds in the front yard, poking their heavy heads through the empty windows. I could almost see her there on the roof with a cigarette in her mouth, smiling, so I turned my head.

My door hovered over me, over the house, over the whole moun-tain, it seemed. All I could see from this angle was the very center— the deepest, darkest part—and only the faintest hint of swirling colors at the edges of my vision. I half expected to see my reflection in the door, but there was nothing. Truly nothing.

When my door first appeared, I wondered if it had taken its shape from my memories of science class in high school. But lying there that night, I realized it had taken its shape from me. I was that darkness in its center. I swallowed everything—all goodness, all light—and gave nothing back. I was the point of no return. All along, my little door had been showing me who I was, like reflecting like.

I felt so helpless then. There was no choice I could think of that wouldn't lead me back here. No way out. No something better.

So I would take my door and I would start again somewhere else. All I had to do was raise myself up and lift my arms and my little door would pick me up like a mother carrying her child and I would wake in a better place.

But I kept lying there on the roof staring up at that endless black. I kept waiting.

I wasn't sure what held me there, but there must have been something wrong. Something I hadn't seen yet.

I waited.

Then it hit me.

I needed to change my socks. They were my least favorite pair—too thin and too high, the threads too tight around my ankle—but they'd been a gift from Granny and I could never throw them away. I hadn't done laundry in a week so they were the only pair I had left. But I couldn't bear the thought of these socks being the socks I started my new life in. What if the world I went to didn't have any clothes? What if they hadn't invented ankle socks there? Or elastic? If I was going to let go of this world, I had to do it comfortably.

So I rolled over and crawled back down the roof to change my socks. But I'd have to do a load of laundry first. So I put some clothes in to wash. Then I realized how hungry I was and I went through the ransacked cabinets until I found some macaroni, which I boiled and drained, then filled the pot with tomato juice. I let it sit for a few minutes so the macaroni could soak up the juice, then I loaded it with salt and ate it straight out of the pot, standing there by the stove in my bare feet with my little door shining outside the window like it was asking me if I'd forgotten what I said I would do.

I hadn't forgotten. I just had to change the laundry over. And as I listened to the sound of the dryer rocking, I realized how much my back hurt, and my knees, and my feet, so I lay down on the couch just long enough to let my good socks dry. And that's where Julie found me the next morning, curled tight as a pill bug under a rock and just as reluctant to be disturbed.

She didn't bother to let the front door shut quietly behind her, but let it slam into place, then whispered "Oh shit" as a screw fell loose from the joint I had repaired the night before. "I'll fix that later," she said.

I tried my best to pretend I didn't hear her. I didn't move, didn't change my breathing.

"I know you're not asleep." Julie rustled around the room. It sounded as though she was carrying fifteen different kinds of bags, all of them too heavy to hold, but she kept holding them anyway. She rumbled around until she stood behind me and said, "Come on now, don't make me do this the hard way."

I cinched my eyes shut tighter.

"Fine then." She sighed. "It's been a while but I still remember how to whoop your butt. I'm the Heartbreak Kid this time."

Then she proceeded to use my own shoulder for balance as she jumped up and landed on my side on her knees. It didn't hurt, exactly, but it did wedge the air out of my lungs so my eyes flew open and the air whooshed out. Julie laughed. She punched me gently along the shoulder and neck, narrating herself like a WCW announcer as she did so and trying to make the sound of a roaring crowd in between. We wrestled just like when we were children in the backyard, rolling down the grass and pinning each other into contorted positions, red-faced and heaving until someone started to cry. Usually Julie, and not because she was getting hurt, but because Carver and I were wrestling too hard and she was afraid one of us would go too far and stop being friends with each other. Julie had been right, just a little late. It would take over a decade before Carver and I learned how to hurt each other properly.

I didn't have long enough to let the sadness grow as Julie pinned my elbow up by my throat and growled "Submit" through gritted teeth.

I tried to laugh, but it was a strangled sound, so I settled for whispering, "Never."

"Aw, come on," Julie said. "This is as close as I've ever come to winning."

I snaked my other arm free, reached up, and pinched the side of her boob. Julie yelped and leaned back, grabbing herself. Her mouth hung wide open, her face the perfect picture of dignified shock.

"Disqualified!" she yelled, looking around the room for a ref.

"Don't be a baby," I said. "You have two boobs."

"And they're both in pristine condition, thank you." She pulled the collar of her shirt and looked inside, cooed to her chest as though she was speaking to two fledgling birds. "If there's any damage, I'll sue. So will all the women who love me."

I laughed then, a loud and proper laugh, and Julie smiled.

She said, "I knew that would work. A little violence always did cheer you right up."

"I'm a simple woman," I said.

Julie looked at me intently. "What's going on? What happened to you?"

"I almost took my door last night."

"What the hell? What happened?"

So I told her about the raid and Uncle Tim and Granny. She'd been gone all weekend and hadn't heard any news out of Blackdamp aside from the flooding, though it wouldn't be long until everyone in the county knew what had happened. I told her about my mom's journal, too, and about Carver, told her everything I hadn't been able to tell her for so long. I toyed with one of the blue flowers as I did, twisting it between my toes, its heavy blue head bouncing against my ankle as I spoke.

When I was done, Julie rubbed her hands over her newly shaved scalp. The sound was like static electricity and it made me shiver. Our legs were tangled together and I picked at a loose string on her yoga pants, not quite ready to meet her eyes. She said, "What made you change your mind?"

"I was wearing the wrong socks."

Julie laughed. "That sounds about right. Back in high school, before things got really bad, I used to think about suicide a lot. I'd come up with all kinds of reasons not to do it. My hair was too long and I didn't want to go to Hell with that haircut. It was the wrong time of year. Once because I had a library book due back at school and I didn't want Mrs. Gross to be sore at me."

"I always liked Mrs. Gross." I smiled, but then it faltered. "So what made you... I mean, when you did, you know, in high school..." I fumbled into silence.

"When I attempted suicide?" Julie said.

I nodded.

"You've never asked me about that."

"I know," I said. "It scared me too bad."

"I'm not sure what was different, exactly," Julie said. "Sometimes… This might sound weird, all right? But sometimes I feel like taking those pills in high school was the first decision I ever made just for myself. Not for you or Carver or the Reverend or even Mom. It was about me. I know people like to say that it's selfish to kill yourself, but nobody ever talks about how many times I *didn't* do it because my socks were too tight or my hair wasn't right. All the ways I fought to stay here. They only think about the time I didn't. And my whole life it's felt like somebody else has been in control so the only thing I could actually choose was how I died." Julie took the loose string from my hand and pulled it hard, snapped it in half. She smoothed down the fabric of her pants.

"That might not have made sense to me before, but it does now," I said.

She nodded. "And listen, I wanted to say I'm sorry for how I handled things this time. I think I've only really known one way to get people's attention. It feels like everybody ignores me until I'm screaming or threatening something. So I went right back to that. Full meltdown. In my defense, it worked. The Reverend is listening now. You listened. But it still wasn't the best way to do things and I know it hurt you."

"Thank you," I said. "I'm sorry, too. I think…I think I was doing the same thing I always do, too. I only have one way of being. I keep seeing it now. One way of handling things."

"Alone?"

"Yep."

"Yep." Julie sighed. "It could be different, though. I'm not my mother and you're not yours. And besides, we don't have to see their legacy as a curse, you know? Maybe it's more like a relay race."

"This ain't field day, Jules."

She smiled. "Maybe it is, though. They got as far as they could. I'm still angry at my mom but I know that she tried, in her way, and I figure because of her I can get a little further. And when I do, it's for her, too, you know? It's not just for me. I want to go where she couldn't."

"I don't hate the sound of that."

"Good," Julie said. "I used to think the Reverend could never change, but she seems different now. She's really listening to me. She wants to help me have the life I want, not just the life she wants for me. If she can change, then me and you can, too."

I nodded.

She said, "That means it could be different with Carver, too."

I groaned. The colors from my little door fell through the living room windows, shifting from green to a deep, rich purple, like it was casting shadows instead of light.

"It could, though," Julie said.

"Whose side are you on?"

"Mine. I don't want to spend the rest of my life hearing you both moon over each other and sigh dramatically when the other leaves the room. Honestly, I just don't have the time for it. I have plans."

"Do you now?"

"I'm going back to school."

"Do what?"

Julie grinned. "I am. I figure I'll start about the same time you do."

"So a decade from now?"

"Hush, Eeyore." Julie reached out and grabbed my hand. "Now, come on. Let's go to the house and get my stuff. Carver's working on something so he won't be there. I'm going to stay with you until Granny comes back. And don't look at me like that. She's coming back. We're going to work things out."

Julie stood up and held out her hand to me. I took it reluctantly, and she pulled me to my feet.

"You're not alone anymore, Maren Walker," she said. "And you don't have to be again, if you don't want. That's up to you." She wrapped her arms around my waist and squeezed me tight, then headed toward the front door. "Hurry up now. I want to get back in time to watch my shows while we clean. And you're buying me a chicken strip basket, by the way. A four-piece."

She was out the door before I could answer, the peach fuzz on her head shining. When I was sure she couldn't look back and see me, I smiled.

chapter twenty-nine

Carver called me the next morning. I had to push Julie out of my way as I headed toward the porch, but she followed me to the door making kissing noises behind my back. My little door shifted as I walked outside, moving away from the house so I could see the dark heart at its center. Its edges were orange that morning, fading to blue near the center. The colors had a liquid quality to them, almost melting into each other as I curled into Granny's rocking chair and said hello.

"Hey," Carver said, and the sound of his voice brought tears to my eyes. I would have made fun of myself if I hadn't had such a bad few days. "Are you okay? Julie told me about Granny."

I shrugged, but then remembered he couldn't see it, so I made a small noise instead.

"Yeah, I figured. Are you taking care of yourself?"

"Julie's making me."

"Have you eaten?"

"Yeah, we had breakfast. Julie made biscuits."

"You didn't let her near the gravy, did you?"

I laughed. "No, I wanted to eat."

"Good."

"What about you? Are you okay?"

"Me? I'm good. Good. Still working on stuff with Pap and the

Reverend. She's been asking about you. She thinks you're a good match for me."

"I don't know if that's a good sign or not," I said. "How's your stuff going?"

"Good, good. Maybe we could talk about it sometime if it don't take up too much space."

I sighed.

"I know," he said. "I'm sorry. It's fine for you to have space. I shouldn't act that way. It's just hard. Is that still what you want? Space?"

"It's what I need."

"All right. But I want it noted that I am not having a good time with this."

"I'll put that in the permanent record: Carver did not enjoy himself."

"You got a notary there to verify that?"

"I am a notary."

He laughed and I wrapped an arm around my knees because I couldn't hug him instead. He said, "Are you sure you're okay?"

"As okay as I can be."

"Yeah. I'm just asking because I don't want to hang up."

"I know."

"I miss you."

"I miss you, too."

"Good," he said, and I laughed. "Well. Now that I made you laugh, I guess I can get back to work. If you need anything, just holler, all right?"

I smiled. "Bye, Carver."

"Bye, Maren."

I walked inside still smiling and helped Julie put the house back together. We cleaned, straightened, patched drywall, filled the gouge in the kitchen floor, found the missing screw from the door hinge. It was easier with help, and louder, too, as Julie sang in every room that she cleaned, and when I asked her why she did it, she said that she was singing the house awake. Singing the life back into things. So I sang, too, though not loud enough for her to hear.

I got a few texts over those days—people asking, in a roundabout way, if I had any pills to sell, but I told them they must have gotten the wrong number. I wasn't sure how I would pay for everything I needed, but it felt foolish to keep selling after the house had been raided. I put Granny's pills back in the high cabinet and shut the door.

It was sometime on that second morning that Julie stood in the kitchen and asked me what the hell I was doing.

"What do you mean?" I said.

She mimicked the way I had been moving—tiptoeing through the flowers, reaching over the blooms that had filled up the sink, the cabinets, sprouting in the refrigerator, so every movement I made was altered by them. But Julie couldn't see the flowers, so all she saw was me moving strangely, avoiding thin air, contorting to fit a shape that wasn't there.

I'd forgotten to tell her about the flowers. So I sat down at the kitchen table to explain, and as I spoke, Julie looked all around the room like it was concentration that kept her from seeing the flowers. She squinted at the sink and waved her hand back and forth in the cabinets, but still, nothing.

"How did you see them when your mom had them?"

"I don't know," I said. "She'd wear them in her hair. She kept one on the rearview mirror for a while. Made the whole car smell like this. I'd forgotten about that until now." I closed my fingers around one of the nearest stems. "I guess she picked them."

"Does that make a difference?"

"Let's see." I twisted the stem to the side with a soft, wet snap, then held the flower up to Julie. Somewhere between me picking the flower and holding it up, Julie's mouth dropped open.

"I can see it!" She clapped her hands together, then held out one cautious finger and touched the flower. I watched it move against her and smiled. "Holy shit. Do that again."

So I did it again. And again. And again. I stopped once we had two mason jars bursting with blue. It was fun, in a way. It made the world feel less small, somehow, not being the only person who could see or smell the flowers, though neither of us fully understood how it worked. Julie carried the bouquets over to the kitchen window and pulled up the blinds. She couldn't see the edge of my little door as it peeked over the eaves, casting lazy pink shadows onto the ground below, but I could. And even though the flowers looked pretty there, they made me feel a little sick to my stomach.

I'd loved my door at first. Loved having something that was mine and mine alone. I even loved the flowers and the way they called me back to Mom. But it was all beginning to feel like a fishing hook caught in my cheek. My door, my flowers—they tugged at my attention, pulled me away from what I was trying to focus on so I couldn't ever really be there in the kitchen with Julie. I was always somewhere else, at least partially. I was surrounded by the past, by Mom and all the choices she'd made, by my future and all the choices I hadn't made. I needed another door to take me away from my door.

I think it was that feeling, more than anything, that made me pick up Mom's journal that night. The next day was Granny's talent show, and I didn't know it yet, but whatever peace I'd had for those two days would end there. I'd talked to Granny on the phone that morning, a stiff, stilted conversation that was so much like talking to a stranger that I nearly cried. She was still angry at me and at the world. I still didn't know how to make anything right, so we were stuck in our own kind of middle, waiting for something to change.

So that night after Julie had fallen asleep beside me and was snoring softly, I picked the journal up and opened it to the last few pages, the last words that my mother had written before she left this world for good.

August 3, 20—

Dear Maren,

I am doing the best I can. I hope that's what you remember when you look back on these days. Or maybe I'll get lucky and you won't remember them at all. That way you'll never come up to me and ask why you spent that one summer at Granny's house or why I disappeared for almost a week and whatever happened to that tall man Thomas, and I'll never have to answer for any of these things that I did.

And the more I think about it, the more I think it wasn't so bad, what happened. Because nothing really happened, did it? I came back. If it hadn't been for Mom overreacting the way she did, then everything would be fine, wouldn't it? There's a reason so many of her children moved away from her. There's a reason Tim doesn't come to visit even when he lives so close, isn't there?

All I know is I'm not going to let that happen to me and you. I'm not going to be a person you have to get away from, Maren. I'll do whatever it takes to bring you home. Even if it means dealing with Mom. I promise.

Love,
Mom

August 7, 20—

Dear Maren,

I get to bring you home this weekend for a visit. I wish it was for good but Mom keeps reminding me it's just for a couple days. I picked up some brownies and ice cream on the way home and maybe we'll rent a movie or maybe I should have gotten a board game. I think we still have a puzzle in a box somewhere. Or maybe Monopoly. I just want us to have fun. I want you to remember how good I can be when I try.

Love,
Mom

August 9, 20—

Dear Maren,

My door is still there. I went back just to see. I told myself that it was on the way to work but it's not really on the way at all and I ended up being late and had to tell my manager that I'd run out of gas. I don't think he believed me, but I don't really care.

It was just the way I'd left it. There we were—a little clay me and a little clay you heading up the mountain and there was Thomas beside us. I went to smudge him in, to make him part of the mountain, but the clay had started to dry. I hadn't noticed it before, but once I did, I saw just how much of it had dried already. I think it started from the bottom. It's the hardest there where it meets the grass, like stone. And then it gets a little softer as it goes up. It's set in place about halfway, so the top half is still changeable. I broke a nail forcing the little Thomas back into the mountain, and I was sweating by the time I was finished, and it still didn't work all the way. I pushed him down enough that you can't tell he was a man before, but now the whole thing looks a little messed up. So much for my dream world.

I guess this is my door's way of telling me I'm running out of time. Doors won't go away on their own but they will make it so that you can't really stand them anymore, or they'll push you a little at a time until you make your choice. I wish my door had found some other way. It feels too much like my life. Freezing in place, nothing I can do to make a change. All my mistakes stuck there where I have to look at them for the rest of my life.

At least now it's just you and me and them pretty blue flowers on my door. The flowers are still growing there too so I picked a few and put them in my purse. I think I'll give one to you when I see you this weekend. Maybe we'll come up with a name for them, like Blue Marens. I like the sound of that.

Love,
Mom

August 10, 20—

Dear Maren,

I don't know what went wrong. I went to pick you up from Mom's today and everything was going fine at first. We were in the living room talking and Mom went out to the car to get some craft you'd made me at school and I bent down to talk to you and you puckered up your face and said that my breath smelled bad. I thought you were joking at first but then you said that it smelled too sharp and told me that your friend Jeremy's dad's breath always smelled that way, too, and he was the PE teacher. I only took a drink before I left because I was so nervous. I needed to steady myself or I was afraid that Mom would think I'd been drinking anyway and refuse to let you come, but it was barely a shot's worth. I heard Mom coming up the steps so I told you to stop talking about Jeremy's dad and you asked me why and what was wrong and you wouldn't stop talking so I hushed you and I grabbed your arm because I was so afraid Mom wouldn't let you come with me and everything I've done would be for nothing.

And you hushed, but you stayed hushed. You didn't say anything once Mom came back in and she was getting worried over you, like maybe you was sick, so I said we ought to be going. I got all your stuff together and went to the door and then you refused to come. You said you didn't want to go with me. That you wanted to stay with Mom.

I thought I'd die right there on the spot. I don't think I would have noticed if someone had run through me with a knife. It couldn't have felt any worse than what I felt right then. Mom saw the look on my face and she tried to talk to you to see what was wrong, to see what made you say that to me. She tried to help, I think, in her way, but there was no helping. I was about to cry so I told her I'd come back in a little while, maybe you just needed some time, and I dropped all your stuff on the porch and I left that little craft you made me. I never even got to hold it.

I'm only writing this now because I've already cried myself out. I don't think I have anything left in me to cry. I thought that last week, too, and the week before that. It's untelling how many times I've emptied myself out over the years but this feels like the emptiest I've ever been. I keep

*trying but it never seems to work. I just don't know what
to do.*

That was the last full entry she wrote. It ended without a *Love,
Mom* as though she might have had more to say. A few lines below
there were some scribbled drawings of doors—doors with windows
and little curtains, doors missing knobs, doors with cracks snaking
all up and down them. And the phrase *pick up, Karen, pick up,
Karen* written five times in a row like some kind of spell. I don't
know if Karen answered her phone or what they might have talked
about. On the next page there was part of what looked like an
address—*133 Chestnut*—but there was no address that matched in
all of Blackdamp. She could have written that on any day, though,
flipping back through the pages to jot something down before
forgetting about it. There was no way to be sure. No clear answer.

I flipped through the last blank pages of the journal, needing there
to be more, but I found my own shaky childhood cursive instead. I
don't even remember writing it or ever having seen Mom's journal
before Karen gave it to me, but there it was. There I was. All I'd
written were three names—Maren Walker, Nell Walker, Iris Walker.

chapter thirty

The rain started back that night and it wouldn't end, really, until most of Blackdamp was flooded. For weeks afterward, people in town would speculate on how it all happened so quickly. There would be many theories, from the lack of snow in the winter to the new logging project east of town to the witch that was said to live at the tip of the old oak tree near Burnt Ridge who had cursed us all and now, finally, the curse had come to collect.

But it seemed more likely that it was just too much rain and that the town was the perfect bowl to catch it, being guarded on one side by the mountain where I lived and on the other side by Burnt Ridge. It was like the dip between two ribs, a perfect place for things to slip through or collect, a place that wasn't so much a place in itself as it was the *lack* of mountain or hill, so it couldn't stand against the rain, couldn't shrug it off. It could only hold all that it was given until it could hold no more.

We saw the first flash flood warning around nine that morning. The rain was coming slow but steady by then, so we doubted much would come of it. This happened, after all, from time to time. Most of the hollers in Blackdamp followed creeks that followed streams up to the mountains, and spring always brought flooded roads and gardens and school closures. It was just part of the price we paid for being so near the sky.

Over breakfast, Julie said she needed to drop by the house before we went into Sterns for Granny's talent show and I faltered, sloshing coffee down my shirt and onto the floor.

"Carver won't be there. I'm not that cruel," Julie said, smiling as I cleaned myself up. "He's doing something for the garage today."

"Is he coming to the talent show?"

"He said he doesn't go where he's not wanted. Which I guess was his weird way of saying that you didn't invite him."

I huffed out a breath and smiled. "Right."

We drove in silence through the rain. The Blue Marens had flooded the mountain, making bright dots of color that shone through the dreary grayness of the day. They swayed along the side of the road and crested the hills beside us and filled the gaps between the trees. They were everywhere, but they somehow made me feel even more alone. I sulked as much as I could without driving us into a ditch, and I tried not to feel left behind. I tried not to think how it was the same thing all over again—how I'd been upset with Mom for scaring me when she'd grabbed my arm so I'd turned her away. Then she'd left for good when what I needed was for her to come back. I needed to know I was worth coming back for. And now I'd turned away from Carver.

Sadness pulsed in my chest in rhythm with my little door spinning over us. The rain ate my door up, falling through it so quickly that it couldn't knit itself back together in time so it was torn apart and torn again.

Someone called me on the way, but the number showed UNKNOWN so I didn't answer. They left a voicemail, too, but when I tried to listen to it, all I heard was static and a muffled voice before the line cut off. It was probably nothing—just a robot or a debt collector—but it still made me feel uneasy.

I tried to stay in the car while Julie went inside her house. I wanted to be broody and sad in the rain, which I felt was my God-given right, but Julie made fun of me until I had to get out of the car and follow her inside to show her that I didn't care.

Of course my caring punished me the minute I walked through the door. Carver was all over the house even when he wasn't there. His favorite coffee mug sat on the kitchen counter beside a solder-ing gun as though those two things made sense together. His sloppy handwriting scrawled across a note on the fridge that I could barely read because he never dotted his *i*'s and I always wondered if that meant something about him. His muddy boots sat by the back door, and he had taken something apart and laid its metal entrails across the kitchen table. I stared down at the pieces, trying to figure out what it was, but I couldn't tell. I knew he could. That somehow, in his mind, he could hold something all at once and all apart, could see how the two were the same, how to put things back together when they'd been separated.

I trailed my fingers along the collar of the blue flannel shirt he'd slung over the chair, and I could see him there, getting too warm as he worked so he'd shrugged it off. It was his favorite shirt even though it was missing a button in the middle. I'd meant to fix that for him when he wasn't looking, sew a button from one of my shirts onto it so he would wake up one morning and find me there, knit into his shirt where he might keep me close to him all day.

"You know I won't judge you if you take that shirt with you," Julie said as she walked back into the kitchen.

"I'm not doing that."

"Why not?"

"Because," I said, but I wanted to, very badly. My fog curled tight behind my ears and told me how sad it was, how pathetic to want something like that, and I knew it was right, I did, but it didn't stop me from wanting it anyway.

Julie sighed. "What if I brought the shirt?"

"Well, that's your business."

"And if you get cold, you can tell me." Julie pulled the shirt from the chair and draped it over her arm. "Because now I have this extra shirt with me that has no sentimental value at all attached to it."

"Well." I sniffed. "All right."

Julie leaned over and kissed my cheek before she headed out of the house. "I sure hope you learn how to be nice to yourself."

"I wouldn't hold your breath," I said as I followed her through the living room and onto the porch. I slipped Carver's shirt out of her hand before we made it to the car and pulled it on and I told myself it was just the rain, just the cold that made me do it, and that it was just the flannel that made me feel warmer the minute it touched my skin.

The roads always made the drive into town a little slow. You couldn't really drive too fast on curves so steep that they almost kissed each other, but the drive was even slower with the rain. We'd been on the road for five minutes when we had to pull over because I couldn't see more than a foot in front of me. The world disappeared inside the water, which poured down so fast and heavy that it was like someone had gutted the sky. I turned on my emergency flashers and waited for the squall to break—it felt impossible for something to keep going like that for so long, like it would have to empty soon, to quiet—but the water kept pouring.

Julie was white as a sheet. She'd never gotten her license and even being a passenger made her anxious most days. We never really talked about how her mother had died in a car—drifting across the wrong lane and into a head-on collision. It had been ruled an accident but everyone in Blackdamp assumed her death had been intentional. Julie sat white-knuckled, clutching her purse to her chest.

"I have to move," I said after I watched a truck creep past, coming so close to us that for a moment the truck was all I could see.

I knew Julie would rather not try, but she didn't say anything as I pulled back onto the road and started the long crawl down the mountain. We passed several cars pulled to the side like we'd been, the dull flash of their lights the only thing that let me know they were there. I tried to keep to the center of the road, jerking over only when I saw what I thought were headlights in the distance. Above us, my door was torn apart into temporary bursts of color, like fireworks shooting from miles away.

Water poured down the driveways and hillsides, turning the pavement muddy and slick. The tires caught and spun beneath us, trying to find something to hold on to, and Julie gripped the console and whispered under her breath. I thought she might be praying, but after a while I could make out the rhythm of a song, though I couldn't understand the lyrics. I hummed along with her when she got to the chorus, and she smiled as we finally reached the bottom of the hill and the rain lightened enough to reveal the town spread out before us.

The Rose Garden was one of the first buildings, sandwiched between the post office and a pharmacy. I pulled into the crowded parking lot and shut off the car. I wanted to get out and run into the building, find Granny and wrap her in a hug, but my body was still catching up to me, some part of it left stuck on the mountain with its fingers clutching the steering wheel. I took a deep, shaky breath and let it out slowly.

"Are you okay?" Julie asked.

"I think so. Are you?"

"I think so."

"We need to get back up that mountain before the rain does."

I laughed. "I think you're right."

She pulled the hood of her jacket over her ears and handed me an umbrella. We half walked, half ran toward the Rose Garden until we were under the safety of the carport outside the front doors. Dozens of people were crowded there, clustered in twos and threes, and it wasn't until we got there that I noticed the school buses lined up outside.

I was looking for Granny and Tim when he walked up beside me and grabbed my arm. "There you are," he said. "I've been calling but I couldn't get through. I was afraid you wouldn't make it off that mountain. We stopped by the house on the way. Granny needed to get some pantyhose but you weren't there."

"We must have been at Julie's. What's going on with the buses?"

"They're transporting all the old folks to the Breckenridge school. They're turning it into some kind of crisis center. Ain't you heard?"

I shook my head.

"The west side of town is flooded," Tim said. "If the rain keeps up, then the whole thing will be under by tonight."

"Shit," I said. The west side was lower than the east. The ground sloped toward the river that cut the shape of the town and kept the mountains at bay, and the grocery store where I worked was just beside the river. "What about the store?"

"Last I heard the water hadn't reached the bottom shelves but it won't be long."

"*Shit.* Where's Granny?"

"Helping Betty, I reckon. I left to go pick up the boys. Suze is on her way here now. You want to go find her? I'd like to get everybody home before the rain picks up again."

"All right." I turned to Julie. "Have you called Carver?"

"I'm trying now. You go ahead. I'll wait for you."

I pushed past the people gathered outside and through the sliding doors of the entrance. The lobby was small. A sitting room on the left was cramped with people who all turned to look at me as I walked in. I waved at them awkwardly and some waved back, then one woman turned around and smiled.

"There comes the sun," Karen said, grinning at me. She opened her arms and I walked into them without thinking. She smelled like Red Door perfume, the same kind that my mother used to wear, and my throat prickled.

"What're you doing here?" I asked.

"I came to pick up a job application," she said. "I always did love working with older people. But things were going south by the time I got here and they could use the extra hands. What're you here for?"

"Granny was supposed to be in the talent show."

"I'll help you find her."

She led me across the lobby to the place where it split in two directions. She pointed to the long hallway to the right. "You take that wing and I'll take the next. Meet me back here in the middle when you're finished, all right?"

I took off down the hallway. The fluorescent lights glinted off every surface—the floor, the framed photos on the wall, the doorknobs—until it seemed the whole place was made of light. I knocked on doors that were half-shut and let them swing open slowly. A woman stood inside one room with a small baby doll clutched in her arms.

"Jenny?" she said as I stepped inside. "Is it time to go?"

I stood there with my mouth open, not sure how to respond, until a nurse walked out of the bathroom beside me.

"It's all right, Mona. We're almost ready for our trip," she said, then turned to me. "Are you looking for someone?"

"Granny," I said, then shook my head. "Iris. Walker. She was here for the talent show."

The nurse smiled. "She was in Betty's room helping her get her bag a few minutes ago. Two doors down on the right. And hurry— the bus is leaving soon."

I nodded and left the room, feeling somehow like I was forgetting something important, something that would be impossible to find tomorrow. I felt like crying suddenly but I bullied the feeling into the furthest corner of my jaw and bit down hard to hold it in place.

I trailed my knuckles along the door to Betty's room as I stepped inside. I checked the bathroom and the closet, but they were empty. Further inside were a single bed and a small table, a television mounted to the wall. There were potted plants in the window, growing wild and green. Everything seemed muted and soft, like I could sink into the air or into the walls if I pushed hard enough. The only thing that really stood out in the whole room was the blue flower lying on the bed. It was one of Mom's flowers, one of mine. The Blue Marens. Tim said they'd stopped by the house on the way, which meant Granny must have found the jar of flowers I'd picked for Julie. She must have remembered them from Mom. My fog threatened to swallow me whole with guilt—what if the flowers had triggered something in her, sent her chasing some memory? I picked up the Blue Maren just as a woman walked into the room.

"Oh," she said when she saw me. "Do I know you?"

"No. I don't know. Are you Betty?"

"Yes."

"I'm Maren. Iris's grandbaby."

"Oh," she said, brightening. "I know you." She walked past me to the bedside table and picked up a pair of bronzed baby shoes. "I forgot my shoes. They were my boy's. I don't know what I'd do if I lost them."

"Is this yours?" I asked, holding up the flower.

She shook her head. "Iris must have left it. She didn't seem to like it very much but she was holding on to it for dear life. She left a while ago."

"Left?"

Betty looked scared for a moment as though she had said the wrong thing. "She said it was all right. She had a ride."

"A ride where?"

Betty shook her head. "I don't know. She said she had something to take care of."

"That's all she said?"

"I'm sorry." Betty's lip quivered.

"No, no. It's all right. I'm just… It's okay."

Someone called Betty's name from down the hall and we both looked.

"It's okay," I said. "You go on."

I stood there for a while once Betty was gone, staring down at the blue flower. I didn't want to tell Tim and Julie that Granny was gone and that I didn't know where or with who. If she really had gotten a ride, where would she go? Some part of me was certain she'd gone to Burnt Ridge. Mom had suspected Granny knew about her door, and if she saw the blue flowers again, maybe that reminded her, and maybe, maybe, maybe... I closed my eyes, needing to shut everything out, needing a moment of quiet, of dark, and when I opened them again, the Blue Marens had caught up with me, working their way through the tiles and growing slow and heavy across the doorway. I walked into the hall and followed the trail that had followed me to the front door, their heavy heads bobbing, their stems still growing, reaching up, up until they brushed the tips of my fingers and curled against my palms like they meant to hold my hand, like they hoped they could make whatever came next just a little bit easier.

chapter thirty-one

Uncle Tim reacted better than I thought he would, and he listened when I said that Granny had probably gone home, even though I didn't believe it. That's why I let him head back up the mountain while I stayed behind and tried to figure out a way to get to Burnt Ridge with most of the roads flooded. I was still holding the Blue Maren when Carver pulled up in Pap's truck with the Reverend riding shotgun. A weathered green johnboat was tied down in the back, tipped sideways to keep the wells from filling with rain.

"Are you all right?" the Reverend asked as she enveloped first Julie and then me in a hug. I was too shocked at the sudden display of affection to say anything when Carver rounded the truck and smiled at me.

"Nice shirt," he said, nodding to the flannel I'd snagged from his house.

I flipped him off behind the Reverend's back but that only made his smile widen.

"I'm so glad y'all are here," Julie said and launched into an explanation of what had happened.

Carver moved beside me and I took a step closer to him. It seemed all the reason he needed to put his arm around my waist and pull me close. He said, "You okay?" and then tightened his arm when I shook my head no.

The Reverend turned to me after a moment and asked, "Are you sure your granny's on Burnt Ridge? We might only have one shot of finding her before the water does."

I swallowed. "No. But it's the best I've got."

She nodded and turned to Carver. "I'll take Maren's car and head the long way to the Ridge, come at it from the north. If there's a chance Iris went that direction, we'll find her. You take the truck and head to the Ridge through the old roads. The truck's the only thing that'll make it. We all have phones?"

We nodded.

"Good. Now give me your hands."

"Reverend, do we really—" Carver began, but the Reverend cut him off.

"Do we have time for the Lord? Always. Now give me your hand."

So we stopped there in the rain, clasped our hands together, dropped our heads, and prayed beneath the shaky light of my little door that somehow everything would be okay.

The Blue Marens led our way. Everywhere we turned, it seemed, they'd turned there just before us even as the roads shifted from blacktop to gravel to dirt. The flowers sprouted through concrete and twisted along thin saplings that were barely rooted to the earth. They bobbed their heavy blue heads in the wake of our passing, so no matter which way I looked, I could see them flooding the hillside, lurking in the shadows beneath the trees. I didn't recognize most of the turns Carver took. Some people thought the mountains never changed, but the truth was that they were changing all the time.

The moment people stopped intruding with their homes or

riding trails or logging roads, the hills closed up like flesh around a wound. The trees regrew, the ground littered with leaves and twigs, the animals reclaimed the space that had been taken from them, so in a year's time what had once been a passable dirt road would be forest again. The trails I knew as a girl were all but vanished, and most of the roads we traveled seemed just days away from growing up, like they might disappear behind us and leave us stranded like two children in a fairy tale. Maybe that would be our trial, making our way across a land we thought we knew, fighting to return home.

The blue flowers watched as Carver drove us over a narrow hill that ran parallel to town. Below, I could finally see what the rain had done. I found the roof of the store where I worked and saw the dark line where the water had marked the brick. There was another pharmacy with its windows boarded and the Dollar General with the lights still glowing. Cars were abandoned here and there, some turned sideways in the middle of the road, the water rushing slowly past the closed windows. There were people, too, sitting on the roofs of buildings, waiting for rescue.

Days of rain had soaked the earth so a few hours could turn the town into this. It was hard to look at and impossible to understand how it could happen that quickly, how a little water could hurt that much. Even as I watched, the rain picked up again. Carver reached out his hand and I took it.

The farther we drove, the harder it was to imagine how Granny could have made it this far. Betty claimed Granny had a ride but all I could imagine was her walking alone in the rain, taking the same path we took now. Soaked to the bone, her favorite dress clinging to her like a second skin. She'd start to shiver, to second-guess her steps. All it would take was one wrong turn, one fumble.

"What if she fell?" I stammered. "Or drowned? What if she—"

"Hey, hey," Carver said, slowing the truck just a moment so he could look at me. "You can't think of that right now. She's tougher than either of us, remember? We won't stop looking until we find her. She's going to be okay."

I nodded. "I'm really glad you're here."

"So am I."

He kissed my knuckles before he turned back to the road. After driving upward for what seemed like forever, we were turning down again. The water collected along the potholes and rushed under the tires so they spun and caught, spun and caught. Maybe Granny really had gotten a ride. There were any number of people who knew her and would have helped. She might have told them that I was stuck on Burnt Ridge and she needed to get to me. She might even have believed it.

And every time the tires got bogged down and Carver had to back up and start again, I knew that we were losing time. Like time was pouring out with the water, rushing down the hills and away from us with every bend and turn. And I hated it then—time. The way it bent and curved around me, brought my mother back in her journal so I could see all the ways we mirrored each other, all the battles she'd lost that I was fighting again. Time that sagged inside Granny's mind and pulled her away from me a little more every day, back to when her children were young and not yet lost to her. Time that brought blue flowers sprouting under our tires and waiting around every curve. Time that urged me toward a choice I still wasn't ready to make.

We crested a small hill that dipped and then rose again, creating a gully in the middle. There had been a creek there once, but the creek was something else now—something bigger and meaner, full of swirling muddy water, ten feet deep and at least twice as many feet wide, that blocked the one road we had left to Burnt Ridge.

chapter thirty-two

"Hold tight now," Carver said as he pushed the nose of the johnboat toward me. I did my best to guide it onto the ground gently, but it still thumped and slid out of my control. Carver nodded as it landed on the wet grass and said, "Good enough."

He hopped down and grabbed hold of the rope that was tied to the johnboat. I followed his lead as he pointed us toward the water, which was moving in quick circles that almost seemed to match the spinning of my door overhead. The water must have come from further up the mountain because it was dark and muddy and moving fast even though the rain had nearly stopped. My little door was mostly whole without the rain to tear it apart, shimmering pink and gold light over our shoulders as we slid down the hill toward the water.

We were almost ready to push off when Carver noticed a puncture the size of my fist in one corner of the johnboat. He walked a slow circle around the boat, cursing everything in the garage that might have caused the hole and himself for not noticing it sooner and johnboats everywhere until he finally came back to where he started and closed his eyes.

"It might not make it across with both of us," he said.

"What if we swim? You're the one who taught me how."

"Yeah, and I barely know how," he said. "And it's dangerous. The water's moving fast enough…" He shook his head. "If we go a little further up and I give you a big push, you should land about there." He pointed to the other side. "You can drag the boat up so it doesn't sink completely. We'll figure out how to get you back once you come back."

I nodded. "I'll be okay."

He said, "I know," but he was frowning so hard that the wrinkles in his forehead nearly cast their own shadows. I smiled at him. "What?"

"Nothing," I said. "I'm just glad you're here with me."

"You said that already."

"Can't I say it again?"

"Yeah, I like it. I'm just mad."

"I know," I said, climbing into the boat. I held on to the narrow seat as Carver lined me up with the water.

"I might swim across after you," he said, his voice low, almost petulant.

"No. I'll be fine. Besides, Granny might not have made it this far. She might come walking over that rise any minute now and she'll need you to be here. I need you to be here."

Carver frowned again, but nodded. I held out my hands, cupped them in the air until Carver leaned forward and placed his face between them. I ran my thumbs over the stubble on his cheeks as I leaned forward and kissed him gently on the mouth.

"I have to go," I said.

He nodded once more, gave me one last set of instructions, and then pushed me onto the water. The boat rocked under me and I had to brace my feet against the bottom to keep from tipping back too far. I watched the hole in front of my feet start to fill with muddy water. It filled faster than I'd hoped as I drifted over the current and my little door drifted above me. Carver followed me down the bank, tracking the boat's every movement. His T-shirt was dark with rain and his hair was sticking to his face and he looked so beautiful standing there, so right, that for a moment I didn't feel so afraid. It felt like things might be okay. That they *could* be okay.

"Hey, Carver," I said. My voice was too high and too tight in my throat. And my fog rose up in me and told me to be quiet and not to tell Carver how I felt, not to hold on to him when I needed him most, but I was so tired of listening to the stories my fog told. I wanted a different story, so I said, "I love you."

"Really?" he said, his hands flying into the air. "You're going to tell me that now?"

I laughed. "Can you think of a better time?"

Carver smiled and it felt like the sun rising. "I love you, too."

The water rose high enough to cover the bottoms of my shoes and I could feel the weight of the boat shifting, everything tilting forward just as the boat hit land, and I jerked to the side. I hurried out and tried to drag the boat behind me, but it was so heavy that I fell to my knees. I turned back for it when Carver yelled.

"That's good enough," he said. "Just leave it. Go find Granny."

"You sure?"

"Positive. Call me as soon as you find her, all right?"

"I will."

"And be careful."

"I will," I called, already stumbling up the hill.

"If you need me—"

"I know!"

"I'll be here."

chapter thirty-three

The flowers were packed so closely together that I had to fight my way up the hill, and every few steps Carver yelled to make sure I was okay. The ground was soggy, slick, and sliding under my feet, so every step felt like ten. I dug my fingers into the mud to try to slow myself down but only succeeded in cutting my skin against the rocks, so every time I sank my hands into the grass my fingers burned. The Blue Marens were just as damp, and they slid under my feet and tangled between my fingers.

I was breathing hard by the time I reached the top of the short hill and waved goodbye to Carver. I knew enough about Burnt Ridge to guess where my mother's door had been and I moved in that direction, slowly. My feet tangled in the flowers every few steps and I stumbled, slipped, fell to my knees more than once. I started kicking them as I walked, but that only made me clumsier. I had to go slowly, had to watch my steps as much as I watched the horizon, looking for the small, familiar slope of Granny's shoulders, the particular knot of her hair, which would be pulled close to her head now, soaked with rain. The thought of her being cold and alone made me feel so sad and heavy that I wondered if I would make it another step.

But I did.

And I made it another after that.

The flowers had far outpaced me, and everywhere I looked, they were already present, their bright-blue heads shaking merrily back and forth as if they were judging my progress and found me sorely lacking.

"Couldn't you have found a more helpful way to pressure me?" I asked my door as I stumbled up another hill and paused, bent double, looking for Granny among the many knolls covered with high grass and thin saplings. My door just spun, as it always did, impassive and impossible and so irritating that I wished once more I could draw back my fist and punch it in the face.

And it was there that I saw her. There was something in that moment that gave me déjà vu, like I had lived this before, like I had known this feeling of relief and sadness swirled all tight together in my chest. Granny was standing on a little hill not too far away, her arms wrapped around herself, her back turned toward me.

I struggled toward her as quickly as I could, wheezing and sputtering, slipping, then clawing my way back up. The flowers swayed in front of my face as I fell so that when I looked up, they were all I could see. Blue and only blue. And I had never hated them more than I did in that moment and hated my door and every door that had ever existed, every door that came and took away what should have stayed here, should have been given its own chance to grow. And I hated everyone and everything that made it so hard to stay here and grow here and love here without suffering, too, without hurting and fighting and clawing every minute of your life until you just couldn't do it anymore.

I must have looked an awful sight by the time I gained my feet again. Covered with mud, drenched with water, like some strange animal emerging from the primordial ooze. I did my best to clean off my hands on my jeans, but it was no use.

Granny turned to face me about that time. Her eyes had that distant, hazy look to them, that faraway gleam.

"Nell," she said, and my heart sank, thinking she was gone again, lost to some other place, some other time. But then she said, "You look just like her, you know."

I blinked. "What?"

"You look just like your mother. Especially now." Granny took a step toward me. Her dress was soaked to her shoulders. I could see the blue trails of veins in her arms and throat. "How'd you know where to find me?"

"Well, your friend Betty was no help whatsoever, but I found the flower in her room. And I figured you remembered and maybe you would be here. I got lucky."

"There's a first."

I snorted. "Maybe things are changing. Are you hurt?"

Granny looked down at her shoes caked with mud. "I don't think so. I don't remember getting here. I remember wanting to be here and being in someone's truck and then you coming up the hill. I think I was thinking of her."

"Who?"

"Nell. I was here the night she left," Granny said. "I never did tell you that. I never told you a lot of things."

Granny looked around like she wanted a chair to pull out, like we might somehow appear in the kitchen back home if she thought about it long enough, but we settled for walking under a redbud tree and I helped her sit on a rock that looked a little dryer than the rest. She took a slow, deep breath and I tried not to listen too closely to the sound of her lungs or think too hard about how sick she might be in a few days. I knelt down beside her and cold water soaked into my knees.

She settled her hands in her lap and looked out over the hills. "I followed her that night. I'd known for a while that she had a door.

You can always tell." She looked at me, a little pointedly, but didn't say anything else. "When I saw her tear out of the driveway that evening, I knew something was wrong."

"I wouldn't go with her."

"You remember?"

"No. I read her journal."

"Oh." Granny shook her head. "She took it too hard. You was just angry is all. And you had a right to be angry. But all she could see was the hurt. So I followed her. I think she was about to leave when I came over the hill like you did." Granny looked down at her hands. "I tried to get her to stay. I offered her everything I could think of. Money. A new car. All kinds of things I couldn't afford."

"There was nothing you could do."

"I was so sure I could fix her."

"She didn't need fixing, Granny. She needed…"

"Better sense. That's what she needed."

I closed my eyes. "You have to stop talking about her like that."

"She was my daughter. I can talk about her any way I need to."

"And she was my mother. She was sick, Granny. And she was lonely and she tried so hard. She tried and it didn't work and she's gone now. She didn't need to be tougher or stronger or have better sense. She was good." My voice cracked on the last word and I looked away. "Why can't you just let her be that?"

Granny shook her head. "It's not that simple."

"Why not?"

"Because," Granny said, "you don't know what it's like to lose your child. To see her walk away. She'd rather have been anywhere than stay here with me."

"Did she say that?" I asked.

Granny looked away.

I winced. "I'm sorry, Granny."

"I look at my children, and I don't know where I went wrong. I tried. I was hard, I know, and I didn't always make the right choices. I should have left Richard after Nell was born. I had all my babies, had everything I needed. But I couldn't survive on my own with four children. I'd never had a job until after Richard died."

"You did the best you could."

"Tim don't see it that way. Neither does Forest."

"Well," I said, "maybe they can now that they're older. Or maybe they never will. But if you want to try, then I'll help you try."

Granny shook her head. "I look at my life and I wonder where it's gone. It's hard enough not having the money to care for myself, needing your help, but losing my memories, too. It's more than I can bear most days."

"I wish it was different, too. I wish I had enough money so you'd never have to worry about anything ever again. But I don't." I dropped my head. "And I need help. I know you don't like having somebody stay with you, but we have to make some kind of compromise. I want the same thing that you want, all right? I want you to have the life you want. I want to help you have it. But I need help, too."

"Will you stop messing around with those pills?"

"Selling them? Yeah. I'll stop. I never wanted to do it in the first place."

"And you won't take your door? You promise me that?"

I looked up at Granny for a moment. My door was above us. Shining brighter than the dim, gray sky behind it, its light the color of a deep bruise, and it lit Granny, too, and softened her edges. There were tears on her face and I looked away. I held my muddy face inside my muddy hands and wondered what Granny had been thinking the night she followed Mom out to the Ridge. If she'd tried to hold Mom back or knock her away or keep her from her door, to stop her from going someplace Granny could never follow. I wondered when any of us would ever get loose of ourselves or if we would always end up here together, soaked through and cold, exhausted, worn down until even a doorway into darkness seemed a better option. And I understood, more than ever, why Mom did what she did. The door wasn't just an escape. It wasn't just about leaving. It was about having a choice that felt hopeful. A choice that made you believe things could be better. And it was so hard to find them here, so hard for us, and my heart broke all over again.

I wish I could say I had some grand revelation there. That I realized the error of my ways or the key to life. Or maybe I realized that I was just made of stronger stuff than my mother and all I needed to survive was my own stubborn will, but I know that's not true. I'm only here because I'm made of the same stuff that made her, and that same stuff made Granny, too. But my life was not my mom's. And I had more than she'd had—even if it was just a few more chances, a few more people, and a little less trouble. But it was enough that when I looked up at my door, I saw a way out when what I needed was a way through. That's all any of us needed. I had a chance for that, even if Mom didn't.

And I wanted a chance.

I wanted to hug Carver again and wrestle Julie again, and I wanted to go back to school and find out what I wanted in life. I wanted to be there to rebuild the town after the waters receded. Nobody had thrown me a surprise birthday party yet and I still hadn't tried curry and I had goats to raise and degrees to earn and new socks to buy. I wanted to be here, even if here was soaked through and cold, exhausted, worn down.

I didn't know how to stop fighting the past. I didn't know how to be here, in this moment, how to hold all this hurt and still keep moving. But I wanted to try.

"I don't want to take my door," I said. "I want to stay here."

"Then stay."

"Then change," I said, and my voice trembled. "Please. If I stay, then things have to be different between us. Even just a little."

Granny nodded and turned her head to keep me from seeing the tear slide down her cheek but I saw anyway. I leaned over and kissed the top of Granny's head and I stood, slowly, my body weighed down with mud and water and memory. My mother's door had been somewhere nearby, and so had she, once, standing here just like I was. I'd spent my whole life missing her, and right then it seemed that we'd never been closer, just a couple decades of time and one choice apart.

The knoll where I stood was covered with sparse trees and shrubs. They'd been replanted years before by the coal company who had stripped the land. But no number of trees would restore what this place had been before. No amount of wildflowers or grass could undo what had been done to it. Still, this place might be something yet. If it had enough time.

"Well," I said, looking up at my door. I lifted my hand and let my fingers trail through its stars one last time, felt the familiar warmth under my skin and shivered. "Go on then."

It happened between blinks.

One minute, the door was there, swirling and soft and impossible, and the next it was gone. When I looked down, the Blue Marens were gone, too. I sat back down beside Granny and wrapped my arm around her shoulders. In a minute, I would call Carver and tell him I'd found Granny, and Uncle Tim would come to help us across the water and we would make it home just after dark, all of us safe. But for a minute we just sat there looking out over Burnt Ridge, over the last place my mother had ever stood, the three of us, together.

chapter thirty-four

Dear Mom,

It's been over a year since the flood. If you drove into Blackdamp today you might not even notice that things had changed, but four people died during that storm, and at least one business closed, and more damage was done than can be accounted for with numbers. I guess not everything survives, but you already know that.

Some good did come out of it, though. That little single-wide task force that John Edward set up sank into the water. All the evidence inside was destroyed. Some people claimed it was pulled into the water by several reckless criminals in johnboats, but no charges were filed. Sadly, John Edward wasn't there to see it happen. He was in Frankfort on the day of the flood, doing a press conference about the great success of his Clean County initiative, which would end shortly after he returned.

The Rose Garden had to close for a few weeks for repairs though the water did little damage. The director still used the flood as the reason to have all the carpet replaced and the walls repainted, so it looked like a completely different place when Karen went back for her first day of work. She texted me a picture of her standing by the front desk. She was throwing up a peace sign and wearing a new pair of glasses with red frames and it suited her, all of it—the glasses, the scrubs, the joy. You would have been so proud of her.

Carver and I got back together on the day of the flood and we've been together since. It wasn't until a week after that he showed me what he'd been working on with Pap and the Reverend: he bought a garage in town. The floor was covered with six inches of mud so he and Julie and I spent a month getting the place cleaned out, organized, and filled with Carver's equipment. The Reverend took us all out to celebrate the grand opening, and it was that night that she asked to sponsor my college education. An investment, she said, in the future of Blackdamp. She paid off my remaining debt and deposited money for books into my account at the start of every semester, and in exchange I sent her pictures of my grade report, not because she demanded it, but because I wanted her to know.

I was able to use the money I'd made selling pills to pay Cheryl to stay with Granny during the day while I was at work. Tim started paying her, too. He came over more often and even Aunt Forest came in for a visit once, though it seems she's happier where she is now. Granny is working with her doctors, doing everything they say, but she still slips into the past every now and again. The last time I went home to visit, I found her on the porch. She called me by your name and I didn't correct her. I just sat down beside her and listened to her talk. She told you all about what I'd done in school that day and how she was worried about the garden. I held her hand and we listened to the whip-poor-wills crying in the dark.

I wasn't sure what I was doing when I started putting all this into words, but I think I've been writing to you all along. I think I wanted to write myself out of missing you. I've spent most of my life thinking that if I could just understand you, understand what you did, that somehow it would ease the ache in my chest, but it didn't.

I still miss you, Mom.

I feel your absence in so many ways. I felt it when Julie and I moved into our apartment last month. With someone there to watch Granny, I was able to finish the last credits on my associate's degree and transfer to a four-year college. Julie applied and got in, too. She's looking at being a massage therapist but I'm thinking about being a drug counselor back home. Just feels right, somehow. We found an apartment near campus that's only a couple hours from home but it's still the furthest I've ever been from Blackdamp.

When we moved in, we barely had enough furniture to fill the place and Julie wanted to paint right away, so I stood in my bedroom and tried to figure out who I wanted to be there. It felt so important to get it right that I ended up stressing myself out. I wanted to turn to you then. I wanted you to pull out a bunch of color swatches and put them on the wall, standing there in the purple dress that I thought was too short, and I'd tell you as much and you'd just laugh and say that God gave you those legs to share, not to hide. I wanted you to be part of my first apartment, my first place on my own. I put your journal on the shelf over my bed with the last of the blue flowers dried and pressed between the pages but it still wasn't enough, Mom.

I wish I could go shopping with you at Christmas, and I wish we could decorate the tree like we used to. I wish I could call you in the middle of the night when I'm lonely. I wish I could hear you bicker with Granny and that the two of you had reconciled and learned to see just how much alike you really are. I wish you had gotten the help you needed and found a person who loved you well and truly, like Carver loves me. I wish you could see Carver. I know you knew him once, but you don't know him now. You don't get to see how he fusses over me or how many times he texts just to say he loves me or how most nights we FaceTime each other and go about our evenings, me studying at the kitchen counter and him sitting at his shop in Blackdamp tinkering with some part, neither of us talking, but both of us happy to have the other one near.

But even with all this goodness, sometimes my heart still trips and stutters in my chest when the phone rings. Sometimes I wake up and don't quite know where I am and I am afraid and my fog threatens to swallow me whole until I walk down the hall to Julie's room and hear her snoring. Then I remember where I am and why I came here. I still check my bank account four times a day and I keep all my receipts in little envelopes and I put those little envelopes in a drawer, and I don't know why, but keeping them makes me feel better. Like my money is a thing with wings that might disappear at the first hint of an opening so I keep it locked down tight. Sometimes when I'm lying in bed and can't sleep, I get convinced that something is wrong with Granny and I can almost hear her breathing stutter in the dark and I think about how I moved two hours away and how she'll be gone by the time I make it home and I can't breathe until I call and wake her up and hear her cough and grumble and I tell her I love her five or six times before she finally hangs up on me.

Life is more different now than it's ever been, but I think some part of me is still catching up to that. I still worry about how far apart I am, how scattered and faraway. I've spent so much time grieving over what happened years ago or worrying about what will happen years from now that I barely had anything left for the moment. But I'm learning a little more every day what I need to let go of and what it's okay to hold on to.

And right now I am writing you this letter because I love you and I will always love you. Right now I'm wearing my favorite overalls and my hair is in a ponytail because some things never change. I'm sitting in a beam of sunlight falling through my open window and drinking a pop that's gone warm and thinking about going outside and sitting in the grass until Julie comes back and we pack up the car to go home to Blackdamp for the weekend. I am warm and I am sleepy and I am sad and I am grateful, too. And I don't know what I'll feel tomorrow or who I'll be a month from now but I know that right now—*right now*—I'm here.

Love,
Maren

Reading Group Guide

1. If a little door presented itself to you, what would it look like? Where do you think it would lead? Would you take it?

2. Money is an obvious obstacle to Maren's continuing education, but are there other things holding her back? How does she handle those other obstacles?

3. When they first start discussing their feelings for each other, Maren tells Carver that what she wants doesn't matter when she compares it to things she must do to survive. How does Carver argue otherwise, during that conversation and throughout the book?

4. Describe Julie and Maren's relationship. Are they on equal footing? How do they negotiate the boundaries of their friendship throughout the book?

5. John Edward's task force strains the Blackdamp community. Do you think raids and arrests are the best way to address issues of addiction? Can you think of an alternative approach?

6. Maren doesn't always love her hometown, but she can't imagine belonging anywhere else. How do you define home? Where do you think you belong?

7. Why does Maren struggle to ask for help, even when she badly needs it? Have you ever been in a similar position? How did you handle it?

8. How would you describe the relationship between Nell and Granny before Nell took her door? What were the unintended consequences of Granny's involvement in raising Maren? How would you support your daughter and granddaughter in Granny's position?

9. What was your impression of the Reverend? Did you change your mind about her at all throughout the book?

10. Compare Maren's experience with her door to Nell's. What do you think was the biggest factor in Nell's decision to take her door? Why didn't Maren do the same?

A Conversation
with the Author

What inspired *Where I Can't Follow*? How did you come up with the little doors?

I've found that the speculative elements in my work are often tied to theme. So I knew I wanted to write a book that dealt with addiction primarily and then a ripple effect of issues surrounding addiction, such as grief, mental illness, choice, and autonomy. The last two were some of my primary focuses, so the speculative element needed to work with that. Doorways or portals offered the ability to explore the relationship between addiction, grief, mental illness, and escape. As I wrote the book, I discovered that even more than escape, the doors present their chosen people with opportunity. A chance. A choice. And so the doors allowed me to deepen that meditation on what happens when we feel like we've lost control of our lives, when we no longer believe that we have autonomy over our futures, when all the choices we have feel like shackles. Then, even in the midst of these difficulties, how do we allow room for change and growth? What helps us to see and act on the choices we *do* have, to break cycles, to stumble forward even when we feel lost?

Nell's support network was very different from the network we see Maren slowly build. How are we shaped by the people who encourage and protect us?

One of the commonalities I see in both of my novels is the necessity of community. I don't think anyone really becomes who they are on their own—we're shaped by so much, including the people around us. That's definitely true for Maren. She has folks in her life who challenge her and are willing to call her out on the behaviors she has that are harmful to herself or others, like Julie and Carver. She knows people who are fighting for her community, like Amanda and Ace. She's able to see people in her life change, like the Reverend and Karen. Everywhere she turns she's being influenced by these people, and in seeing their choices she's reminded of her own. One thing Maren realizes at the end of the novel is that she also lives in a very different time than her mother. She has a few more opportunities, a few less obstacles. That, combined with the support in her life, is enough to help her overcome the challenges she's facing.

Maren and Carver disagree frequently, but their relationship still comes across as incredibly tender. How did you balance their conflicts and their care for each other?

We meet Maren and Carver at an interesting point in their development. I feel like they're at a place where they're almost ready for each other but not quite, so we get that friction as they try to outgrow old ways of being and relating to each other and step into a new chapter. I think they have to outgrow old expectations, which is hard to do when you've known someone for so long. They end up making room for each other—Carver's tenderness allows Maren to soften some of her edges and begin to rely on him, and Maren's faith in Carver and her desire to see him set boundaries helps Carver believe in himself enough to reach for something he wants. To me, those two go hand in hand. The conflict they have is part of their caring, how they treat each other when they're annoyed or tired or stressed out, how they come back from feeling hurt or betrayed, how they offer and receive forgiveness—those things can make or break a relationship. And so does their willingness to love each other through the good and bad, to believe they're both trying. Those are the kind of relationships I'm drawn to—two imperfect people trying their damnedest to love each other—and I think that's what Maren and Carver build throughout the book.

Karen warns Maren that you can lose your whole life trying to make sense of the past. How can we learn from the past without losing sight of the future?

I think that's one of the driving questions of this book: How do we honor our past without feeling as though we're trapped within it? I'm especially motivated by a generational perspective because I think part of the way we imagine our future is based on the adults in our lives—we know what's possible for us based on what was possible for them. So when Maren sees so many of the women in her life struggling just to feel like they have autonomy, it makes her doubt her own future. It's hard to forge your own path when you don't feel like you have guideposts to help you, and with Maren, there's also guilt, because pushing forward into a new life feels like leaving the people she loves behind. Even though that's supposed to be the dream—for each generation to improve on the one before—there can also be a feeling of loss that comes with going where no one else in your family could go because of their struggles. I'm not sure I have a single answer for this question, but I think Julie touches on it when she tells Maren that she wants to go where her mom couldn't and, in doing so, carry her mom there in her heart. So it's not just about the loss of the past; it's about acknowledging how the people before us helped carry us, too, even if they didn't get as far as they wanted. And it's how we pick up where they left off, how we make sense of ourselves as part of a whole, and how we draw strength from that lineage in moments of doubt.

Despite all she dislikes about Blackdamp, Maren feels like she's perfectly suited to it. Do you feel that way about your hometown or where you live now? Do you think there's a difference between loving where you live and *belonging* there?

I've definitely felt like one of Darwin's finches when it comes to my home, and it's a feeling I've heard echoed from a lot of my friends who have moved away from Appalachia without ever really leaving it behind. There can be this sense of not fully belonging anywhere—when I leave home I'm marked by the accent, the habits, the perspective of my home, but when I return now, I'm also marked by the ways I've changed so I don't feel I fully belong there, either. It can be a lonely kind of in-between. I think the difference between love and belonging is part of coping with that in-between feeling: knowing that you can love your home without living there, that you can honor its place in your life and what it's given you even from somewhere else.

You write about addiction and mental health with great empathy. What do you want readers to take away from your characters' struggles with these complicated topics?

I think empathy is probably my greatest goal—to make a space where readers can consider these issues from a different perspective. There are a lot of narratives around addiction and mental illness that I believe are harmful, like the idea that mentally ill people are dangerous when, statistically, they're actually more likely to be the victim of a crime, not the perpetrator, or the idea that addiction is a choice people make, an act of pure selfishness, which seems a very simple view of a very complicated issue. I want, more than anything, for people to sit in a space of empathy, which I think is a space of curiosity: to wonder what influences in a person's history—their family, their community, their society—might lead them down certain paths and how even if we disagree with someone's choices or don't understand them, especially in the case of addiction or mental illness, that we can still treat them with compassion and respect.

If you had a little door of your own, what would it look like? Do you think you could easily decide whether to take it?

I'd like to think that, at this point in my life, my door might look like the opposite of Maren's. Maren's door is based on a black hole, which comes after the death of a massive star, so I'd like to think my door would be a living star instead. And if the door plucked the image from my mind, then I think my door would look like Betelgeuse, a red supergiant, part of the constellation Orion, and my favorite star. We know Betelgeuse will die, or go supernova, sooner rather than later. "Soon" is in astronomical terms, so that could be a hundred thousand years from now or more, but it's possible this will happen in our lifetime. There's something about Betelgeuse that just makes my heart break—the thought of this star existing out in the dark of space, bigger and older than my mind can possibly comprehend, its death imminent, and in its death, its final act, it will seed new life, new stars. I'd like to think my door would let me carry Betelgeuse with me for a while, and as much as I'd be tempted to touch the star, I wouldn't. There have been many points in my life when I would have taken a door—any door—to leave this world. But I have worked very hard to build a life I don't want to leave. So as beautiful as my door might be, and as curious as I might feel about what lay on the other side, I know I could let it go without regret.

How did writing *Where I Can't Follow* compare to your last book, *Every Bone a Prayer*? Were you surprised by any similarities or differences between the two stories?

I'm not sure the writing process could have been more different between these two books. I didn't use an outline for my debut, but I did for this novel. I drafted my debut very slowly over a few years, while I drafted this novel on a much shorter timeline during a global pandemic that kept me indoors most of the year. Even the craft elements I focused on were different and the goals for each book felt very distinct. Although even with all those differences, I can still see so many of my obsessions in each: the impact of trauma on our lives and our core beliefs, the importance of support networks, the struggles of poverty, and the same mix of darkness and light, difficulty and hope.

About the Author

Ashley Blooms is the author of *Every Bone a Prayer*, which was long-listed for the Crook's Corner Book Prize and which NPR says "bears within its pages striking beauty and strangeness in equal measure." She's a graduate of the Clarion Writer's Workshop and received her MFA as a John and Renée Grisham Fellow from the University of Mississippi. Her fiction has appeared in *The Year's Best Dark Fantasy & Horror, Fantasy & Science Fiction*, and *Strange Horizons*, among others. Learn more at ashleyblooms.com.

Every Bone a Prayer

Misty's holler looks like any of the thousands of hollers that fork through the Appalachian Mountains. But Misty knows her home is different. She may be only ten, but she hears things. Even the crawdads in the creek have something to say, if you listen.

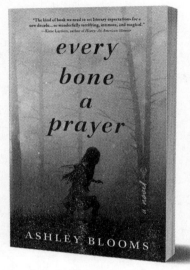

All that Misty's sister, Penny, wants to talk about are the strange objects that start appearing outside their trailer. The grown-ups mutter about sins and punishment, but that doesn't scare Misty. Not like the hurtful thing that's been happening to her, the hurtful thing that is becoming part of her. Ever since her neighbor William cornered her in the barn, she must figure out how to get back to the Misty she was before—the Misty who wasn't afraid to listen.

This is the story of one tough-as-nails girl whose choices are few but whose fight is boundless as her coping becomes a battle cry for everyone around her. Every Bone a Prayer is a beautifully honest exploration of healing and of hope.

"Blooms has taken the voice and names of Appalachia, tended, and evolved them, and created a book that is at once haunting and hopeful."
—NPR

For more info about Sourcebooks's books and authors, visit:
sourcebooks.com